to Gayth
with Best Wishes

STEAM AND STRATEGEM

CHRISTOPHER HOARE

from
Christopher Hoare

Steam and Stratecem

Christopher Hoare

TYCHE BOOKS LTD.

STEAM AND STRATEGEM

Published by Tyche Books Ltd.
www.TycheBooks.com

Copyright © 2013 Christopher Hoare
First Tyche Books Ltd Edition 2013

Print ISBN: 978-0-9918369-7-0
Ebook ISBN: 978-0-9918369-8-7

Cover Art by Tretiakov Alexey
Cover Layout by Lucia Starkey
Interior Layout by Ryah Deines
Editorial by M. L. D. Curelas

Author photograph by deJourden's Photo.graphics Ltd; Lethbridge

Library and Archives Canada Cataloguing in Publication

Hoare, Christopher, 1939 -, author
Steam and Strategem / Christopher Hoare.

Issued in print and electronic formats.
ISBN 978-0-9918369-7-0 (pbk.).-- 978-0-9918369-8-7 (pdf)

CIP information has been requested

DEDICATION

With my thanks to all who have made my writing readable; my wife, Shirley, who is always the first reader and set of eyes looking for my errors and omissions; my fellow writers and critiquers at the Crowsnest Novel Writers' Group; my publisher and her staff for adding all those quality bits; friends who helped with sources of research; and everyone else who has read, edited and commented on my work over the years; and to all of you followers of all things steam, I dedicate this work to you all.

CONTENTS

Prologue
Unwelcome Proposal

Roberta waited in the drawing room for the summons from her father that threatened to change her life forever. A typical Newcastle day poured down rain in blasts and squalls off the North Sea which the fire in the grate did a poor job of countering with warmth. The house had been a great advance from the cottages she'd been raised in, but she fretted that her father had paid more for the lease than the house warranted. Not that the "Father of Railways", George Stephenson, could ill afford it with the number of orders for steam locomotives and expert consultations for new railways that poured in. She knew hers was no more than the ingrained caution of a young woman who had been lifted into the gentry by a father's rise in the world.

A man who had risen from the mines of Northumberland had to step carefully in the society of England in 1810, a difficult and competitive world that could take away as easily as it gave. The calumny of the dispute with Sir Humphrey

Davy over the invention of the miners' safety lamp still hung over them, even after the Commission had exonerated her father from the charge of stealing the design. That all the mines of the North Country used her father's rather than the Davy lamp did not exclude them from jealous gossip.

And now, her father looked to preserve the business he had built for the future—one to be inherited by a son, if Heaven had granted him one. Roberta tried to still the fear that threatened to rise in her throat—for the only reason Martin Postlethwait had visited them today was to discuss the running of a business that, through the legal conditions of the partnership, could only be inherited by *her* future son, and administered until his majority by the partners and the child's father.

Roberta tried hard to read the pamphlet in her hand, a tract on an investigation into the efficiency of paddle-wheels employed in the propulsion of steamships, but her mind kept slipping away into the discussion that must be ongoing, out of earshot, in her father's library. Hadn't she done her best to be the son her father wanted? She had been raised with steam, and possessed a great deal of experience in interpreting that knowledge into material products. Martin Postlethwait might be a reliable engineer in her father's locomotive shop, but he was no manager. She knew herself more capable in that role than he.

The sound of the library door opening came to her and she almost dropped the pamphlet. Footsteps in the corridor signalled the time had come. Her father appeared at the door. "Would you please go to the library, Roberta? Mr. Postlethwait would like to speak privately with you."

She would have felt no worse being invited to step onto the gallows. Her father did not wait for her to leave the room before settling himself into the best armchair with the latest newspaper—he had clearly given his approval for the matter.

Her Aunt Nelly, sitting by the fire, caught her eye briefly as Roberta walked to the door, but could offer no hope of assistance. Unmarried herself, she had no support in life save as a servant to her rich brother.

Roberta steeled herself a moment at the library door and then marched in resolutely. "Good morning, Mr. Postlethwait."

Martin Postlethwait stood to offer her a Cheshire cat smile that made his narrow face and close-set eyes look even more like that of a rat peering out of a cream churn. His bony frame told of an upbringing much like her own, with sparse rations in hard times, and a cough that spoke of too many nights huddled over a coal fire to catch every chance of warmth. Not that she despised him for his modest upbringing—it was the way he had accommodated to it that grated on her nerves.

"Do come in and sit near me, Miss Stephenson."

Roberta walked to the centre of the room and took a seat somewhat farther away than the one he had offered. Yes— offered, as if he were already master of the house.

Postlethwait looked at his chair and eschewed it in favour of crossing the room to stand near her seat, looking down at her. "My dear Miss Stephenson. I am so glad to have this opportunity to unburden myself to you after such a lengthy . . . and indeed gratifying discussion with your father. I have no doubt but that you have some inkling of the nature of our conversation about the continued prosperity and, indeed, profitability of the Stephenson Engine Works and the manner of carrying that success into a second and a third generation."

Roberta merely regarded him with as little expression as she could muster and gave no sign that she had heard his words.

"I owe my every success in life to my employment with your father these past five years—years that have seen me give all my energies and loyalties to the continued advancement of the business. I must admit that the honour your father has presented to me in his address has gone straight to my heart—it is far more than I might have . . . indeed, had any right to expect . . . Words fail me to frame the gratitude and utmost respect I feel in return for his faith he has expressed in me. He has given his opinion to me that he feels that I . . . above all the others he could name . . . offer the greatest prospect of solid and enduring management to the business. What do you think to that, Miss Stephenson?"

"I hope you and the business will be very happy together, Mr. Postlethwait."

Postlethwait's shoulders slumped. "I did not mean . . . I must assure you that I did not assume . . . You must surely understand that the management of the Stephenson Engine Works must be placed into the hands of a new manager at some date in the future. It is most assuredly in your interest as well as your father's that this manager shall have had a long and successful history of participating in the enterprise as a member of the family. In his long experience and wisdom, your father has determined that the best man to entrust the future of both family and Engine Works is into the hands of myself. Am I to understand that you wish to dispute your father's judgement?"

Roberta strove to keep her voice steady. "And was there any suggestion in the discussion with my father that the management of the Stephenson Engine Works might possibly include the management of the owner's daughter? Myself? Am I included in the business? Did the two of you consider your suitability to undertake *that* task?"

"Why, Miss Stephenson. Dear Miss Stephenson—that the conclusion of the business could only be resolved by this discussion with yourself, was in no doubt. I thought it has been quite clear for many months that I hold you in high esteem . . . . I admire your beauty and your amiable

4

qualifications. I assure you that I can offer you my complete and undivided devotion, and that my protection of yourself will always be as important to me as the regard I shall give to the business. I will never be ungenerous and negligent in my care of you when we are married—"

"Mr. Postlethwait, you must realize that you are too hasty. You have not yet been so generous as to offer me a proposal—a proposal that I must emphatically refuse."

"Refuse?" His face reddened. "I assure you that my intentions toward you carry the utmost respect for your feelings and situation."

"Thank you for making your intentions so clear to me, Mr. Postlethwait. I fear your expressions of devotion lack only one thing—that you may have the feelings of a suitor toward the object of his affections. But perhaps you have done that . . . in your own way. I thank you for this interview but it is over and will never be repeated under any circumstances. Good day."

Roberta closed the library door behind her with a great deal less force than her mood demanded, but she heard its thud answered by sounds of movement in the drawing room. She turned away from that direction and set her foot on the staircase, not pausing until she reached the next floor and entered her own room.

There, she refused to succumb to the despair of throwing herself on the bed. Arms crossed, she stood in the window, looking out at the modest grounds in the rain. Her outrage, not directed at Martin Postlethwait but squarely at her father, brought bile to her throat. How could he? She suspected she would very soon find out.

The voices from downstairs mapped the conversation that must certainly be ensuing from her departure. She heard the library door open and close twice. She heard the sounds of Martin Postlethwait receiving his hat and coat from the housekeeper and leaving by the front door. She stepped away from her window so she did not have to watch him leave. Footsteps ascending the stair alerted her to the knock on her door well before it came.

"Come in, Father."

George Stephenson walked into the room and seated himself in a chair near the head of the bed. At forty-four, he was a fine figure of a man, clean shaven and with threads of silver in his hair. His face spoke of sober and well-judged consideration, but at the present moment troubled with a great deal of perplexity. "What did you say to Mr. Postlethwait, Roberta? I have never seen him so agitated."

"You are concerned to see him agitated, Father? What about my agitation?"

"I do not understand why that should be so. I have considered long and hard how best to make my dispositions for the future. You are twenty-two and unmarried . . . and seem to take little interest in the young gentlemen of our acquaintance. It seemed to me that it would be an excellent measure to find a good engineer—"

"To take on both tasks! Yes, I heard those words repeated by Martin Postlethwait. Did it not occur to you that I refuse to be bartered about as nothing more than the controlling interest in the shareholders' meeting?"

"But you cannot inherit in your own right—Stephenson Engine Works is not some little sweetshop in the High Street. I am doing the only thing that makes business and social sense—please see that."

"Damn Stephenson Engine Works. Leave it to your brother and his sons. I want no part in it if it means I shall be required to share a marriage bed with whatever oaf has the ability to start a steam engine."

"I can see you are in no mood to discuss this sensibly. I will leave you alone and hope you will be in a better frame of mind at dinner."

6

Roberta watched as he stood to leave but went to him before he could reach the door. She took his hands in hers. "Father, you know I'm a better engineer than most of the young men in the works. I was not being facetious yesterday when I asked to be considered as manager for the steamship works you are planning on the Clyde. I and a dozen of my ladies from school have the ability to start that enterprise for you. Promote as many of your young men here as you wish into the manager's position—give them all a chance at the post. And if I should find one of them I might come to love . . . or even just to respect . . . I will marry him if you wish it. Just do not rush me into some ill-favoured relationship that might serve your present business circumstances. You are a young man yet—there is no reason for haste."

Mr. Stephenson regarded her gravely. "Thank you for relating your feelings to me, Roberta. We will speak more at dinner."

CHAPTER ONE
FOUR YEARS LATER

Julian, Lord Bond stood beside the steersman at the wheel of his private yacht, staring astern at the vessel coming up on the horizon. Definitely a French sloop and intent on overhauling them before they could reach England. In an easier sea, he might hope the *Foresight* would out distance the Frenchman, but in the present heavy swell the larger vessel had the advantage.

He had placed his report in a waterproof oilskin package in the event he might still hope to get it to the Admiralty, but he had also placed it in a heavy iron skillet as a weight, in case he had to throw the evidence of spying overboard. The report was the fruit of his recent visit to the Low Countries—in this summer of 1814, a possession of France under the Emperor Napoleon—gained at substantial risk and expense in the ongoing war, and clearly not without an equal risk this blustery afternoon. Where was the Royal Navy when he needed them?

It had been foul luck that caused the early morning mist to rise before they sailed out of sight of land. Equally unfortunate that some sharp-eyed coast watcher must have noticed the *Foresight's* gaff rig and foresail on the horizon and decided it looked like an English fashion. Damned bad luck, just when he had vital information about Napoleon's latest preparations to invade England—as well as the first solid information of the Emperor's new wonder weapon that very well might make it possible.

His sailing master came up on deck from the tiny midship cabin. "Are we making headway, My Lord?"

"Not a bit. I fancy they have gained a cable's length while you've been below. How wet is it in the bilge?"

"Ne'er so wet that yon pump might better it. 'Tis that small leak near the prow, I fancies, but worse now us must take the sea at such a heel." Bloggins paused to shade his eyes and peer at the approaching sloop. "I has put they two Dutch cabin boys at pumpin'. Likely they will keep pace with 'en."

"How long before dark? Dammit! Why cannot the weather offer us a respite with a squall and a thick mist?"

Bloggins hawked and spat overside. "I thinks we'll be within range of his bow chasers afore we might expect night to hide us, My Lord. Shall we heave to and let him board us?"

Lord Bond smacked a fist into his palm. "We shall see. We're not done yet. The navy must have blockading ships somewhere close."

"Aye, My Lord, but they has a divil of a big coastline to watch."

Indeed. After Nelson's victory in '05 the Royal Navy had few enemy battleships to fight. But their tight blockade from the Baltic Sea around the coast of Europe to the Kingdom of the Two Sicilies took almost every ship to maintain. Every ship that hadn't been sent across the ocean to blockade the

Americans. It had looked as if the Navy's task would ease when Napoleon took the risk of invading Russia, but even that repulse had not ended his power when he'd been able to wait for spring to march his army out of Moscow. The allies thought they had him at Leipzig in 1813 but he managed to better their larger army and break the alliance against him. Now Prussia was a vassal, Austria hard pressed, Wellington on the retreat back to Portugal, and a new French army gathering on the Channel Coast to invade England.

The fruit of England's naval efforts still denied the French Emperor the supplies needed to build and equip a new battle fleet, but Lord Bond's information must warn England of a stratagem whereby Napoleon might succeed with an alternate plan. He fumed and fretted—if only he could escape this pursuit and reach England.

Christopher Hoare

CHAPTER TWO
A SECOND VOYAGER

Miss Roberta Stephenson reached the starboard engine room as her artificers finished rigging a hose pointing at the overheating bearing. She ducked her head to walk into the reek of steam and hot oil, and the thunderous racket of two hundred horsepower unleashed into the confined iron space. She and her staff were no strangers to the wonders of steam propulsion—they had worked for her father on railway locomotives for years, and she had grown up with an oil can in her hand. He still planned railways and built locomotives, but she had moved to Glasgow where she and her best women engineers had brought about an economical and reliable force of steam to the Country's maritime needs.

Reliable most of the time, but pressed hard on this voyage. The Admiralty had offered her a test to take the *Spiteful* into Napoleon's lair and prove her ship was up to Naval requirements. Engineer Lieutenant Worthington followed her into the engine room to judge if that was the case.

"I should suppose ye'll have to stop the engine and let it rest, Ma'am. If that journal gets hotter it'll throw the piston rod all abroad." Engineer lieutenants in the Regency Royal Navy were not and did not sound like gentlemen—and neither were they welcomed into the officers' messes; being but men promoted from the Black Gang for their experience with the foul and dirty devices they tended.

"We shall see, Lieutenant. My engines have a better bearing metal than you might be used to. We have crossed the North Sea with more water pouring onto the engines than going into the boilers more than once."

Worthington wagged his head doubtfully. "I'm told your arrangement of stern paddlewheels allows the vessel to proceed on a single cylinder."

Roberta nodded. "Aye. We can stop both and couple the two wheels if we need, but it will not be necessary." By this time she had arrived at the pounding cylinder and reached between her artificers to test the bearing with the back of her hand. It was hot but not enough to blister. "As long as we have this much water pouring on the bearing it will not fail," she said confidently. "Let's return to the weather deck."

On their way through the main deck she detoured to the engineers' quarters and knocked on a door. Elizabeth Grandin opened the door and peered out, easing it closed somewhat when she saw Worthington standing behind Miss Stephenson. Elizabeth had her boiler suit partly unbuttoned.

"I have checked the main bearing on the starboard engine, Elizabeth, and instructed the artificers how to deal with it. Perhaps you will inspect it again when you start your watch."

"I will do that, Chief. How far are we from England?"

"In mid-Channel; perhaps five hours steaming to Dover."

Elizabeth nodded. "Aye. Our phosphor bronze will handle that." Elizabeth was one of the women Roberta had schooled with at Miss Mather's Academy for Girls. The late Miss

Mather had believed in training her girls to be helpmates for their future husbands and thought a woman's patience and care over minutiae fitted them perfectly as reckoners and figurers—and so filled their heads with Euclid, algebra, and other mathematical things. It had born fruit as the girls had become the office staff for the compilation of Stephenson's railway designs; for the improvement of the construction metals; and the assembling of a set of steam tables that allowed the more efficient employment of steam. From that start it had been quite a small step for them to become the design team for Roberta's steamships.

Up the companionway they climbed from the hot and humid below decks to the brisk wind and flying spray of the weather deck. Roberta took account of the fly of the Royal Naval ensign at the peak of the mainmast to determine if the wind had changed. An elderly sailing master served as her first officer for his experience in sailing ship handling and rules of the sea, but Roberta reserved the executive authority as her own captain. The *Spiteful* was a new type of vessel, and no one in the country had more experience than she in its handling.

The steam galley was long and slender for its tonnage with three short masts rigged for gaff sails when winds were fair and coal could be economized. The two boiler chimneys were as high as the masts, for good furnace draw, and stood side by side between the main and mizzen masts. A short quarterdeck rose but four feet above the welldeck to give better visibility forrard and more headroom in the cabins below. The quartermaster and the ship's wheel stood in the centre of this deck just ahead of the conning tower—an iron redoubt to serve as a safe post in action. *Spiteful* was a warship of a new and secret type, designed to sink enemy ships with its iron ram bow once its superior speed and manoeuverability under steam propulsion brought it within striking distance of the enemy.

Roberta hoped to prove the vessel's worth for home defence to the Lords of the Admiralty, and gain orders to build more at her Glasgow shipyard. With a crew of only 60 seamen and officers and a hull of iron, the design promised to economize on scarce naval stores for wooden sailing warships, ease manpower difficulties, as well as offer much shorter building times. *Spiteful* had taken but 200 days from keel laying to its first harbour departure on proving trials. It was the only warship in the world designed to carry no cannon, but had launching rails at the bow for Congreve rockets that could assail an enemy with fire and explosives as they approached to ram.

She and Lieutenant Worthington made their way up the companionway to the quarterdeck, leaning with the roll of the waves and hearing the pounding and dull noise of the machinery below through the thrum of the wind in the rigging. MacRae, the master, came forward to them as they reached the binnacle. "Come to lee side a moment, Madam. Your ears are younger than mine."

"What do you hear?"

He answered with a shrug as they followed him. At the rail he cocked his head to the wind. "Is that my imagination?"

Roberta did as he did and strained to hear what the older man fancied. The noise of ship and wind made it difficult, and she was beginning to imagine sounds as she waited for evidence.

At last, the dull boom of a distant cannon came to her. She looked at Worthington, who nodded to confirm her judgement. "That's a cannon shot, Mr. MacRae. You do not imagine it. Change course—we will go to investigate."

Chapter Three
Three Vessels

The Frenchman's first two shots splashed down well astern, the third hit the water close enough to the port quarter to send spray over Lord Bond and Bloggins as they stood beside the steersman. Bond glanced up at the ensign flying at the top of the mast to judge the wind. If he ordered a turn away they would be running closer to the wind and their fore-and-aft rig would lose some advantage and speed.

He turned to the steersman. "Turn two points to port."

Bloggins looked at him doubtfully but said nothing as they stood watching the Frenchman for another telltale cloud of powder smoke. It seemed the Frenchies took an eternity to reload—not unusual, for their navy had little experience because they skulked in port to avoid being caught by the Royal Navy's blockade.

At last, the flash and gout of smoke came and they tensed as they waited for the fall of shot. The Frenchman was firing at near maximum range so their wait seemed to last forever. A gout of spray flew up from a wave away on their starboard side. He had guessed right—the gunners had corrected to their position before the change of course and the shot had gone wide. Bloggins shrugged and smiled.

How long could they keep this up? They'd not fool the French all the time. There was an added problem—this course took them farther rather than closer to England.

Lord Bond moved away from the others to stand beside the stern lantern. The Frenchman hadn't copied their change of course, but would still shorten the range. They would stay on the wind for a while, where their square sails gave their greatest speed.

As he stood watching the distant craft, still a mile distant, he fancied he could see a dark cloud or possibly a squall coming up from the southeast. Odd that it should seem to be coming against the wind.

The fifth shot from the Frenchman's bow chasers hit the starboard side of the *Foresight* at the midship rail. Two of the stays of the standing rigging parted and the mast began to totter. Lord Bond, Bloggins, and three crew members rushed to lower sail and repair the hit with a new splice of rope. While they worked feverishly, the vessel slowed with only the fore staysail propelling them. The Frenchman came noticeably closer, even though their steersman changed course to keep the yacht moving.

Another shot hit them in the hull just above the waterline. If they tried to turn toward England the damage would be underwater and they'd ship the sea through the hole. As Lord Bond moved from the splicing to set the seamen to raising the sail again he realised they had sustained only the one hit while they'd worked. The Frenchman must have held his fire, thinking they intended to heave to and surrender.

He waited for a signal from Bloggins before ordering the hoist, and remembered the squall cloud he'd seen astern.

Indeed, it was still visible—even getting closer. It looked more like smoke now. How could that be?

Bloggins waved that the splices were tight and Lord Bond grabbed the halyard. "Together now—hoist." The two seamen with him hauled for all they were worth; they had been in his employ for many years and could not be more loyal if they'd won a royal pension. The hoist went smoothly but the Frenchman's cannon shot sounded before the sheet reached the peak. Lord Bond didn't hesitate his heaving but could not help flinching as he heard and felt the cannonball strike home.

"Where were we hit?" He looked toward Bloggins and saw him staring horrified.

Swinging around, he saw the steersman tumble to the deck in a spray of blood.

He and Bloggins ran aft as the yacht began to broach without a hand at the wheel. Bloggins grabbed and threw his weight against the spokes. Lord Bond fell to his knees beside the steersman to lend assistance . . . or would have if the poor fellow still lived. He dragged the body away to give Bloggins room to work as another cannon shot sounded. Damn them, but they seemed vengeful at what they'd supposed was a feint. A few more shots would finish the *Foresight*.

Two more cannon shots came hard on his thought. Both hit the hull, sending flying splinters and whole planks spinning into the air. The spliced mast stays began to unravel as the mast sustained damage below decks. The yacht lurched as water, pouring in through holes in the hull, sloshed about below.

Lord Bond walked deliberately to the mainmast. His duty told him he must haul down his colours to save the lives of his crew. He stood a moment before untying the halyard. His frustration and regret at the failure of his spying mission blinded him for a moment from the sight on the horizon.

Then he stared. He stopped fumbling with the wet rope.

The Frenchman had turned broadside on to them. Did the devil intend to finish them with a broadside? Hardly, the cannon ports were still closed. What was the fool doing?

He swung his head farther to look astern and couldn't help his mouth from dropping open. The source of the squall, or the smoke, was clearly visible—a steamship at full speed, its Royal Navy ensign streaming in the wind of its passage.

The French sloop tried desperately to get away but every new maneuver failed against the greater maneuverability of the steamer. The Frenchman's cannon fired several times and the steamer replied with what looked like rockets that exploded in the sloop's rigging. Bond left his Union flag flying and joined the others in the stern to watch the fight as the *Foresight's* hull lurched and settled deeper into the water.

"We'd better launch the gig," he said, but no one moved. All eyes were on the warships.

The steamer made a turn at speed that no sailing ship could match without losing way . . . which was exactly what happened to the Frenchman. The steamer didn't stop or turn away.

"By God," Bloggins cried. "He means to ram."

Surely not, but Lord Bond had to change his thought. The steamer hit the sloop amidships; the mainmast of the Frenchman fell overside, and for several minutes the two ships were locked together. Then he could see the paddlewheels in the English vessel's stern change their rotation and the steamer pull clear. The rest of the Frenchman's masts fell into the sea as the shattered hull listed.

But *Foresight* continued sinking as well, and dipped its bowsprit underwater. "We'd best get to the gig," Bloggins said as the water reached the scuppers.

Chapter Four
Foresight Farewell

Roberta Stephenson watched the French sloop drift broadside-on to the wind and list only long enough to determine their fight was finished. She could see its crew scrambling to launch the ship's boats.

Lieutenant Worthington groaned, but she guessed he mourned the loss of prize money that a captured ship would earn them.

"I'd suggest as we not try to pick them up, Ma'am. They'd outnumber us three to one, easy."

"I had not planned to. I do not doubt but they'd rather chance their luck rowing to France than spend the next few years in Dartmoor Prison." She walked to the other rail as MacRae stopped the engines in preparation for going ahead again. "Where is that English yacht? Is it still afloat?"

Worthington pointed. "But barely. We'd best be quick."

The crippled yacht was just minutes from sinking when the *Spiteful* hove to beside them. The men aboard barely glanced up as they struggled to get a boat in the water. Roberta took the engine room telegraphs in hand and ordered one cylinder stopped and the other slow ahead to bring them alongside.

"You are English?" she called down to the men, now staring at them as if at a conjuror's illusion.

"Aye," answered a grizzled seaman, half into the small gig. "Lord Bond's yacht *Foresight*. And ye be . . . ?"

"The steam galley *Spiteful* out of Clydebank—on Admiralty business."

Another, taller man stepped forward, holding an oilskin package in one hand and what looked like a cast iron skillet in the other. A funny time to think of cooking. "Would you like to come aboard?" Roberta asked as she walked to the entry port.

This man inclined his head and bowed. "If you please. I fancy it will get rather wet aboard *Foresight* very soon. I can pay for our passage."

Roberta heaved a rope ladder over the side. "No need. We are bound for Dover, would that suit?"

"Admirably! Go on, Bloggins. You first."

The older mariner, three crewmen, a cook, and two ship's boys all climbed the ladder as the tall man held the bottom of the rope. As the last boy reached the deck, the yacht lurched once more, and began to roll over. The tall man, still holding his package and the skillet, jumped for the bottom rung of the ladder and scrambled to safety.

He reached the deck and regarded Roberta for a whole minute before bowing slightly. "Please convey my earnest thanks to the captain, Madam."

Roberta stifled a pained sigh. "I am the captain, Sir. This is my ship. And you are?"

He stepped back and looked around as if for someone to make introductions but Lieutenant Worthington held back. The man shrugged. "I am Lord Bond. On the Prince Regent's service."

"And I am Miss Roberta Stephenson, proprietor of the Stephenson shipyards and engine works at Clydebank."

Lord Bond blinked and then smiled—almost a laugh. "Well met, Ma'am. Your father and I were introduced at an Institution of Mechanical Engineers function in London a year ago. You have saved us from a very long swim to England . . . . Our gig had been holed by cannon fire. I must request that you make all possible speed as I must get to the Admiralty as soon as possible."

Roberta was just about to answer when Elizabeth Grandin arrived on deck and interrupted her. She held out something sharp and black with oil. "Take a look at this, Chief. I've shut the starboard engine down—our last manoeuvres have finished off that bearing."

"Damn. Couple the paddlewheels, we'll have to limp home on one engine."

Roberta noticed Lord Bond trying to hide a smile. She doubted he was offended by women who swore mildly, but her claim to being a lady had been betrayed by her ancestry in the Black Country. Well, damn him too. She was no man's servant—she had her own life to lead. "I must apologize for the inconvenience, My Lord. We'll not make Dover before midnight."

CHAPTER FIVE
FIVE HOURS LATE

The crew and passengers had a late supper as the *Spiteful* made heavy weather of the journey on one engine. They took their seats at the first bell of the first watch, 8:30 pm to landlubbers, and numbered forty officers and men, two women, and eight rescued from the *Foresight* seated around the trestle tables in the great cabin. Roberta followed the yeoman farmer custom of all the help eating with family, which caused Lord Bond's eyes to rise almost into his hair. Her other custom of having the junior lads off watch take steaming hot pots to the sixteen men and one woman on watch before eating made the rest of the strangers shake their heads in grudging approval.

Lord Bond sat at the head of the main table beside Roberta and blinked as the cook's helper set a steaming kettle of stew before her for her to help herself. When she had done so, she offered Lord Bond the ladle. "As you see, My Lord, we do not have domestic servants aboard the *Spiteful*. All crew members are expected to attend to their own wants."

"Indeed," Lord Bond replied, taking the ladle in his hand as if grasping the tail of a snake. "And how long have you all been . . . shipmates on the *Spiteful*?"

Roberta answered while brushing aside a loose red lock of hair—she denied dressing more carefully for her guest, but one needed a certain standard. "We began the ship's trials at Clydebank two months ago and began our voyage to Chatham to show the vessel to the dockyard superintendent just two weeks hence. Our present voyage to the coast of the Low Countries and back is presently approaching four days old."

Lord Bond looked around the table at petty officers, able seamen and engine room artificers drinking strong Scottish ale and ladling stew into their mess tins while talking and laughing about their fight with the French sloop—all the signs of a happy ship. "And for what purpose did you bring the ship to Chatham?"

"I have had a communication from the Lords of Admiralty that they would consider my proposal to supply Their Lordships with a number of vessels of like design to constitute a squadron of steam galleys to operate in coast defence. The superintendent looked over the ship and then appointed Lieutenant Worthington," she paused to nod at the lieutenant sitting opposite, "to sail with us and report on the utility and reliability of the vessel's engines."

Lord Bond inclined his head sympathetically. "And here we limp back to Dover as cripples. Bad luck, my dear."

Lieutenant Worthington looked up from his stew. "If I may'st interject a word or two, My Lord—"

Lord Bond smiled and nodded.

"Thank you, My Lord. As I were going to say . . . what I have seen h'indicates no great disadvantage to Miss Stephenson's vessel or engines. They have performed harder service than those on any ship I served in previous. I'd venture to say that there is likely no steamship built that could have performed half so well. The bearing that have failed only did so under the extreme stress of dire action. Even then, it have not caused major damage to the engine which can likely be repaired in a few days at a royal dockyard."

Roberta took a relieved breath and exchanged smiles with MacRae. Worthington had seemed an honest and steady fellow before, but now she thought him one of a very rare breed. Most men would have asked for silver before offering such a recommendation. "We too are required to travel to the Admiralty to report our findings upon return to England. Perhaps you would consider offering a few words about your recollection of the fight with the French sloop, My Lord."

"A pleasure, my dear. Your timely assistance requires no less. It was an impressive action."

Worthington appeared encouraged by His Lordship's permission to enter the conversation. "We was ordered by the Admiralty to sail close to French shores, My Lord, as a provocation . . . but we expected to find no civilian yacht doing likewise."

Lord Bond's expression soured. "Quite."

Roberta hurried to the Lieutenant's aid. "I feel quite sure His Lordship was not in dangerous waters heedlessly, Mr. Worthington—as I am sure he is not at liberty to speak of it. But his need to reach the Admiralty as soon as possible suggests his journey has been of the utmost importance."

Worthington's eyes lowered to his stew. "Yes, Ma'am. I apologize, My Lord, for my foolish question."

"No harm done. I would assuage your curiosity if it were appropriate. I have a question for your captain. Were you instructed to be on the lookout for French steamships, Madam?"

Roberta smiled. "I fear we were not. I take it you are of the opinion that their existence is not an unfounded rumour. No one will give us an official answer, but we hazarded our time, energies and money on offering our ship as a counter to those things that have been spoken of so often in gossip."

"But you must have had some certainty to undertake such an expensive endeavour, dear lady."

Roberta shrugged. "My father had certainty of a steam vessel that served on the Seine at Paris in 1783, My Lord. Called, I believe, the *Pyroscaphe*."

Lord Bond nodded. "A steamship of that name did sail in that year in France, but the river was the Saone and the experiment was not a success. However, I can see the truth is very important to you so I will amplify the story further. The Emperor saw fit to have the experiments repeated in more recent years, and the rumour of the experiments refer to vessels that can tow barges—that are called, after the original, pyroscaphes.

"That could tow invasion barges across the Channel, My Lord?"

The whole company stilled their conversation and watched, wide-eyed, to await His Lordship's answer.

"I believe that is the intention, but I can say no more . . . here. However, if we are both to travel to the Admiralty, Their Lordships might well consider it appropriate to enlarge upon the discussion between us in their secure surroundings."

The other diners resumed a buzz of conversation—now directed, no doubt, on the possibility of further clashes with the French after their successful one just a few hours past.

Lord Bond set down his ale mug. "I know it might, in some circles, be considered improper—even scandalous for a man and woman who have not been properly introduced, but it could be a wise undertaking for us to travel in company to London, Madam. We both have information that could be considered confidential. You were intending to take the train?"

"Yes. Lieutenant Worthington and I were intending to take the last train today, but I fear we will be too late for it. I would be pleased to have a double escort for a journey on tomorrow's six o'clock departure. I believe the urgency of our wartime business outweighs normal considerations of propriety."

"Then I will look forward to your continuing company, Miss Stephenson. I hope you will see fit to apprise me more of your remarkable ship. Was there damage to your prow from the ramming?"

"No, My Lord. The scantlings were designed for the duty. We could safely ram a vessel more than twice our tonnage." Roberta was not completely reassured at his turning the conversation to technical matters. His address had been somewhat provocative—and she was quite sure she recalled hearing of his less than exemplary reputation with the ladies. She felt secure in that she was no impressionable girl to have her head turned by the company of a peer of the realm—heir to the Marquess of Tiverton—and not in need of more than customary prudence in her manner.

Christopher Hoare

CHAPTER SIX
SIX O' CLOCK TRAIN

Lord Bond and Roberta stood in the concourse of the Dover station while Lieutenant Worthington went for their tickets. A few early morning travellers drifted in with the morning mist from the street, but the station seemed mostly empty. Well, it was. The plans for the South Eastern Railway had been formed and put into action during the brief truce in 1802 for the Treaty of Amiens, when all the rich and fashionable had taken channel packets to a Continent they'd had to abjure for ten years. Alas, the truce only lasted a year and by the time the rails reached Dover there were very few passengers en route for Calais.

Roberta listened most inattentively to Lord Bond's monologue of pleasantries as they waited, merely nodding her head and smiling at those junctures when a response seemed expected. Passengers at train stations always took on an air of adventure and mystery—so many people to whom one had not been introduced, all preparing to enter upon the inconveniences and possible alarums of these next few hours of being whisked, at speeds far in excess of thirty miles to the hour, across the face of England. She, of all people, should be used to it, but the thrill of a new journey never left her.

That well-dressed couple awaiting their manservant's arrival with their luggage were surely bound for London to visit with their newly married daughter and her husband. The soberly dressed fellow with a bible under his arm must surely be an evangelical low-church preacher destined to reduce some chapel congregation to spell-bound silence with the power of his oratory. Those two stiff-necked gentlemen half obscured by the porter's trolley of parcels seemed to have something foreign about them—nothing overt, perhaps only the impolite way they had of surreptitiously observing herself and Lord Bond in the centre of the concourse.

Worthington returned to them. "I fear the authorities has placed an obstacle in the path of my duty, My Lord. They agree that they can h'accommodate the three of us in their train for the journey, but only two of you in First Class for the fee of four and twenty pence. They do not entertain our paying the difference to upgrade my own travel warrant from the Navy from Second Class for me to accompany you."

Lord Bond's eyes glared across at the ticket wicket under lowered brows. "Did they not, indeed? What rot. I shall see about that."

The three of them advanced upon the official behind the window like a French column assailing an Austrian brigade.

"Listen here, fellow. My name is Lord Bond and I am determined to travel to London aboard your train in the company of this lady and this naval officer. I surely hope you do not expect us all to ride in Second Class to accomplish the plan. I demand to speak to the Stationmaster. Fetch him at once."

The Stationmaster duly arrived and stood in respectful

silence as Lord Bond entered into a lengthy dissertation on the dismay that would be caused to the Chairman and Directors of the South Eastern Railway, with whom he was personally acquainted, when they learned of the most unsatisfactory and niggardly treatment meted out to respectable passengers by their stationmaster and staff at Dover station. Roberta eased her embarrassment for the poor fellow by watching the two stiff necked gentlemen, who seemed gratified to learn the identity that Lord Bond announced loudly to the whole gathering.

As a result of Lord Bond's complaint, Worthington was invited to upgrade his Royal Naval travel warrant and join the others in the best First Class compartment that could be found for the honoured guests of the railway. "It was no wish of mine, My Lord, to impose an inconvenience upon the Officer or on the Royal Navy—that Heaven knows has kept the terminus viable these past years with their official traffic between the city and the Squadrons based in the dockyard and harbour. Merely a difficulty with the manner of reporting the ticket sales to the accounting office—which I'm sure I can account for with a personal letter to the comptroller."

"Excellent." Lord Bond regarded his fellow travellers. "Then I suggest we take our seats."

"I will have the head porter show you the way, My Lord," the Stationmaster assured them. "I would venture to enquire if you were able to breakfast before setting out this morning. I will have an attendant from the First Class dining room bring tea and some Chelsea buns for your journey."

"Thank you, my good man. Most accommodating of you."

They followed the head porter to the First Class carriage of the waiting train. Just before she stepped up through the door the worthy held open for her, Roberta glanced along the platform long enough to see the two stiff necked gentlemen climb into the nearest Second Class compartment in the second carriage of the train.

Lord Bond looked about their railway compartment while the porters stowed their meagre luggage on an overhead rack. This carriage was one of the non-communicating kind that he preferred. It had a door giving egress to a station platform on each side, but no means of connection to the rest of the train. He handed the departing porters a generous shilling each, feeling anything but the perfect peer of the realm, despite his exaggerated outburst at the station. If truth were told, he *was* acquainted with the Chairman of the South Eastern Railway, but each despised the other. He took off his travel soiled gloves to place on the seat—he would have to visit his club as soon as he arrived in the city to take a bath and access the fresh clothing he always kept there.

The head porter put his head in for one more piece of information before wishing them a pleasant journey and closing their door. "I must h'inform you that there will be a *slight delay* near Tonbridge, My Lord. A goods train have suffered a minor derailment which is h'expected to cause a late arrival in London of about seven minutes."

"Thank you for the information." He looked at Miss Stephenson as she took her seat with her back to the engine, opposite him and Worthington who shared the other. What arrangements she might make for her own accommodation in the city? As the head of a prosperous manufacturing business, and daughter of another, she was certainly not poor—worth a thousand a year, he surmised. Attractive too, with her red hair, pleasant face, and a slim, well-shaped figure—enough of that—he had Admiralty business to attend to first.

"Do you need advice on accommodation in London, Miss Stephenson? I presume our business with the Admiralty will not be of mere hours duration."

"My father retains a few rooms for company officers on city business at an establishment in St. James's Square, My Lord. I expect to find lodging there."

"Excellent location," he replied as the train jolted into motion with a great huff from the locomotive. "And you, Worthington?"

"I expect to find a room at the Army and Navy, My Lord."

"That will be on Pall Mall, quite close to Miss Stephenson."

"Yes, I suggest Miss Stephenson and myself might share a hackney carriage to travel from the Bricklayers' Arms—if that would suit you, Miss Stephenson?"

"I thought we might all share a growler to take us into town from the station," Lord Bond remarked, "but there is plenty of time to discuss that on our journey. I suggest our first call in the city will be at Admiralty House to arrange our appointments."

"Of course, My Lord."

"If I may divert the conversation a little," Miss Stephenson interjected. "I wonder if we might remark upon some of the fellow passengers who boarded the train at Dover."

Lord Bond noted her slight colouring as she spoke. "If you wish, my dear. What did you find remarkable about them?"

"I expect you were attentive to the two gentlemen near the porters' cart, My Lord?"

"Two cavalry officers by the look of them. Yes, but I didn't pay them particular mind."

"Possibly cavalry officers, if you say so, but I thought that from their manner they were not English gentlemen. They seemed impertinently inquisitive about us."

"Really? What do you suppose that signified?"

"Well, as a lady . . . I should say they would give reason for her to take care for her accessibility and seek some reliable company while they were present. Purely a woman's concern you may think, but we *are* in possession of important information that unsavoury individuals might seek some profit from."

"Hmm. I would not dismiss your concern for a moment, Miss Stephenson. I always give regard to a lady's intuitions." He offered her an encouraging smile. "But this train has, as you see, no connecting corridor, so we need not bother ourselves until we leave it at London. I would venture that if they do entertain some unwelcome concern for our business, it might only be significant at our destination."

She looked at him uncertainly. "But what if they're . . . French—or possibly other Europeans in French service?"

"The only way they can reach us would be over the carriage roof—a perilous journey that might well attract the attention of the train's guard and ticket inspector." He smiled again, a little less serious this time and gestured toward the door. "If we should note a pair of feet descending from above, we should promptly let down the window and seize them. Worthington, you might take that door and I shall take this."

"You are both laughing at me," she said with some heat. "I presume you are armed, My Lord?"

He nodded casually. He always kept his Jover & Belton repeating pistol close to hand when on Royal service. He could not help but draw back in surprise as the lady withdrew a nasty little over-and-under pistol from her muff. Made by Henry Nock of London, by the look of it. "What about you, Worthington? Do you conceal a naval cutlass beneath your Officer's breeches?"

"No, My Lord. I apologises, but can add no armament to our defence."

"Ah, no matter. Miss Stephenson and I could bring down a brace of Frenchmen, should they fly past. I thank you for your shrewd observations, my dear. As long as we keep our eyes open I feel sure we will arrive safely at the Bricklayers' Arms terminus."

Miss Stephenson replaced her pistol in its hiding place,

although her dark expression suggested she felt an urge to discharge one barrel at him. Ah, he had always liked spirited young women.

Chapter Seven
More Strikes Against
His Lordship

As the train left the environs of Dover and made for the entrance to the first part of the Shakespeare Cliff tunnels, the three of them set about the refreshments provided at Dover station. Lord Bond was condescending enough to hand out the plates of Chelsea buns while Roberta poured aromatic Lapsang Soochong tea into china cups decorated with a blue willow pattern.

Lieutenant Worthington held up his cup to peer at the contents, clearly dismayed not to find his usual beverage of black tannin smoothed with cow's milk. He offered no comment, but Roberta had to smother a smile—her own workmen would likely down tools if fed the same genteel brew.

Roberta only gradually calmed her pique at the cavalier response her warning about the strange gentlemen had garnered. Earlier, His Lordship had intimated to her in private that his ill-fated trip had been in return from spying upon the French invasion preparations. Surely he had not been so careless about possible threats to his person while in the Low Countries? If his attitude meant he was not prepared to accept her concern, she resolved to pay close attention to any approach to their compartment door while the train was standing in the stations along their way. Luckily, that would be no more than four times, in the major communities along the route—this train being placarded as being in "express service."

The compartment darkened as they entered the first of the Shakespeare Cliff tunnels—a small oil lantern above one door making itself visible with a dim glow that had not been evident in daylight. She looked out the window to see sparks from the engine flying past in the invisible smoke as the locomotive driver used steam to draw more air into his boiler fire to raise the combustion rate. Oh, leave it, girl. You have lived too long with steam—take this opportunity to engage in the kinds of conversations heard when quality meet.

"More Lapsang Soochong, My Lord?"

"Thank you, my dear, if there is enough."

"No more for me, Miss Stephenson," Worthington said quickly. "You and His Lordship may have mine."

Lord Bond shrugged. "I believe the train stops long enough at Tonbridge that you'll have time to find an urn of working-men's tea on the platform. I must own that there are times when I have welcomed such a brew."

"I agree, My Lord," Roberta said with a smile. "There were nights in my father's machine shop when some repair simply could not wait until morning, and a brief rest and a mug of hot, sweet tea served to set us all up for another prolonged effort."

Worthington broke into a cheery smile. "Aye—there's nowt to beat a nice 'ot cup o' tea."

Lord Bond shook an indulgent head. "But do you intimate that you toiled with the workmen, Miss Stephenson?"

"I must admit it, even if you should think the less of me for my apprenticeship. My father always wanted a son that the Good Lord did not send him, and so he determined that I should roll up my sleeves and serve in a son's place."

"Ah, I could see that you was well taught in mechanical arts, Ma'am. It do show to one who 'as took the same road."

Lord Bond stared. "Good Lord. I would never have supposed a young lady to be expected to engage herself in such a thing."

The train emerged into a brief daylight before plunging into the second tunnel. The grey smoke from the locomotive descended so low as to completely obliterate the view through the windows.

"It was no hardship, My Lord. I enjoyed it—as I must presume do ladies of quality who take the art of horsemanship seriously and ride to hounds. They must be no strangers to rain and mud—and to the proper care of horses."

"Well, I do have a sister such as you describe. I swear sometimes that she likes to busy herself in the stables while the family is inside the house at whist or being entertained with a musical soiree."

The loud panting of the locomotive eased soon after they left the last tunnel, an indication that they were soon to stop at Folkestone. The smoke lessened enough for Roberta to catch a glimpse of the Channel where two gun brigs beat to windward across East Wear Bay. Was the whole of the war taking place on the other side of the strand?

About twenty more passengers joined the train as it stopped for hardly more than two minutes at the Folkstone station. Roberta offered the excuse of easing her stiffness for standing to look out their station side door's window. One white-haired gentleman with a small leather portmanteau and a rolled up newspaper climbed into the compartment ahead of them while a young couple with a nanny and four small children took possession of the one behind.

She didn't feel one whit reassured to see one of the foreign cavalry officers watching the arrivals and their new locations while leaning out his own open window.

The guard stepped down from his position at the end of the train with his green flag in one hand and a pocket watch in the other, in preparation to waving the train on. A porter walked down the length of the train toward him crying, "Six oh four h'express from Dover an' Folkestone leavin' platform one for Asf . . . ord, Ton . . . ridge, Ri . . . gate, and London Br . . . k . . . lays Arms terminus. H'all aboard. Mine' the doors." The guard blew his whistle, waved the green flag, and stepped back into his cubbyhole as the train lurched into motion. The foreigner leaning out of the window in the carriage behind seemed to smile broadly at her as he withdrew inside.

Such impertinence—Roberta pulled herself back and hoisted the window closed with a degree of irritation and more force than was necessary.

Lord Bond raised his head from a small notebook as she withdrew from the door. "Anything interesting, my dear?"

"That foreigner smiled at me. I told you they were neither English Officers nor gentlemen."

"Ah well. Did you perhaps consider that they could be Portugals or Spanish allies? I have met a few such since the war re-commenced." He inclined his head in infuriating reassurance. "We will reach Ashford in thirty-five minutes. I will go to make their acquaintance while the train rests at the platform if it would calm your fears."

"They are not fears, My Lord. Only expressions of caution."

"Yes, of course."

The next thirty-five minutes passed in near silence—save for the clack of the train wheels on the track and an occasional hoot from the locomotive whistle. Roberta reached into her portmanteau to find a notebook with her own notes for the Admiralty visit and buried her nose in it until the train rumbled across the bridge over the Great Stour as the locomotive slowed for the station.

No mention was made of His Lordship's visit to the foreigners as they waited for the guard to blow his whistle. Lord Bond pretended not to have remembered while Roberta held a strong resolve not to favour his negligence with a request. She did keep her eyes on the door and listened for approaching footsteps but refrained from showing any interest in passengers and railwaymen who walked past.

During the run to Tonbridge, Lieutenant Worthington must have been fighting off boredom, for he worked to keep conversation going almost the whole way. "A great loss of your yacht, My Lord. Had y'owned it long?"

Lord Bond looked up from his notebook. "Yes. Pity, that. I was growing quite fond of the old girl."

"I suppose the Admiralty maught recompense you?"

"Oh, I doubt it. Their Lordships have a great many expenses far more pressing than mine."

"You'll be lookin' to replace it, then. I'm sure Miss Stephenson could recommend a good steam launch that would suit fine."

Roberta looked up with a valiant attempt to maintain a neutral expression. Lord Bond could not restrain a laugh.

"I see you have an excellent salesman for your shipyard there, Miss Stephenson—once peace is declared. Do the Lords of Admiralty approve of your practicing your peacetime interests while on duty, Worthington?"

The Lieutenant coloured deeply. "I meant nothing inappropriate, My Lord . . . Miss Stephenson. I meant nowt but an innocent remark, I assure you."

Roberta came to the rescue again. "I believe His Lordship

is being facetious, Lieutenant. I believe we all know that the building of private pleasure vessels is forbidden during the war."

"Indeed it is. Which was why I had to purchase the poor old *Foresight* on her way to the breaker's yard. She was at the end of her life when we left Ramsgate on our way to the Low Countries. But come—let us speak of happier things. When peace comes, what steam monster would you attempt to beguile me with, Miss Stephenson?"

"For coastal use or able to sail to the Costa Brava?"

"Ah, now you do tempt me. Is it possible for a steam vessel to range so far?"

"Steam and sail for certainty, but one day I believe a steamship could power itself across the ocean to America."

Lord Bond pretended to cough, no doubt hiding an expression of great amusement.

"That be a powerful long way, Ma'am. 'Twould take a mighty pile o' coal—enough to sink most ships."

Roberta felt a flash of annoyance—every time she felt her opinion of Lord Bond rising he managed to demolish her judgement with another chauvinistic assault on her intelligence or her breeding. "I did not mean any ship or steam engines in existence today, Sirs, but projecting forward the improvements in efficiency we steam engineers have attained in the past ten years, I think the prospect to be anything but a subject for amused dismissal."

Lord Bond seemed to find difficulty in breathing. "We steam engineers . . . we . . . ? You must . . . certainly design me a steam yacht, my dear. I wait with . . . great anticipation to see your best work."

CHAPTER EIGHT
AN EXTRA DELAY

Tonbridge was visited and departed with little of interest, save Lieutenant Worthington managing to find a pot of tea to his liking and rush with it to their compartment as the train began to move.

"Thank you, My Lord," he gasped from the doorway as Lord Bond closed the door he had held open.

"Capital show! You ran a fine race and didn't spill a drop," His Lordship allowed as he returned to his seat.

Roberta had to smile at the two of them—like small boys rejoicing over a raid on an orchard to scrump some apples.

The train left Tonbridge town but its acceleration seemed much less than had been usual at other departures. The smoke from its chimney had reduced remarkably—enough that Lord Bond went to the door again and let down the window to look out.

"There appears to be a flagman at the side of the track," he announced over his shoulder.

"The accident to the goods train, I presume," Roberta offered.

"I am sure you are perfectly correct," Lord Bond agreed. "We are very close to Chiddingstone Causeway, I'd wager. Perhaps the soft ground there had some culpability in the derailment."

Lieutenant Worthington joined His Lordship at the window as they slowed some more and reached a place where the sounds of busy clanging and hammering came to them. Roberta had a glimpse of something being raised by a steam crane mounted on a goods wagon, but the two men almost obscured her view. The train went only a hundred yards farther before stopping completely.

"I thinks they mus' be buildin' up the track, afore us ventures farther, My Lord."

"I believe you're correct."

As soon as the train squealed to a stop, Roberta's nerves began to tense. Was this the location the Frenchmen—or whoever they might be—in the second class carriage had waited for? She looked at her male companions, engrossed in the repair of damage to the track and the rescuing of the tumbled wagons. Neither of them watched the other access to their compartment.

She turned on her seat to face it. At that moment the door started to open.

She barely had time to grasp the pistol in her muff before someone outside flung the door wide. A man with a kerchief over his lower face clambered up from the track level, a pistol grasped in one hand.

He stopped, half in and half out, as he saw her. He raised the pistol.

Behind her she heard her two men scramble away from their door. She could not wait for them; the man was about to fire.

She took aim on her largest target, the middle of his chest, and squeezed the trigger.

The powder smoke of her shot hid her target for a moment. What if she'd missed? The man's pistol discharged.

Smoke cleared in time for her to see the weapon fall from his hand as he fell backwards out of the doorway.

"Good shot, my dear." Lord Bond rushed past her, his own pistol in his hand. Lieutenant Worthington was beside her the next moment, bending over solicitously. "Were you hit, Ma'am?"

Was she? She'd felt nothing.

Lord Bond leaned out the open door to fire a shot. Over his shoulder he called back to Worthington. "Look up, man. The ball went wide."

Roberta and the Lieutenant glanced upwards to see a small patch of daylight in the roof.

"Get out your door, Worthington, and round up some railwaymen. I winged the other blighter but he's limping away westwards. Lead a party to catch him, there's a good fellow."

Roberta was almost afraid to ask. "What about the first man?"

Lord Bond graced her with a smile as he turned to let himself down. "You'd best stay in your seat, my dear. Should you feel in need of a restorative—you do look a trifle pale—you will find a flask of the best French brandy in a pocket of my overcoat. Take what you need—I'll look to your opponent."

She felt that was good advice, she did feel queasy already, but this was a time she needed to be strong. She stood and walked to the carriage door to lean out. Her view of her victim was somewhat obscured by Lord Bond, but not enough to hide a great deal of blood on the sleepers and gravel roadbed. "Is he . . . ?"

"As a doornail." He glanced at her over his shoulder while his hands went through the man's pockets. "If you are as good an engineer as you are a pistol shot, I'd grant you could design

47

a really cracking new ship."

Roberta didn't answer, being concerned with settling some unease in her stomach. The dead man was the foreigner who had smiled at her. A voice came from behind, through the open door Worthington had left behind himself.

"Wot's goin' on in 'ere?"

She turned to see the guard from the rear of the train. "Some foreigners attacked us," she said, standing upright and walking toward the door. The faces looking in backed up hurriedly and she realised she was still grasping her pistol. "Awfully sorry about that," she said as she put it away. "You are the train staff?"

"Aye, Lady."

"Please go to the engine driver and ensure he does not prepare to leave until we have secured our assailants. Lord Bond has one on the other side of the train. The man is dead, but the other one is attempting to run away."

Lord Bond found nothing on the dead man's person—in itself a strong indication these two were trained desperados and not some amateur footpads. He picked up the discharged pistol. A military issue that could be from an English or French armoury after twenty years of war.

He looked up as Worthington and the railwaymen returned with the limping fugitive clasped between them by a dozen arms.

"I am innocent victim." The man pointed at Lord Bond. "This man has murdered my brother. We were in need of help. Our door fell open. My brother fell out. We look for assistance."

Lord Bond held up the pistol. "With this?" He looked toward Worthington. "Did he carry a weapon?"

Lieutenant Worthington held up another pistol. "This one,

My Lord. Prussian made, by its markings."

The train guard appeared, wearing a worried frown. "We mus' continue our journey, My Lord. We shall put the whole railway all behind else."

"Very well. I need a few items for your attention. Firstly, I need this body and the prisoner loaded into your goods van. Second, I want you to find those English sailors who boarded the train at Dover and order them to report to me at the aforementioned van. Third, I want someone to sit with Miss Stephenson in our compartment until the Lieutenant and I return to her at Reigate. She could be upset after the shooting affray, so some steady matron or a clerical gentleman would be appropriate."

The guard duly reported "Yes, My Lord" after each order, and stared down at the corpse.

"Well! Get on with it."

With the help of the railwaymen he and Worthington carried the corpse and prisoner to the guard's door and hoisted them up. The sailors arrived soon after, a bosun's mate and three seamen who had been detailed to collect a draft of pressed crew from the poorhouses in London. "For the brig-sloop *Penguin*, My Lord. Fittin' out at Dover."

"Good. We have this prisoner to hand over to the Admiralty in London. I believe him to be a French spy. Take this pistol and load it. You report to Lieutenant Worthington, here."

"Aye aye, My Lord."

When the train prepared to resume its journey, all was in the order Lord Bond had directed. The spies were secured in the goods van with their naval escort, and after a quick search of their vacated compartment, Lord Bond rejoined them. The train guard waved his green flag and blew the order to leave, and the locomotive responded with blast of its steam whistle. The engine driver waved to the working men at the side of the track and they replied with waves and huzzahs: so began a triumphal progress anointed by the defeat of the French attackers.

"Remove all the clothing from the body and search it thoroughly for hidden items," Lord Bond instructed the bosun's mate. "Worthington, you and I are going to do the same for the live one."

The man regarded them with alarm as they approached. He gave out a heavy groan and clapped a hand to his bloodstained thigh.

"I only winged you. Don't make such a fuss, man. We will dress your wound once we have searched you—if you have cooperated."

When Worthington pulled off the man's jacket, Lord Bond turned it inside out and began ripping the seams with a small folding knife he kept in a pocket. The prisoner groaned in dismay when the knife found a weaker seam where Lord Bond located a folded paper. He opened it up to look at ten blocks of meaningless letters arranged in a square pattern.

"Instructions in a secret cypher," he remarked in a jovial tone to the sweating captive. "Enough to hang you."

CHAPTER NINE
CHAPERONES

Roberta wanted to help the men apprehend the fugitive spy, but her nerves would not cooperate. The hand that had fired the fatal shot would not cease its trembling. Striving to keep her senses and entertain only thoughts compatible with logic, she insisted to herself that this must only be an effect of the pistol's discharge and its recoil against her wrist. Even so, she decided it would be wiser not to expose herself in this distressed state and remained within the compartment.

She did look out when she heard the men return with the prisoner, but withdrew inside and closed the door when they prepared to lift the body and carry it away. As a consequence, she expressed surprise when the train guard arrived at the other door to her compartment with two middle aged ladies and some track navvies with a makeshift set of steps.

"His Lordship h'instructed me to bring these ladies to ride with you . . . on account of how he will not be able to return until the next station stop."

"Oh. Is there something wrong with him . . . or perhaps Lieutenant Worthington?"

"Not as I knows, Ma'am. I h'understands he will be h'interrg . . . h'interr . . . ah, questioning the prisoner in the goods van."

The steps were set in the doorway and the first of the ladies helped to ascend. When she reached the compartment she bobbed in a polite curtsey—which Roberta reciprocated.

"I am Miss Pollard, until recently governess for the grandchildren of Lord Arundell, My Lady—oh, and this is my sister who also served in the same household."

"I am pleased to make your acquaintance, Miss Pollard—Miss—"

"Mrs. Milton, My Lady. Lady's maid to the late Countess."

"Mrs. Milton." Roberta responded to this lady's courtesy. "I must confess to not meriting the title My Lady, as I am a commoner—the daughter of Mr. George Stephenson the railway locomotive engineer."

"Oh." The two sisters exchanged knowing looks. "Then, His Lordship . . . ?"

"Lord Bond and Lieutenant Worthington were accompanying me to London on Admiralty business when we were assailed by those two French spies."

The two ladies' eyes went round as they found their seats. The sound of the improvised steps being removed came from outside and the train guard appeared in the opening, reaching up for the door handle. "If everythin' is in order, Ladies. I will close the door—the train will be departin' in another two minutes."

Roberta smiled at him. "Yes. All in order, but you might be so good as to take Lieutenant Worthington the pot of tea he bought at Tonbridge. I fear he was not able to drink a single drop."

"Right, Miss. Us can hot it up in the guard's van."

When they were left alone, Mrs. Milton took up the question that had clearly been burning on her tongue. "French spies, Miss Stephenson? How terrible. Did they . . . ?"

Roberta smiled slightly, still piqued at the thought Lord Bond had considered her in need of nursemaids, but acknowledged she would be pleased at the resulting opportunity for conversation. "The brutes did not succeed in gaining an entrance—although one of them tried—" Here she stopped at a resurgence of the nervous distress she thought should have left her.

Miss Pollard immediately rose to her feet and came to her. "There, my dear, it's all over now. Dear me, you've gone quite white."

"I have some smelling salts," Mrs. Milton said, proffering a small cut glass vial.

"Oh, I don't think it necessary. I will be perfectly recovered in a moment."

"No, my dear," Miss Pollard said, taking the vial from her sister and opening the cap. "Take a sniff of this."

Roberta did, and immediately sat back to cover her face with a handkerchief as she sneezed and spluttered. The locomotive had whistled by the time she recovered her composure and the train set off on its delayed journey once more.

"There now," Mrs. Milton said, "that'll set you to rights. It always worked for the dear, late Countess."

"I suggest we do not discuss these intruders any further, my dear," Miss Pollard decreed. "It will be better to take your mind off the whole distressing business. I wish we had a tot of spirits to offer you. It might do a power of good."

"Perhaps you are right. His Lordship has a small silver flask in the pocket of the overcoat on the rack. He offered me as much as I needed—we had a tot aboard our Stephenson Company vessel in the Channel last night."

Mrs. Milton stood and turned around to put a hand up to Lord Bond's heavy frock coat. "In here? I hope he will not miss a drop for us all."

Roberta laughed. "He did suggest he would have offered my crew and myself a whole cask of brandy, but unfortunately it went down with his yacht."

Mrs. Milton turned with the silver flask in hand. "His yacht?"

Miss Pollard craned her neck, her eyes gleaming. "Your crew? I hope you do not mind our impertinence, but it seems that you have been in a great adventure. Do tell."

Roberta imparted as much of the adventure of the past twenty-four hours to her listeners as discretion advised—and they sat in rapt silence. They wiped the blue willow pattern cups and each sat sipping at a small measure of His Lordship's generosity.

"And His Lordship's yacht was wrecked?" Mrs. Milton exclaimed.

"Sunk by the cannons of a French sloop of war in the middle of the English Channel."

"The beasts," Miss Pollard said as she clenched her fists. "I hope the Good Lord will punish them for their outrage."

Roberta shrugged. "When last we had seen them they were in longboats rowing for home—not a certain journey. Their sloop was rolling bottom up in preparation to joining many of its fellows in Davy Jones' locker."

"Indeed? The Royal Navy came to your rescue?"

"I cannot say much more of the affair, but our ship, the *Spiteful*, put paid to the Frenchman—before we hurried to the stricken yacht to rescue its crew before it too vanished below the waves."

"Your ship? It must be a ship of war, then."

"Of a new and secret kind—of which I cannot speak."

"And your father was the commander—?"

"Or perhaps, Lieutenant Worthington?" Mrs. Milton broke in.

"Actually, I am the principal officer of my Father's shipyard. The executive position aboard was mine . . . ," she offered a slight smile. "I must suppose the Admiralty will record the Captain of the victorious vessel as myself."

"Well I never," the two ladies said almost in unison.

Chapter Ten
Noon Appointment

Lord Bond rejoined Roberta in the First Class compartment at Reigate station—the sisters would have returned to their previous compartment, but he assured them he had already upgraded their tickets for the previous part of the journey.

"Thank you, My Lord," Miss Pollard replied. "I hope we are not trespassing upon your privacy."

"Not at all. You do us a great service by remaining—since Lieutenant Worthington has remained in the goods van in charge of the prisoner and escort."

The two sisters glanced from His Lordship to her, but made no comment about their new role as chaperones.

"What business do you ladies travel upon," Lord Bond asked conversationally.

"Our previous employer, Lord Arundell, has given us our liberty to engage upon a family matter, My Lord," Miss Pollard replied. "Our brother has been the proprietor of a haberdashery in Woolwich for a number of years. Recently he has been unwell—he is much older than us—and has asked that we should come to help him in the business."

"Indeed. I hope your arrival will aid considerably to his recovery."

Roberta listened to the pleasantries with only half an ear as the train reached some new building activity at Purley. Mrs. Milton joined her to look out of the train window.

"More new houses! How the countryside does change, so."

Lord Bond nodded. "Indeed. If you watch as we enter the city you cannot fail to see how the city grows. Every one of the towns and villages is spreading its habitation along the railway, so that it appears likely that eventually they will all meet as if one enormous city."

"And has the railway done that?" Miss Pollard asked.

Roberta took up her father's explanation. "It happens wherever the railway extends. More people can make longer journeys than ever before. They can even work in more distant communities—they can live in the country while attending to their business affairs in the city."

Lord Bond's expression soured. "I agree. It must be of great advantage to them, but I fear the countryside is becoming far too crowded in the process. The coverts are either cut down or filled with folk out walking. It is becoming difficult to find a place to shoot." He forced a smile. "No doubt the pheasants and partridge consider it a great boon."

Roberta decided their ongoing plans needed discussion. "Will Lieutenant Worthington not join us in the city?"

"Eventually, he will. He will be taking our prisoner for incarceration aboard a prison ship moored in the Thames. I propose to hire him the growler for his task—it will be sufficient for him, the prisoner, and part of the escort. The petty officer will convey the other Frenchman . . . ," he paused to peer carefully at her, "to St. Mary's Churchyard on

Congreve Street."

Roberta looked casually away. She no longer felt disturbed by the recollection, but why did His Lordship and the two sisters watch her so intently? "Do we ride alone to the Admiralty?"

"If you would permit me to accompany you—it will be busy in the city in the late fore-noon. I believe these ladies will not wish to cross the river, since their destination is on the Southwark side."

Miss Pollard looked apologetic. "If that would suit you, my dear."

Roberta considered the propriety. Walking a city street in His Lordship's company would not be a cause for scandal—so sharing a hackney in broad daylight would hardly ruin her reputation.

"I dare say the convenience would suggest my approval. I was hoping to arrive at the Admiralty in the Lieutenant's company as he is personally acquainted with the Engineer Officer we must meet."

"I doubt he will arrive long after us. If I know my Admiralty, it will take a great deal of waiting before you are passed from clerk to clerk and eventually meet with the responsible party. I will do as I can to smooth your passage, but my business is with . . . ," he glanced at the ladies, "an inner cabinet at Admiralty House."

The train continued through the suburbs and between the rows upon rows of new-built housing adjacent to the track until it reached the city proper at Peckham. The locomotive slowed as it threaded through goods yards and engine houses on its way to the terminus. Here the single track of the main line became three, and even as many as four lines; where she saw the Dover bound train waiting for the transfer of the staff to move onto the track they vacated.

The terminus of the South Eastern Railway was shared by

other main lines beside theirs and so the platforms were thronged with waiting passengers, sightseers, and friends awaiting departures so they might wave farewell to the travellers. When they met Lieutenant Worthington, Roberta was pleased to see the sailors had fashioned a light wooden box for the . . . deceased, and had it on a railwayman's cart to push through the streets.

Lord Bond handed the Lieutenant enough money for the transportation and a few shillings for his naval escorts. "Please join us at the Admiralty when you have handed over the prisoner. Please impress upon the prison ship's commandant to make all diligent care to secure the prisoner—who has, doubtless, much more information to impart before he makes his rendezvous with the hangman."

"Aye, My Lord. The hulk is moored at Greenwich, so I may be late in the city. I wonder if we should arrange an appointment for tomorrow, Miss Stephenson?"

"I expect to wait upon the convenience of the Admiralty, Lieutenant. I doubt Their Lordships of the Board will consider our business as pressing as Lord Bond's."

The two sisters came to say goodbye, having found room upon a horse-drawn omnibus that could take them to Woolwich. She stood beside the omnibus outside the station portico speaking with them while His Lordship found a vacant hackney. She looked across the street at the station's namesake, an imposing hostelry under the sign of the Bricklayers' Arms—the armorial badge presented when the guild had been founded.

The party split up to go their separate ways, and Roberta followed a porter, conveying her and Lord Bond's luggage, to the hackney at the front of the line at the kerb on the Old Kent Road. She was surprised to see it was one of the newest two wheeled carriages with the driver located behind and above the passengers, affording them a fine view of their progress over the withers of the draft horse.

They set out up the Old Kent Road for Great Dover Street and London Bridge in a veritable Derby Day throng of cabs, coaches, and drays. Roberta felt quite the lady sitting beside His Lordship, who regaled her with his knowledge of the premises and districts as they passed through them. As they started across the river, a brisk wind gave her quite a chill. Lord Bond produced a travelling blanket from under the seats to spread across her person. Her gratification became interrupted by concern and embarrassment as his hand rested a moment on her knee, but her alarm lasted but a second before he smiled and moved it to smooth the folds.

Over the bridge they entered the city proper. Roberta tried to find a name but could not remember one. "This is . . . ?"

"Eastcheap, home to more than eight hundred thousand souls, my dear."

It seemed as if they must all of them be riding today in cabs and coaches that came swerving past as Roberta stared fascinated at the passing scenes, and while their hackney carriage made its way through the thronged streets of the city.

A smartly dressed man—a foreigner by the look of his dress—stopped to look at something in a window and a porter, running behind, bumped into him. The man did shout a "by your leave," but far too late to prevent a crash. It was a wonder she heard the words—uttered in a momentary lull in the racket of carriage wheels—through the din and clamour of hundreds of tongues, postman's bells, street organs, fiddlers and tambourines of itinerant musicians, and the cries of vendors of hot and cold food on every street corner.

On another street a crowd of beggars, sailors, and urchins came around a corner. A stout gentleman leaning on a cane shouted, "Stop, thief!" Everyone ran to press forward, perhaps to catch the thief, perhaps to steal a watch or a purse themselves. A young woman appeared from a doorway to accost a rich man in cravat with lace in his cuffs. The bawd smiled and said something Roberta could not hear, but when she took him by the hand and he turned to follow, she did not need to hear the words.

At the next corner the rattle of carriages and drays ceased momentarily behind a drove of oxen—the gilded carriages of the aristocracy and the coal wagons with their blaspheming draymen all brought to the same immobility in a street darkened by a floating pall of congealed smoke. So they moved slowly until the animals turned off to Smithfield and their hackney became freed to climb the hill to St. Paul's.

Down Fleet Street toward the Strand they met another delay under the arch of Temple Bar. "Would you rather walk?" Lord Bond asked. "We are quite close to St. James now."

Roberta smiled. "I would, but I can see more from here. I was a child when last I came to London—it frightened me with its turmoil and didn't strike me as such a fascinating sight as it does today."

Lord Bond returned her smile and placed a hand gently over hers. "Then enjoy it all, my dear. I feel as if I have never seen the city in its true glory before, as I do with the guidance of your eyes."

Roberta took great notice at his words—and at his hand on hers. She did not attempt to have him remove it.

She hardly noticed their passage through the traffic and into Whitehall with her mind on Lord Bond and his attempt at gallantry. What did it signify—a genuine regard or some passing fancy? Oh! All this consternation because they were never properly introduced and given her father's approval of the growing friendship. For friendship it must certainly be named—his actions far exceeded the requirements of common politeness.

And what was she that his attention should so discommode her? What was his title, after all? She knew good, honest young fellows on Tyneside whose address was every bit as gentlemanly and who didn't attempt to hasten their acquaintance. No. She must be firm. She moved her hand away from his.

At that moment their driver called down to them. "Here's the Old Admiralty, My Lord—or dos't want Admiralty House?"

"Stop beside the main entrance to Robert Adam's screen. I must first escort the lady to her appointment."

Roberta was pleased to have him assist, but felt she was interfering with his duty. The hackney stopped and Lord Bond alighted and turned to offer her his arm. "Thank you, My Lord, but I must not delay your own business. Please leave me at the entrance hall to make my own enquiries."

He seemed to agree but escorted her through the gate and across the courtyard, greeting several gentlemen by name as they passed them. Once inside he took her to the central desk and insisted the clerks should send word for the Commander of the Engineering Directorate.

Only when a clerk arrived to escort her to the correct office did he take his leave and hasten to the doorway leading to Admiralty House, the residence of the First Lord of the Admiralty. She watched him disappear within as if he were a customary resident—perhaps he was—and she felt suddenly smaller and less sure of herself at his absence. She was, after all, only a suppliant here—attempting to convince the Board of Admiralty of the benefit of her invention—as so many had done before her.

By an hour after noon she was glad to have spoken with a dozen clerks and attained an appointment to see Engineering Commander Ripley at noon the following day.

Christopher Hoare

CHAPTER ELEVEN
THEIR LORDSHIPS

After breakfast the next day, Roberta prepared herself for the interviews by selecting a conservative Polonaise dress of dark red gabardine, ankle boots buckled at the front, and added just a dash of femininity with a jaunty bergere hat with coloured lappets in red and blue. She had found the hat in a milliner's on Pall Mall the previous afternoon.

Promptly at eleven, Lieutenant Worthington called for her—they had decided to walk to the Old Admiralty, it being a fine summer day. Crossing Pall Mall they followed a footpath to St James's Park and entered the Admiralty through the Park entrance. They waited in an anteroom to the offices assigned to those ill-favoured practitioners of steam and coal until Commander Ripley sent a clerk to fetch them.

They had barely entered his office and seated themselves when he looked at them across his desk with a small degree of agitation. "I would start our interview at once—except I have been notified of a change in venue. It really is most unusual, but I hope it signifies that our business is regarded with somewhat more favour than matters of steam propulsion usually receive."

Roberta well knew the Admiralty was the abode of salt water sailors who had a great reverence for masts and sails, and little regard for the dirt and grime of coal and steam. She inclined her head and smiled. "Indeed, Commander. What is the nature of this change?"

"I have been instructed to wait upon a summons for us to go across the entry hall to Admiralty House. I am led to believe that the First Lord of the Admiralty wishes to be present at our assessment of your ship's performance."

Roberta glanced at Lieutenant Worthington, whose face had taken on a markedly red hue. This was indeed some remarkable event to her mind—as it was astounding to an Engineer Lieutenant who was generally never received by the post captain of a ship into his Great Cabin. She had to suspect this prodigious event had something to do with Lord Bond's interview in Admiralty House the day before.

Sure enough, when they were escorted through several corridors to the room in which the Board of Admiralty customarily met, she saw His Lordship seated with four distinguished gentlemen around the conference table. The clerk who had brought them announced their names to the gentlemen and then introduced them to the First Lord, the Second Viscount Melville, seated at the head of the table; Sir Joseph Sydney Yorke, the First Sea Lord; a Mr. William Dundas, perhaps a relative of the First Lord; and Lord Henry Paulit—another Sea Lord, the designation indicating an experienced seaman and admiral rather than a civilian politician in office.

Sir Joseph began the discussion, taking the reading spectacles from the bridge of his nose. "I must congratulate you on your timely and successful action the other day in the Channel, Miss Stephenson. Not only did you come to the aid of a gentleman conveying vital information to this Board, you have distinguished yourself as the commander of the first steamship to defeat a French warship in action."

Roberta felt the gravitas of the occasion—not only did Their Lordships have to acknowledge the success of a despised ugly duckling, they had to recognize the part played by a mere woman. Would that incline them more to their favour of her business or less? "I thank you for your kind words, Sir Joseph. I understand that, due to the confidential nature of my proving voyage, it may not be convenient for the Lords of the Admiralty Board to disseminate the particulars of my vessel's action."

The First Lord smiled. "Very perspicacious of you, Miss Stephenson. Indeed, it would be as notable for the action not to be recorded in the minutes of the Board as for the commander and captain of the successful vessel to be identified as . . . a lady."

"And secrecy is important at this juncture," Lord Bond added, with a warm smile at her.

Lord Paulit nodded gravely. "The French must be allowed to believe their supremacy with these steam pyroscaphes for as long as possible. Any consideration by the Board for the purchase of these steam propelled rams of yours hinges upon their nature being a surprise."

Roberta recognized the truth immediately, but there was already a problem. "But surely the crew of the sloop we sank will report their action with a steamship?"

Sir Joseph inclined his head in agreement. "Unfortunate, but not an irredeemable problem. We . . . that is, the Board, wish to identify the victor of the action as one of our steam tugs. The Master will be identified as one of our steam tug commanders—only as long as the secrecy must be maintained. When allowable, you and your crew will be given every credit due. Do you find that fair?"

Roberta looked around at the serious faces of the Board. No doubt they would wish to conceal every success of steam over sail, but she had to accept their reasoning. "With one exception, My Lords. My own vessel has a sailing master named Hamish MacRae. Since his ship handling was more than the smaller part played by our officers, I think it appropriate for him to be so identified."

"That seems to be possible, Miss Stephenson," the First Lord said. "We will need his particulars of qualification."

Mr. Dundas spoke for the first time. "Since vessels of your type of ram could possibly—if we secure the government's agreement to offer the Stephenson shipyard a contract—could possibly, be engaged in other actions during their introduction we might use Master MacRae's identity to mask the number of vessels involved."

The other Board members nodded their agreement. Their attention was drawn to Engineering Commander Ripley by his discreet cough. "If I may take the liberty of suggesting, My Lords, that before such considerations as possible contracts for further vessels of this type, it would be appropriate for Lieutenant Worthington to give his full report."

"He hasn't already done so?" the First Lord exclaimed. "By all means, give your assessment of the vessel's machinery at once, Lieutenant."

With his face as bright as a night-time beacon, Lieutenant Worthington launched into a detailed recitation of the report he had prepared. Their Lordships were not conversant with some of the engineering details and so Roberta and Commander Ripley clarified the technical points as he read from the pages.

For many minutes, the boardroom of the Board of Admiralty was filled with the intricate details of the world of steam. Commander Ripley seemed on top of the world, while Worthington gradually gained confidence and lost his ruddy glow. Only Lord Bond seemed to appreciate the overturning of the old world with discreet amusement that he conveyed to Roberta with a sparkle in his eyes whenever she looked in his direction.

The problem with the engine bearing was examined in detail. Roberta explained the difference between her shipyard's use of phosphor bronze bearing metal and the customary white metal, and agreed with Commander Ripley that she would be glad to receive a revised specification from him for a more durable design in the next engine produced. The Board members watched this exchange with some astonishment—no doubt the first time any of them had heard a woman discuss anything within this room, let alone on a topic they themselves barely comprehended.

With the technical matters dealt with to the satisfaction of the Engineering Department, and the clarification of the improvements required before the Board could recommend the purchase of a number of such ships to the government, the Engineering officers stood to leave. Roberta stood with them, but the First Lord shook his head. "Please stay, Miss Stephenson. There are further matters we must discuss and Lord Bond suggests you may be able to assist us with them."

Somewhat surprised, she resumed her seat and smiled at Commander Ripley and Lieutenant Worthington as they stood to attention at the door and saluted. They clearly desired further discussion with her as well, and she nodded her assent before they left.

When the door closed behind the engineers, the First Lord turned to Lord Bond. "I would like you to tell the assembled board the information you gave me yesterday. Your new intelligence of the French indicates we are clearly at a juncture in the conduct of the war." He regarded each in turn, even Roberta. "The strategy we have always used to prevent a successful invasion of England across the Channel has met an implacable counter. I must consider this to be the greatest threat this kingdom has met in three hundred years."

CHAPTER TWELVE
MORE DAYS IN LONDON

Lord Bond stood and walked to the large globe in the window before starting to speak. He spun the globe slowly as he marshaled his thoughts.

"Having friends of my family in Amsterdam since the alliances between England and the United Netherlands in the last century, I began my spying mission in that city. I remained there long enough to establish my identity as an American and my business as a sot-weed factor."

"You possessed a passport as a neutral, My Lord?" Mr. Dundas enquired.

"Not at first. Through friends, I acquired the passport of a Gideon Paine, a citizen of New Bedford. I still have it and believe I could safely use it again—should the need arise." He exchanged a knowing look with Viscount Melville. "It has one defect—that it includes the accompaniment of a wife. I must admit that I have never made the acquaintance of this lady, who seems to have left Mr. Paine's bed and board for parts

71

unknown during the past year."

"And the trade in tobacco?"

"I was able to obtain part of a cargo of that weed from a merchant vessel taken as a prize by the Royal Navy in the Channel."

Miss Stephenson showed signs of having a question. "Yes, Miss Stephenson?"

"Where does your yacht, the *Foresight*, come into this?"

"I used the vessel to go to Amsterdam. I ordered Bloggins to remain there, sheltered by friends, until I sent word where to meet me for my return to England."

"The Hollanders can be trusted?" Sir Joseph asked. "Ever since Napoleon's brother became king—and then the country's annexation to France—the French grip on the populace has tightened."

"My friends are patrons of a small but dedicated resistance. I do not fear for their loyalty, but I do take precautions against their discovery by Napoleon's minions."

"I think we might profitably put those concerns aside for the moment, Sir Joseph," the First Lord said. "Please continue with your observations on the continent, Lord Bond."

"Yes, My Lord. My first destination was Flushing, where the construction and gathering of barges for the invasion has been in progress for a year. The required number is recorded to be two hundred and fifty, but the number of completions is reputed to be between one hundred and twenty and two hundred—with the lesser number more nearly correct. The same is true for the gunboats under construction—of one hundred gunboats ordered, less than fifty are completed."

"So the French will need another year for their preparations," Lord Paulit commented.

"Just so, My Lord. However I learned something unexpected while observing the activities at Flushing. One of the rumoured steam vessels appeared—I presume on a trial run. It became apparent to me that the vessels are being built at Antwerp."

"What did you understand from your sighting of the vessel?" Sir Joseph asked.

"I did not get a good view—the day was rainy and the vessel turned about to return up the Westerschelde before it reached the open sea. However, I estimated it to be a steamship with two low masts, and of about a hundred and twenty feet on the waterline, travelling at times about six knots and upstream against the current at about the same rate of progress."

"The current being?" the First Sea Lord asked.

"Two knots, Sir Joseph—making the vessel's true speed to be perhaps eight."

"What do you think, Miss Stephenson?" Viscount Melville said with a smile.

"If the vessel was indeed on a trial run—which seems likely from its brief visit to the waters off Flushing—I would suppose its commander to be running at half power; perhaps two thirds of its maximum speed."

Lord Bond watched her thoughtful manner and her omission of formality with interest. This was a woman of considerable self-possession and logical deliberation—unlike any other he had known. And that included Elise, who had fulfilled the requirement for a Madam Paine during his time on the Continent—another cool head who could be relied upon to dare any danger and to expect her measured response to be exactly what the situation required. He wondered, with a little apprehension, how she had fared when they split up at Gravelines and she took the east road with the carriage to decoy away any following Frenchmen.

"Hmm," Sir Joseph muttered through his steepled fingers. "Its capabilities in sheltered waters gives us little knowledge of its stability in the open Channel."

Miss Stephenson had a ready answer. "The information about the original *Pyroscaphe* my father gleaned indicated it was long and narrow, like a canal barge—not a very stable form for the open sea. Did you form any opinion of this ratio of breadth to length during your observation, Lord Bond?"

"It turned about only the once, and at its greatest distance from my view, but I would venture to say that my impression was of a somewhat sloop-like form, but that may have been exaggerated by the presence of its side paddle-wheels."

"And its burthen? Would you say greater or lesser than my own, *Spiteful*?"

"Somewhat lesser. Perhaps nearer five hundred tons than *Spiteful's* eight hundred."

"So we come to the point, Miss Stephenson," Viscount Melville said. "Can your vessels, built to the same plan as the *Spiteful*, catch and destroy these pyroscaphes by ramming?"

"I am certain that they can, My Lord. We have our kinetic energy in favour and can match the speed of twelve knots in sheltered water."

"But in the open Channel?"

"That would be a function of the seaworthiness of the pyroscaphes, My Lord. I need to know their freeboard, their centre of pressure against the waves, even the capacity of their boilers to provide sufficient steam to work up to full speed in a rough sea. Estimation is a poor substitute for hard figures and precise calculation."

Lord Bond almost laughed as he caught the look that passed between the two Sea Lords—accustomed to judgment founded upon years of experience rather than measurements and figuring. They were as far from their element as a ploughman on a First Rate's quarterdeck, and so, as a matter of fact, was he. But where the Sea Lords' reaction was to surrender the field of discourse he felt challenged to understand more. He was not about to let Miss Stephenson escape to her Clydebank shipyard without engaging him in a great deal more discourse. He glanced at her figure—still youthful though she must be all of twenty-five—and recognized he felt other interests as well.

"I think we must now turn to your discoveries in Antwerp," Viscount Melville suggested.

"Yes, My Lord. I was unable to penetrate the workshops and slipways of the shipyards along the river, but my first observation was that there were no fewer than five pyroscaphes in the river, under various stages of completion."

"Can your shipyard match that production, Miss Stephenson?" the First Lord enquired.

She smiled at him. "That depends upon the premium the Admiralty is prepared to pay for an accelerated rate of production. The *Spiteful* was completed in two hundred days. If the contract were signed immediately, my yard could complete three more by a year hence. If the premium were enough I could contract production in three more neighbouring yards—say another six ships."

All the men around the table chuckled at her ready answer and cool demands. "And we understand that you have no husband to perfect these pecuniary negotiations upon?" Viscount Melville said with a smile.

Miss Stephenson's expression suggested great forbearance. "My answer was merely founded upon my knowledge of the business, My Lord—and some calculations I made in preparation for this interview."

"Excellent. I hope you may furnish us with a detailed summary of the considerations for our request to Parliament."

"Are we ready for the last discovery of my journey, My Lord?" Lord Bond enquired.

The First Lord's humour stilled and his face grew a serious mien. "Yes. We are ready now."

"While I was not able to penetrate the shipyard or see

anything of the vessel I must report, I did have access to a senior official who knew the project, for a day and a half." He did not explain that such time was as long as Elise was able to keep the man drunk and besotted with her person. "The French have embarked on a new and entirely novel form of warship that they are constructing at Antwerp. It is, in brief, a steam powered battleship protected with iron plates from the impact of hostile fire."

Everyone stared—even Miss Stephenson.

Viscount Melville placed his hands palm down on the conference table. "I have considered this at length since Lord Bond apprised me of the project. We will, of course, conduct much more discussion of the matter over the next week or two. That will be the time I estimate for the Government to deliberate on the proposal we submit for the procurement of the steam rams. My most forceful impression is that this vessel, if practical as completed, would circumvent our blockade of the French Emperor's line of battle ships—their escape to sea would be unnecessary. It would constitute a new threat to our inshore craft and frigates that must constitute our last line of defence against a hostile invasion."

"What is the force of this ship, Lord Bond?" Sir Joseph asked.

"I will relate what I was told, My Lords. This is not my assessment of the information—merely what I gathered from our interrogation of the official. They have taken two hulls from vessels previously under construction and cut them down to a single gun deck. Into these hulls they have loaded the steam machinery and a battery of twenty-four pounder cannon. On the outside of the hulls they will affix plates of iron of sufficient thickness to repel the impact of enemy cannonballs. The coal supply for its steam power will be sufficient for this vessel to remain at sea in the Channel while the invasion fleet makes its transit, and protect it from our warships."

"Can your *Spiteful* fight a vessel such as this, Miss Stephenson?" Mr. Dundas asked.

She stared down at the table for several minutes before looking up at the two Sea Lords. "Two vessels of such strength in the decks that can carry these cannon; add to that the weight of a very powerful steam engine and that of the iron plates—what tonnage would you suppose?"

Lord Paulit looked at Sir Joseph. "My first supposition would be that two vessels of fifteen hundred tons would be the basis, though I have no conception how they might be joined."

Sir Joseph nodded his concurrence.

"I could not undertake to set the *Spiteful* against a ship more than three times its size, My Lords."

"A larger *Spiteful* could be built?" Lord Bond suggested. "Perhaps doubling the calculations that have gone into the smaller?"

"Scaling up a design is a practical measure, My Lord. Increasing the size generally reduces seaworthiness considerations. The engines might be a different matter."

Viscount Melville wagged his head. "But you could offer the Board some concrete figures—in the time it takes the Cabinet to digest the information we will be presenting it. Say, fourteen days."

"Rather sketchy figures, My Lords. I would need to know much more of this French project first. Its size; its speed; its handling in a seaway; the strength of its iron plates—and whether they are merely added on or whether they add strength to the hull. The best I can do is provide an upper and lower limit for the design of a ship to meet it."

"Which must all be accomplished by this time next year," Viscount Melville said, putting his head in his hands. "My suggestion I made yesterday, Lord Bond, must become a certainty. How soon can you undertake to prepare another expedition to Antwerp to investigate this French Leviathan?"

"My own preparations would extend only as far as procuring a suitable vessel to return to Amsterdam, My Lord. The more difficult task would be to locate a nautical engineer capable of accompanying my expedition to render the necessary expert evaluations."

CHAPTER THIRTEEN
ITEMS TO UPGRADE

Roberta left the meeting with her composure in a most uncertain state. The likelihood of success with the contract for as many as ten new ships of *Spiteful* design was more than she had ever hoped. The expression on Lord Bond's face as he spoke of his need to be accompanied to the Continent by a competent marine engineer made her fear he intended to make an assault on her . . . if not virtue, at best her independence.

His manner about her position as an engineer had heretofore been somewhat patronizing—nay, very patronizing. Suddenly his opinion had taken a totally opposite course? Not without some incentive known for certain only to himself, but she was not without her suspicions.

However, she must consider her duty to her country. She felt confident of her ability to judge the qualities of this French warship if given solid information. She also saw the advantage of her making this assessment herself as she prepared a design to better it. She knew of no man who had both the knowledge and the youth needed to bear the hardships such a journey of espionage would entail.

That did not mean such a one did not exist—she must write to her father to ask his opinion. She had written him last night, describing her voyage and its unexpected ending . . . as well as the death of the French spy. She planned to wait a few days before letting him know about the interview at the Admiralty and the order for ten ships—better to wait until its certainty grew. She need not tell of her suspicions of a part for her in the espionage—merely ask if he could offer a name she might present to the First Lord and Lord Bond.

Feeling somewhat more at ease with her suppositions, she hurried to the renewed meeting with Commander Ripley.

Commander Ripley stood to greet her when she entered his office. When she told him of the tentative order and Their Lordships' words to her, his face positively glowed. "I must be the first to offer you congratulations on such success in the conference, Miss Stephenson. Ten steamships . . . a personal recommendation of the First Lord! Such a triumph that the Engineering Department has ever seen."

She seated herself in front of his desk beside Lieutenant Worthington. "Thank you, Commander, but I feel constrained to wait until I learn how the Cabinet has received the request."

"Ah, I see you have a canny head on your shoulders, but a personal recommendation from the First Lord—and from the First Sea Lord—almost unheard of."

Lieutenant Worthington seemed overawed by his experience as the first engineering officer risen from the Black Gang to participate in a conference at the Admiralty with the First Lord. Roberta felt any advice or opinion he might offer would reflect his present state of mind.

Roberta allowed herself a smile for both, but she wanted to get these details settled so she could leave and begin making plans. "If you gentlemen are ready, I would like to begin our discussion. I have five issues that I wish to improve upon in the next vessel to be laid down. I believe, Lieutenant, you had nine when we last spoke."

Worthington took up a large journal from the desk before him. "Indeed, Miss Stephenson, but I has one more concern about protection for the crew . . . as the vessels approach to ram the enemy. That makes a new total of fifteen items to consider."

Lord Bond spent more time with the Board members as they discussed the strategy for a renewed spying mission. He turned his chair at the boardroom table to glance at the huge dial of the wind indicator on the front wall. It showed a strong west wind in the Channel—a guarantee the French could not embark any invasion fleet to threaten England today.

"The army is engaged in espionage of a military nature," Viscount Melville said. "Determining the order of battle of the French army around Boulogne and Montreuil."

"Our blockading ships keep a count of the movement, numbers and anchorages of the French invasion fleet," the First Sea Lord added.

Mr. Dundas offered Lord Bond a conspiratorial grin. "So you see; you very much have a free hand for gathering intelligence about the shipping being prepared in the region of Antwerp and Flushing. Would you look to entering Europe in the vicinity of Amsterdam again?"

"If a suitable craft can be found, I would prefer entering the Schelde," Lord Bond replied. "My *Foresight* was probably recognized as a very English-looking vessel when they came inshore for me near Gravelines."

"I will put out an order to the Prize Courts to send particulars of all the smaller Dutch craft seized and still awaiting disposal," the First Sea Lord said. "Will you stay in London awhile? I can inform you of possible vessels for your examination."

"I had hoped to be about the country on business, but I can have my sailing master, Bloggins, come to London to be available. I trust his judgement implicitly in the surveying of sailing craft."

"As you would prefer to trust the judgement of Miss Stephenson in the matter of steamships I see," Dundas said with a smile.

Viscount Melville looked at both. "What are you two considering? I judge Miss Stephenson to be a very respectable young woman—I would be sorely vexed to see you pressure her to become a spy."

The First Sea Lord looked over his spectacles. "I'm sure an engineer of the male sort can be found. You can take Ripley, if you wish."

"A woman would fit the particulars of my American passport better, My Lords."

Viscount Melville raised his chin. "I must own to recalling your saying it proved unnecessary to include a Mrs. Paine in your last mission, less than an hour ago."

"Yes, My Lord. I admit that I did, but my statement was intended to spare Miss Stephenson any embarrassment. I did take a young woman into my employ as an assistant to myself, and she proved invaluable in drawing the French intelligence away from me so I could take ship for England."

"And this young woman could perform a similar service for your next mission?" the First Sea Lord asked.

"I would have to locate her first. I am awaiting word from my friends in Amsterdam about her fate. I fear she may have been captured."

"Good Lord! And you contemplate taking Miss Stephenson to the Continent in her place?" Viscount Melville said in a tight voice. "I would advise you that she has considerable knowledge of our steam developments and plans. I strongly advise you to abandon the intention you seem to entertain."

Lord Bond lowered his head and shrugged. "I merely pursue the most effective plan for my next mission. I agree that Miss Stephenson would need far greater security for her person than Elise did, but then, that young woman has been in and out of trouble many times before. I would admit to no surprise to find she has talked her way out of all suspicion in France and is now on her way back to Amsterdam."

Mr. Dundas exchanged a pained look with him. "These loyalists from the time of the Batavian Republic must be under considerable pressure of French investigations. Can you rely upon their reports to you?"

"I am in communication with more than one agency of resistance to French rule in the Netherlands. I look to their incongruences to alert me to suspected French interception."

"Hmm," Viscount Melville uttered as he shook his head. "I leave such treacherous business to you—I hope you know what you are doing. I would strongly advise our investigations to keep Miss Stephenson in England—possibly at Chatham where she will be in close touch with both the Admiralty and the seaborne communications from the Continent. I will arrange another appointment with her to explain our intentions."

"Thank you, My Lord, but I would hope to have the opportunity to discuss the matter with her first. It is evident that she must return to Clydebank as soon as the *Spiteful* is repaired in order to commence the preparations for building the new ships—"

"If the order is confirmed by the Cabinet," the First Sea Lord interjected.

"Nevertheless, My Lord, my knowledge of engineering business tells me there are preparations that must be made at the earliest possible moment. It is generally known that the enterprise that has begun to fulfill a contract before it is tendered is often the one to win it."

"I can certainly offer some money in advance from discretionary funds," Viscount Melville mused, his eyes on a ledger before him. "Enough to start the procurement of materials."

"That would be most generous, My Lord. I hope you will allow me to inform her of the offer."

"When would you do this, if she returns to Scotland and you conduct the business 'in the country' you spoke of earlier?" Mr. Dundas asked.

"Quite soon—I need to make further arrangements for my yacht crew, whom I left aboard her ship in Dover harbour. I would take the opportunity to ask her advice about sources of information for my edification." Lord Bond smiled. "I see that I have a pressing need for further instruction into the technicalities of steamships before I return to the Continent."

Chapter Fourteen
The Missing Hanoverian

Five days later, when Roberta and Lord Bond had spent the morning in the Steam Directorate assessing the information about the French steamships, the First Lord sent word for them to meet him for luncheon in his private apartment upstairs in Admiralty House.

The family dining room was of modest size and had ample room for the two guests and the family—today comprising the Viscountess and a teenaged daughter with whom they exchanged a few pleasantries as they seated themselves. "What was the verdict on the configuration of the French Leviathan?" Viscount Melville asked them, even before the first course arrived.

Roberta set down her water glass after taking a sip. "The two hulls mentioned seem to baffle everyone, Your Lordship, but logic demands that they could only be hulls joined beam to beam. The other option of stem to stern would be too susceptible to dangerous hogging. They could break apart in heavy seas."

"Yes, of course," the First Lord said. "I was trying to envisage taking the timbers of two vessels to make a very large ship—sufficient to carry the heavy steam engines, but it would require years to finish such a giant and fit it out for sea."

Lord Bond paused from buttering a roll. "As Miss Stephenson says—it is only logical that they are affixed beam to beam . . . and as she also suggests, likely with the paddlewheels, otherwise vulnerable to our cannon fire, secured out of danger between the hulls."

The First Lord nodded and then directed a family question at Lady Dundas; the first course was brought in and little was said until the soup was finished.

"How was today's Cabinet meeting, my dear?" Lady Dundas asked her husband. "I hope they are not fretting about the Naval Estimates again."

The First Lord laughed. "No, not today. The strangest thing was all the concern for a missing secretary—but then he is one of the Hanoverians, and they don't want His Majesty the King to become disturbed."

Lord Bond gestured with a hand. "No, Lord forbid. Poor old gentleman must be kept from harming his health with such worries. Who is it, My Lord, someone attached to the King's German Legion?"

"No, the Duke of Cambridge visited several days ago and anxiously informed the Prime Minister that a secretary with the Hanover Privy Council was missing from their offices in St James's Palace. No one had seen him for about four days."

"Anything missing with him?" Lord Bond asked.

"Apparently not."

Roberta delved into her memory for the topic of discussion. King George was the Elector of Hanover as well as King of England and his German Legion was a force of troops raised from the King's German subjects. She had never heard of the other organisation.

Luckily, neither had the young Lady Dundas. "What is the Privy Council, Papa?"

"It is the government in exile of the Hanoverians, my dear. They have been in London since the French invaded the place in 1807 . . . or was it in 1810? One or the other."

"What governing do they do?" Lord Bond said.

"Very little, I expect, but they insist on maintaining diplomatic ties and finances separately from the government in Whitehall. You had a relative connected with the King's German Legion, did you not?"

"The late Earl of Silchester was Colonel of one of the Dragoon Regiments," Lord Bond said. "The Dowager Countess is my Aunt Caroline."

"Hmm, I wonder if I should advise Lord Liverpool to involve the German troops in finding Gottliebe?"

"I might suggest I call on Aunt Caroline. She is quite familiar with the senior officers and might be able to suggest a name or two you could pass on to the Prime Minister."

"Thank you. It could be helpful."

"I was to escort Miss Stephenson back to St James's Square this afternoon, but perhaps you would like to come along, my dear? Aunt Caroline lives opposite the new Regent's Park and is always an entertaining old bird—time you started meeting more people in the city."

Roberta felt suddenly unprepared to meet any of his relatives, but she could hardly refuse. "I did have work to attend to this evening, My Lord, but if you would take me to Number Six to change into something suitably fashionable for such a visit, I would be pleased to accompany you. But I still have no one to chaperone me."

"That was one matter I might discuss with Aunt Caroline. One of her late husband's sisters might suit."

"I would not like to put anyone out, but I have been too

long unaccompanied here. My aunt is on her way from Scotland but may not arrive for days."

"Then I will ask my aunt for her recommendation." Lord Bond smiled. "That's settled then."

As it happened, Roberta was to meet two countesses. The younger was the wife of the present Earl, son of the elder, the Dowager Countess of Silchester. While the younger's attitude showed her complete disinterest in meeting some commoner, the other showed a very embarrassing degree of interest in any young woman in her nephew's company.

"Miss Stephenson is almost a colleague, as it were," Lord Bond said airily when the young countess had made her excuses for leaving them alone. "We are both involved in discussions at the Admiralty."

Despite a very severe visage and a tall, rather lanky frame that seemed to consist entirely of bones, the Lady Caroline issued a barrage of questions with a very good natured, if somewhat ironic, manner. "So what led you to suppose you would excellently serve in the role of chaperone, Julian?" She shifted her gaze toward Roberta. "We must quickly ensure no one else sees you alone in the company of this ne'er-do-well nephew of mine. Have you no relatives in the city?"

"No, My Lady, but my aunt is on her way from Scotland to be my companion."

"Did no one anticipate that need beforehand?" Lady Caroline's expression seemed to denote a mind delving fruitlessly for a word suitable to describe a parent so lacking in good sense.

"I suppose not, Your Ladyship. My meeting with Lord Bond at sea was not something we planned for."

"Meeting at sea? You were on a sea voyage unaccompanied?" Nothing would serve but a recounting of the complete story of the sinking of the *Foresight* and the journey to the Admiralty. "So, young lady, do you mean to tell me that you hold a position of some authority in your father's business . . . and are even qualified to make . . . decisions?"

Roberta lowered her chin to present a smaller image. "I am manager and designer of my father's shipyard, Your Ladyship."

"Good Heavens." Lady Caroline's face went from horror to something more akin to sharing a scandal. "You have a man's role in the works—! How wonderful! You have achieved something that generations of women have had to secure by marriage and by a deal of superhuman subterfuge and patience. How I envy you."

Arriving at the discussion Lord Bond had planned for the visit had to be postponed until after several similar detours and a lengthy and convivial tea had been dealt with. While the Countess' questions showed a complete lack of knowledge about steam and ships, she was very shrewd in her pronouncements on business and the way one must approach politicians if one needed something from them.

"Lord Bond mentioned to the First Lord that you were very familiar with the officers of the King's German Legion, Your Ladyship," Roberta said after she noticed him showing signs of impatience.

"I was, while my husband was alive, but what interest can you have with them?"

Lord Bond saw his opening and quickly took advantage of it, relating what they had learned at lunch.

"Hmm, yes. I can see some dark stormclouds in any number of teacups, but why is it a concern of yours?"

"Because of the French agents, and more importantly, the likely existence of a spy in the Admiralty—whose information about my activities may well have led to our shooting affray on the train to London."

"I still do not see any connection to this missing Herr Gottliebe."

Neither did Roberta, who waited for Lord Bond's explanation as avidly as did the Countess.

"Do you not think it suspicious that this disappearance should have occurred within a day or two of Miss Stephenson's and my information reaching the Admiralty? I am suggesting that this Herr Gottliebe could be the correspondent of the spy's information, and that he thought the situation was becoming too dangerous for him when one of the agents he set on me was shot and the other was in custody and subject to interrogation. He has gone into hiding."

"It does seem more than a casual circumstance when you look at it that way," Roberta said. "But does that mean the content of our discussions is on the way to France?"

"It could . . . as could also be the disclosure of the presence of yourself, a woman, at the Admiralty—something that has never happened before. The French will surely notice that." He turned to his aunt. "I have promised the First Lord to obtain your assessment of the politics and rivalries in the King's German Legion, Aunt Caroline, and also the relationships within the Hanoverians—both the soldiers and the Privy Council."

The Countess leaned back to study the ceiling a moment. "Quite a tall order, Julian, but I will tell you as much as I can."

Chapter Fifteen
Admiralty Warrant

Roberta and her Aunt Nelly had barely finished their breakfast in the small, private sitting room in the annex of No.6 St. James's Square when one of the downstairs maids knocked on the door to inform them they had a visitor waiting for them in the front drawing-room of the main house. "Who is it, Ruby?" Roberta asked the girl.

"The same gentleman who visited two mornings a . . . ah, Lord—"

"Lord Bond?" Aunt Nelly queried, her eyebrows rising. "Has he taken upon hi'self the propriety o' visiting a single lady to whom he has never been properly introduced, Roberta? I must declare that my arrival by the Scotland steamer has not come a jot too soon. What are you thinking, my dear?"

They rose to follow the maid into the first floor passage connecting the annex to the main house. "Hush, Aunt. I sent a note for him to come to meet you as soon as I learned you were about to arrive in London. And while I admit of a small impropriety in our acquaintanceship—it seems of small account in comparison to our meeting in the middle of the English Channel. I take every mark of his attention to be no more than evidence of gratitude for my part in saving the lives of him and his crew."

Aunt Nelly looked at her with a stern eye. "Aye, you may find it natural, lass. But I ha' seen young gentlemen's gratitude expressed in diff'rent ways."

They reached the staircase hall and descended to the main floor to follow the maid across the tiled floor to the double doors of the drawing-room. She opened the door and moved aside to let them enter. Lord Bond stood in front of the ornate chimneypiece with his hands behind his back. He smiled and bowed when he saw them. "I hope I have not arrived at an inconvenient time, Miss Stephenson."

Roberta curtsied in reply, while Aunt Nelly took the senior relative's prerogative and merely bowed her head. "Not at all inconvenient, My Lord. We have just finished breakfasting. I would like to introduce my aunt to you.

"Lord Bond . . . Miss Eleanor Stephenson."

"Ah, nay, lassie. No one knows me by my Sunday name. 'Tis Nelly Stephenson, My Lord—a pleasure to meet you, I'm sure."

Lord Bond bowed again in greeting, and this time Aunt Nelly attempted a slight curtsey. "Well met, indeed. Upon my soul, I had barely begun to recover from my surprise at learning England possessed a Miss Stephenson, when I find there are actually two of them. I hope you will allow me to call you Miss Nelly?"

That lady tittered, as her cheeks reddened. "Aye, My Lord. I am not one for ceremony—I'm an engineman's daughter an' does answer to any name what leads me to the dinin' room."

"Oh, Auntie. You have no call to excuse yourself, as I'm

sure His Lordship recognizes. He is well acquainted with the Stephenson family—has met your brother on business—and knows us to be solid English working stock."

"Well said, Miss Stephenson. We need not put on airs and graces here—we are . . . I hope . . . among friends." Lord Bond waved a hand to the furniture. "Would you ladies like to be seated? I have several things to say."

Roberta took a small chaise to one side of the empty fireplace while Lord Bond sat beside Aunt Nelly on a larger one opposite. A slight noise from the doorway reminded her then the maid had not yet left. "I'm sure Lord Bond would like to take tea with us, Ruby. Could you please bring some Lapsang Soochong."

"Yes, Miss. Right away."

The door closed and Lord Bond directed his attention to Aunt Nelly. "So you lately came by steamer from Scotland, Miss Nelly?"

"Aye, this past week. By Clyde Puffer through the Firth and Clyde Canal to Grangemouth where I took the coastal steamer. 'Tis but a three day passage all't way to the Pool o' London."

"I hope you are not tired from your journey. Perhaps I should have waited another day before bothering you here."

"Nay, My Lord. 'Tis not a bother. If truth were told I found the voyage most restful . . . the sea were calm, an' I did a power o' sleepin' in the ladies' saloon."

Roberta watched the interaction between the two. Lord Bond's words seemed to convey the perfect truth—he betrayed no trace of condescension and spoke to the older lady with the same easy familiarity he used with his sailing master and with Lieutenant Worthington. Aunt Nelly seemed to warm to him. Perhaps acceptance of his ready conviviality was the reason she found herself less critical of him than she had intended to be when they first met.

Lord Bond leaned forward to speak to her. "And when will you be departing for Scotland in the *Spiteful*, Miss Stephenson? I daresay the repairs to the bearing are completed by now."

"Yes, My Lord. I received a letter from Miss Grandin, my senior engineer, yesterday to inform me that they had given the repair a trial voyage and found it satisfactory. I will return to Dover as soon as I have definite word of our business from the Admiralty."

"Perhaps I can settle the matter of the definite word this morning." He reached into an inner pocket of his coat. "Lord Melville gave me this to bring to you. It comes from the Admiralty discretionary funds and I hope it will be sufficient to allow you to begin the shipyard preparations for the pending contract."

He handed over an envelope which Roberta opened with an act of more outward calm than she felt inside. The envelope contained an Admiralty warrant for fifteen thousand pounds sterling. She strove to push aside her indecent thrill at this evidence of her success. A few moments' thought suggested it sufficient to order the first ironwork for three new spitefuls, as well as enough to claim priority placement in three neighbouring shipyards for the slipways to build three more.

She took a deep breath. "Indeed, My Lord. It will allow me to make most of the preparations I need."

"Then I am most happy to have brought the warrant to you. I was not at ease in my own mind if it were sufficient for the task—I really must admit to being somewhat at sea with the details in this new regime of steam invention."

"Only natural, My Lord. Little of the business particulars are given to those outside the companies engaged in the improvement of steam propulsion. The level of confidentiality separating our enterprises likely approaches the intensity of that between nations at war."

Lord Bond sighed. "I suppose that means that my own further enlightenment is beyond accomplishment. I was hoping to improve my grasp of the particulars of steamships before going to the Continent again."

"I wrote to my father to ask if he could suggest a suitable engineer to accompany you, and have his reply in my room."

"Why, that was extremely thoughtful of you, my dear. And was he able to suggest such a person?"

Roberta could not completely suppress a chuckle. "I must admit that the names were of principals in companies we consider rivals—and that their absences would, no doubt, prove beneficial to our own affairs. They are all competent engineers, but I must admit to skepticism that any would volunteer to join your mission."

Lord Bond looked less disappointed than she had expected. He even smiled slowly. "With your permission, I will take the names to Lord Melville. Perhaps he will use the leverage of patriotism for persuasion—or even the suggestion of some ennoblement, should the mission prove a success."

"I'm sorry I could not offer you anything more, My Lord."

"But perhaps you could offer something indirectly more useful to my mission, Miss Stephenson."

Aunt Nelly looked very guarded. "I hopes this request is something of a conventional nature, Your Lordship."

"Oh, I assure you it will prove so to be, Miss Nelly." He turned a somewhat persuasive expression to Roberta. "My yacht crew is still aboard your vessel and we must come to some agreement over their victualing, but I would first like to ask which course you intend to take on your return voyage to Clydebank. Will it be by the south and west channels?"

"I will travel by the English Channel and the Irish Sea, My Lord."

"Then would it be too great an inconvenience for you to

convey them as far as Falmouth, where the Admiralty has offered a Dutch prize as a potential replacement for my lost *Foresight*?"

Roberta paused a moment when Ruby appeared with the tea and began to serve. "I understand from Miss Grandin's letter that your crew has become great friends with those of the *Spiteful*, My Lord. They have offered much assistance in the way of taking watches and conveying passengers and goods across the harbour. I would be prepared to make them welcome for the Channel passage."

Lord Bond smiled. "Excellent. But I have a further request to make—if it should offer no inconvenience."

"Please continue, My Lord."

"I would appreciate your including myself as one of the travellers—and offering me the opportunity to observe . . . even more . . . participate in the conduct of the voyage in order to afford me some much needed insight into the operation of steamships. Whatever engineer the Admiralty should locate and engage for my mission, I feel the more I understand, the more secure our cooperation shall become. I know that whatever I might learn will be of insignificance compared to that I might acquire from a . . . working . . . visit to the Stephenson Shipyard, but I do not wish to impose myself upon you."

"Well I never," Aunt Nelly exclaimed.

"Your request is not beyond my inclination to grant, My Lord, but you are correct to suppose any insight would be merely superficial. In view of your need for a prompt return to the Continent to obtain the information we need to counter this French ship, I do not see that sufficient time is available for you to acquire any deeper understanding. You must leave England within weeks, I presume?"

"That is my intention—however, I have to await a reply from my contacts on the Continent. That may not be expected before a month has elapsed."

"Then I might be able to suggest some information of value we possess at the shipyard that you may find useful—"

"Nay, lassie. You must speak with your father before suggesting inviting any visitors to Clydebank. He was ver'a insistent in his words to me."

"Then I should write him today." Roberta even surprised herself at her intention. Why did she look so favourably on entertaining Lord Bond at the shipyard? "The information we have there on other steamships would give you some grounding in engineering comparison—and should you have the proficiency in mathematics that would be expected in a man of your education, we can refresh your abilities to make competent estimates based upon what you learn. There are some items of vital information that a successful design to counter the French vessel must be founded upon, and I am most anxious that we might discuss these thoroughly."

"I find your offer most generous, Miss Stephenson. I assure you that you will not regret making it. I believe this assistance will contribute a great deal to the outcome of the mission."

With that, the serious business was ended and they turned to lighter things as they drank their tea. Aunt Nelly was quite subdued in comparison to her earlier open cordiality. She spoke only when spoken to and laughed little, not revealing the thoughts in her mind until their guest had departed.

"'Tis well you should write your father to ask his approval. I see the need for his presence in our establishment during His Lordship's visit as well. I don't presume to judge your thinking about ship and steam matters, but I do have a judgement for your social welfare. I suggest you are more favourably impressed with this heir to a noble peerage than a girl of more modest ancestry has any right to be. Be careful what you wish, my dear. There is many a lassie that has had her heart broke by a gay cavalier."

"Impressed, Aunt? What makes you say that? I merely respond to the cordiality he shows toward me."

"Aye, 'tis the cordiality I notices."

"Well, I must say that the respect he shows for my father and myself is more welcome than the Tory contempt we received from those of his class over the dispute of Sir Humphrey Davy's lamp a few years back. I would be made of stone not to feel such, but I may never see His Lordship again once the ships are built and sold. I will not be endangered by a week or two of his presence in Clydebank."

CHAPTER SIXTEEN
WHO'S FOR DANCING

Roberta felt a twinge of apprehension as she waited with Lord Bond and Aunt Nelly in the panelled and richly draped anteroom for admission to the Summer Fete presented by the aldermen of the City. The entertainment was taking place in the same rooms where the ultra-fashionable Almack's balls were held during the height of the London season. The season had ended almost three weeks before; just as well, for she knew a manufacturer's daughter would never have been accepted by the Lady Patronesses who passed judgement and doled out "tickets" on those who might be deemed suitable to attend Almack's.

Aunt Nelly wore a smart gown of burgundy muslin for the evening, as befitted a matronly woman of fifty, while Roberta had acquired a ball gown of the latest Circassian fashion for the occasion, although she feared it to be too extravagant even for His Lordship's company. The robe of pink gossamer net over a white satin slip did not arouse her approbation, but the peasant's bodice of satin, fastened in front with silver, and the calypso helmet cap, were fashions popular among young women possessed of far more social allure than she credited for herself. Perhaps she should have bought a different gown that merely supported her stalwart North Country femininity.

From inside came the sound of an ensemble tuning up, and a hum of voices. The door opened and a man in powdered periwig, grey jacket, knee breeches, and white stockings looked out at them. "Can I help you, Sir?"

"You certainly can," Lord Bond said in a testy tone. "Please admit me, Lord Bond, and my guests, Miss Stephenson senior and Miss Roberta Stephenson. We are expected."

The doors spread wide and the man drew aside. "Certainly, My Lord. I apologise for not recognising you."

"No harm done; I've not been here for a year or two. It's Budd, isn't it?"

"Budge, My Lord. So good of you to be so generous." He smiled broadly as he dipped in decorous bows to them all.

Lord Bond waved a hand nonchalantly as he took Roberta's arm and started into the ballroom. She hesitated enough to signal a warning to Aunt Nelly that she was not expected to respond to the servant's courtesy and cut off a curtsy that could have brought them some embarrassment.

"Is Mr. Holmes here yet?" Lord Bond asked, clearly providing cover for their need to delay.

"I believe you will find him at the furthest end, My Lord. It is certainly a pleasure to see him in the ballroom."

"Yes, quite."

Lord Bond started walking again as he turned his head to Roberta. "Impudent fellow—however I must admit to admiring them. The scum of the Earth as the Field Marshall calls them, our London cock-sparrers are the lifeblood of the country."

Roberta smiled, a little uncertainly. The "Field Marshall"

would surely be the Marquess of Wellington, England's commander in Spain and Portugal, but she hardly gave a thought to the accusation of impudence while they advanced down the side of the dance floor and she looked about the ballroom. The ceiling was quite high—enough to allow room for the double tiered chandeliers spaced down the length of the room—surprisingly retained instead of the new gaslights she used in her own factory and offices. The ornate decorations of the walls, with curtains and hangings interspersed with statuary, in her estimation, compensated for the lack of modernity. Both sides of the ballroom, lined with couches sparsely occupied at the present hour by a colourful scattering of young and not so young ladies; and gentlemen in dark formal attire with the obligatory knee breeches and stockings, rang with a great deal of merriment and conversation, giving an air of sparkling life and fashion to the establishment.

Aunt Nelly made an effort to recover from her near mistake. "'Tis a grand place ye have brought us, My Lord, although I must admit to not understanding your accusation of impudence. I may be completely beyond my depth, but the man seemed very civil to me."

Lord Bond gave her one of his patient smiles—as Roberta judged them. He always seemed to indulge her lack of social graces with the gentle air of an instructor in etiquette. "Ah, Miss Nelly, you cannot be expected to catch the inference. It might be said that Mr. Holmes visits the gaming rooms at Watier's far more often than he is seen in the social salons."

"Ah. I hope he does not lose too much—him being a friend of yourself."

Lord Bond laughed. "Actually the truth is much the reverse. He wins more than is good for him—I fear he will make a bad enemy one day."

Roberta looked up at the balcony, where the ensemble

appeared to be almost ready to begin playing, and smiled absently. She had been surprised the day before when, after a final meeting at the Admiralty, Lord Bond had invited them both to this social function . . . something of a grand ball for those who lived in the city and yet might not, like her, gain admittance to an Almack's ball. Her curiosity was raised to a degree of suspense when he had added that he would be introducing her to a friend there, and then offered no further explanation.

She looked about as if she might pick out this Mr. Holmes by his very appearance as they walked to the far end of the hall. When she saw they were headed for three gentlemen near the refreshment table talking and sharing snuff from the box one of them held out, she immediately picked the tallest to be their objective. She was gratified at her intuition when this gentleman turned at their approach and greeted them with a deep bow.

"Good evening, Julian. Just in time, I see."

Roberta studied him as Lord Bond made the introductions. Not only tall but almost gaunt, with a not unpleasant, hatchet face and thinning black hair. With very formal gallantry he took her hand and kissed it when they were introduced.

In turn, he introduced his interlocutors. "Mr. Arthur Bentley and Mr. Mortimer Haigh, my card partners and Names at Lloyd's—I must confess we were talking business."

"Enough with that, Symington," Lord Bond answered. "Tonight I shall expect you to help me amuse these two ladies from the North Country. Miss Stephenson, here, saved me from a long swim in the Channel."

"Ah, Julian. You will get into these devilish scrapes."

Mr. Bentley laughed and joined in. "I hear you had a shipwreck but neglected to have your journey insured."

"I would have asked you for a quote; however I was not engaged upon slaving business."

Symington Holmes slapped him on the shoulder. "Really? You must have raised the amount of the pittance you pay to your poor, long suffering, Bloggins to have foresworn slavery."

Mr. Bentley frowned. "Slavery is becoming a poor investment. This past week we learned of two more ships seized by American privateers—both insured by Lloyd's and with a significant exposure for myself."

Mr. Haigh joined in. "Yes, please tell us, My Lord—what measures are your friends at the Admiralty taking to tighten the blockade on the American ports?"

Lord Bond shrugged. "The demand for ships and crews has far exceeded the Royal Navy's ability to meet. Two huge blockades to be maintained at once—if the American war is not settled soon . . . well, I hate to think what will come of it."

Symington Holmes smiled mischievously. "I swear I heard two Members of Parliament propose a new taxation levy upon the maritime trade and Lloyd's. A measure to raise a source of funds for a subsidy to the Czar for a reinforcement in—"

The two Names drew back in shock. "A new levy? A tax upon Lloyd's?"

Lord Bond laughed. "And all for a fleet of ramshackle Russian frigates? Symington—your jest is without credibility."

Mr. Bentley shook his head angrily. "I should know enough not to take your bait, Mr. Holmes. I have absolute certainty of your integrity in saying nothing of Admiralty business in social circles. Two Members, indeed!"

Lord Bond turned to Roberta with a smile. "Mr. Holmes has a post in the Admiralty. A post for which you might consider befriending him—although I agree with Mr. Bentley's suggestion that he is scrupulously careful of any business that has passed over his desk."

Mr. Haigh turned to her. "He has a senior position in the financial affairs of Admiralty—signs notes for many thousands of pounds with as little qualm as a land holder might disburse a hundred."

Symington Holmes chuckled. "It does not happen regularly, and I must own that it is easier to disburse when the specie is not mine."

"You are the head accountant, Mr. Holmes?" Roberta asked.

He smiled at her. "Not exactly, Miss Stephenson—my post is actually as a technical advisor. I am a mathematician by education . . . a tripos at Cambridge. My duty for the Admiralty is to assess the services it acquires and to approve or deny the price the supplier has placed upon them."

Lord Bond smiled broadly at her but said nothing. She hardly needed to ask his meaning—she was in the company of the gentleman who had the final word over the payment for the steamships the Stephenson Shipyard would supply the Royal Navy. Here was the man who might make or break her enterprise.

Lord Bond and the gentlemen led her and Aunt Nelly to some vacant couches under a window where they seated themselves just before the ensemble struck up the introduction and honours for a longways dance.

"Do you ladies know 'Wildboar's Maggot'?" Mr. Bentley asked.

Aunt Nelly inclined her head. "I assure ye that my niece and myself are well acquainted, Sirs, but I haf'ta observe that we have the lack of enough young ladies."

Mr. Bentley smiled. "I do believe you are correct, but isn't that your sister over there, Mr. Haigh? Perhaps she might join us."

Mr. Haigh looked about. "Ah, I see her. Excuse me a moment."

It took but a few minutes to welcome a rather tall and horsey young lady with her brown hair in ringlets to their company.

"Are we ready to join the dance?" Mr. Bentley said jovially, his eye on Miss Haigh. However, it seemed she had made a resolve to dance with her brother.

Lord Bond remained seated. "I'll sit out the first dance, if you'll do the honours for me, Symington."

"Delighted," he answered, offering his arm to Roberta. Which left Mr. Bentley no alternative but to smile gallantly at Aunt Nelly and escort her onto the floor.

An unspoken decision selected Mr. Holmes and Roberta as the senior couple, while Mr. Haigh and his sister took the next senior position. Roberta listened carefully for the fiddles and winds to reach the repeat of the opening bars for their entry into the dance while Mr. Holmes regarded her with an expectant expression. At last the repeat came and they set off heying down the group.

As they turned about Aunt Nelly and Mr. Bentley at the end to dance together back to the start position, Mr. Holmes smiled and said, "So you have known His Lordship a matter of weeks. I trust he has been good company . . . ."

They parted to their positions before Roberta could answer, leaving her with the question hanging. Was there some hidden meaning? Why had he asked Mr. Holmes to partner her in the first dance?

When next they had the chance to speak, Roberta claimed the first word. "Does Lord Bond suppose your company better than his own?"

Mr. Holmes smiled. "My company might be a little less constrained, although I fear I have the disadvantage of not having been rescued by the charming lady captain and her vessel."

"Is that considered to be a better introduction than a courtesy call upon her father?" Roberta responded at the next opportunity.

"Decidedly more memorable. I fear I could never match

Miss Stephenson in her charm and her manner of deportment."

"I take it you suggest carriage, Sir?"

"Well taken. I wonder what beguilements I must needs offer to be entertained in the Stephenson Shipyards . . . ." The dance parted them before Roberta might answer.

The last repeat began, which would see them end back in the senior position. Roberta decided on boldness. "Am I to suppose you have an inclination to learn the secrets of steam, Sir?"

He chuckled. "I must tell you a secret first, Miss Stephenson."

"Go on, by all means."

"There is a rumour that the Admiralty is considering me as the person who might best observe the Frenchman's nautical wonder."

The dance ended with the dancers honouring their partners, and Roberta returned to her seat with Mr. Holmes. "Your words suggest to me that you have some familiarity with steamships, Sir."

"Some, but not a great deal. I did resolve a dispute over the contract conditions of some harbour tugs, but I must confess that to be poor preparation for Lord Bond's task."

"He has spoken to me of visiting Clydebank to learn more at the Stephenson yard. Will you be coming too?"

"I do not know." Holmes frowned. "He did not tell *me* that."

CHAPTER SEVENTEEN
AT THE END OF A ROPE?

Roberta had been plagued by periodic palpitations ever since boarding the train that morning. It had only become worse since they alighted at Tonbridge station and she took a carriage to the magistrate's estate with Post Captain Montague and Lt. Worthington. The captain, sent by Their Lordships of the Admiralty, had been reassuring the whole way, but three days before, an official message had notified her that the enquiry into the death of the French spy had been well-nigh dismissed by the Lord Chancellor. The very fact that they were here standing on the threshold of the mansion told her that something was definitely not well at all.

The butler opened the door and guided them to Sir Totham Wootenbury's justice room at the rear of the ground floor. "The people from the Admiralty, Your Honour," he said as he ushered them in.

The Justice of the Peace was seated behind a large oak desk, wearing a white periwig on his head and a black gown wrapped around his spare frame. His dour face gave no sign of welcoming them. "We are here to investigate the report of the death by shooting of an unknown man at Chiddingstone Causeway on July 14th 1814, as reported by a Mr. Bateman in an affidavit I have to hand here."

"Mr. Bateman rode in the next first class compartment aboard your train," Captain Montague whispered to Roberta. "He undertook to carry out his citizen's duty as required by the law of the land to ensure that a possible crime was investigated."

Sir Totham frowned at the interruption. "Which of you was present at the affray?"

Lieutenant Worthington stepped forward, appearing as disturbed as Roberta felt, his face reddening. "I were present, Your Honour, as a witness to the affair . . . and as—"

"Name and occupation, if you please," Sir Totham rasped.

"Royal Naval Engineer Lieutenant Alfred Worthington, stationed at His Majesty's dockyard Chatham, My Lord."

When Sir Totham finished writing this down in a ledger he looked up at Roberta. "The complaint about the shooting mentioned the presence of a young woman . . . are you that young woman?"

Roberta's voice came out as a mere whisper. "Yes, Your Honour."

"Speak up, speak up. Are you that woman?"

"Yes, Your Honour," Roberta said loudly.

"State your full name and family heritage, if you please."

"My name is Roberta Stephenson; I am the daughter of Mr. George Stephenson of Wallsend in the county of Northumberland; the inventor, railway engineer, and proprietor of—"

Sir Totham waved a hand. "Yes, Miss Stephenson," he said as he wrote, "I believe I am familiar with your father's business affairs."

His face, that had almost seemed well disposed as he took her particulars, now turned dour again. "You do realise that I am bound by my duty as Justice of the Peace for this western borough of the county of Kent to determine if there is sufficient evidence to remand you in custody until the next Assize Court to answer for an indictable offense . . . namely that of murder?"

Captain Montague cleared his throat and stepped forward. "If you will permit me to lay before you the documents provided by the Lords of the Admiralty, Sir Totham, we can bring this investigation to a timely—"

"No Sir! Indeed, I do not give you leave. This is my court and it is not under the jurisdiction of any high London office, nor any department of Parliament and Crown save only the pleasure of His Majesty the King."

"And, I presume, His Royal Highness the Prince Royal, as his father's regent?" Captain Montague responded in a forceful voice. "It so happens that I have a letter here under his Royal Highness' signature requesting the Civil Power to honour the concerns of Admiralty in the matter of Naval espionage and the good order of the service. If you will be so good as to read it."

Sir Totham scowled, and delayed as long as was prudently possible before replying. "I will examine this letter, Sir, and take note of your own name and position."

Roberta had been aware of the delicate relationship between the government in London and the civil powers, the regional magistrates in the counties, but had never understood the extent to which it affected the ministries actually at war. Now she did.

"I am Captain Howard Montague, assigned directly to the First Lord of the Admiralty, Viscount Melville, and responsible for domestic legal matters . . . such as those issues as may arise between the Admiralty and the various branches of the Crown."

Roberta watched as Sir Totham received the letter from Captain Montague and settled a pair of spectacles on his nose to read it. The galling thing here was that the Justice was probably a Whig, like her father and all their family, using his local power and partisan instincts to discommode the organs of the Tory government. He seemed to read with exaggerated deliberation, as if memorising the letter's contents and, by the motions of his eyes, re-reading a number of passages until satisfied as to their contents.

Finally, Sir Totham looked up from the letter. "You are alleging that the murdered man was engaged in some foreign espionage?"

"Yes, Sir Totham," Captain Montague answered.

"Very well, I will have the witness give his account of the matter."

Lieutenant Worthington drew himself upright and launched into his recollection of the affair. At one point he mentioned "His Lordship" and Captain Montague had to explain to the court that the identity of this person, in the Service of the Crown, was being withheld.

At the end of the recitation, Sir Totham fixed his eyes on Roberta. "Am I to understand that your part in the matter was as a person under the command of a senior officer of the Crown?"

"Yes, Your Honour."

"Would it not have been more appropriate for the Naval Lieutenant to have been the armed person on guard against surprise intrusion?"

"Well, Your Honour," Worthington spoke up, as if to take the onus upon himself. "I were not carrying a weapon, while . . . our senior officer . . . had h'ascertained that both he an' Miss Stephenson was armed. They could bring down a brace o' Frenchmen was his words . . . as I remembers."

Sir Totham glared at them. "So the possibility of an affray was discussed?"

"Only because I had noticed these two men, two men of military bearing, watching us as we boarded the train, Your Honour. I believe neither Lieutenant Worthington nor . . . the other gentleman . . . took my concern seriously."

"Hmm. Do you have any proof that these men were French spies, Captain?"

"I do, Your Honour. There were documents in cypher that appear to have been received from someone in an official position in London . . . and also some letters of identification that were discovered in their lodgings in Dover when, as a result of the interrogation of the other man, they were identified and searched."

Roberta looked in some surprise as the documents were handed over. She had not been told anything of the later investigation of the man held in the prison hulk at Greenwich. Sir Totham regarded the papers with a frown, as if about to complain that they appeared to be in a foreign language. "Can you explain what the documents say, Captain?"

"The names of the two men are the first items underneath the crest of the French cavalry regiment; I understand the text officially records their being detached from the regiment at the Emperor's orders, and that their pay will be the responsibility of the Minister of Foreign Affaires, Charles Maurice de Talleyrand-Périgord, prince de Bénévent until such time as they are reassigned to their regiment. This makes the documents very valuable to the Crown," Captain Montague said as he took them back. "They are effectively passports to the Continent."

From that point, Roberta's nerves began to settle and the enquiry ended with the assurance that the local judiciary would take no further measures into the incident. The three of them took a glass of wine and some refreshments with the

Justice of the Peace before leaving. But Sir Totham could not resist one last admonition to Roberta.

"I must impress upon you that, in future, your duty is to remain in your father's house and pursue only maidenly graces and *certainly* never take it upon yourself to discharge a pistol at anyone, as long as there are able bodied gentlemen at hand to perform the task."

Roberta thanked Sir Totham for his good advice.

CHAPTER EIGHTEEN
THINKING OF YOU

"There, my dear lady," Captain Montague said as he left them at the Old Posting Inn on his way to catch the next train back to London, "I must relay these words of apology from Lord Melville at the distress this matter has caused you: 'We are duty bound to respect all matters of law within the country we vow to protect, no matter how onerous and inconvenient.' I can only assure you that you should have no further trouble from the civil authorities in this matter."

"Thank you, Captain."

He climbed back into the carriage and turned to speak. "I am entreated to inform you that Their Lordships will send out orders to all naval stations informing the commanders of your status as an officer of the crown in the matter of your assistance to the defence of the realm. We cannot, of course, commission you . . . . It would hardly be appropriate for one of the fair sex, but you will receive a special warrant that should accomplish much the same thing."

Roberta inclined her head and shook the captain's proffered hand. "Thank you, Sir," she said again as the carriage door closed and the coachman shook the reins.

Lieutenant Worthington took her arm as they turned to go into the hostelry. "A warrant from th' Admiralty. That should prevent any more o' these troubles, Miss Stephenson. 'Tis sure this day have been most painful for you."

They no sooner entered the hostelry than Aunt Nelly appeared with Mr. Holmes in her wake. "Ah, my dear girl . . . I was so worried . . . not that Captain Montague did not assure us it was but a formality." She threw her arms about Roberta with enough enthusiasm as to almost prevent her breathing.

Mr. Holmes approached and bowed. "All's well that ends well . . . eh? The officialdom is satisfied and you are a free woman again?"

She unwound herself from Aunt Nelly and gave a slight curtsey. "I believe so, Mr. Holmes, but I almost believe Sir Totham has warned me not to leave my father's house without an armed escort of gentlemen, lest I should besmirch my reputation—with the magistracy, at least."

He smiled. "That's the spirit. And speaking of spirits, we have a small luncheon arranged in a private parlour, and I do believe there is a bottle of Portugal's finest waiting to dispel whatever unpleasant feelings the morning appointment has inflicted."

With that he interposed himself between Roberta and Lieutenant Worthington, took her arm and escorted them all back to the private room.

After a couple of small glasses of excellent port and a fine chicken pie, the whole memory of the inquisition in the magistrate's gloomy justice room faded into the distance. She could hardly believe herself so easily freed from such a brush with the law . . . a brush that would have resulted in certain transportation to Botany Bay, or perhaps even a hanging, if she were still no more than an engineman's daughter. How much more pleasing was England when a girl had such powerful friends.

"We've received word from Lord Bond that he will meet us at Falmouth," Mr. Holmes announced over the port. "He has entrusted me with the task of asking all the foolish questions on the voyage from Dover, if you will be so kind as to accommodate my ignorance."

"He is called elsewhere?" Roberta asked. She had to admit a touch of disappointment that his plan of joining them on the evening train had been changed.

"He has to call upon the Marquess," Holmes said with a haughty mien and dignified voice.

Aunt Nelly let out a laugh that she quickly tried to hide. "Oh, Mr. Holmes. You must not be so cheeky."

"Ah, Aunty . . . not as cheeky as all that. His Lordship, the Marquess, has lectured me enough in years past—I must admit to relishing the thought of Lord Bond facing the music in his turn. Although I do not know what he has done to warrant it."

He said this last with his eye on Roberta, which gave his words a tinge of mystery rather than humour. A mystery that seemed connected to her.

"What train will we take to Dover, then, Mr. Holmes?" Lieutenant Worthington wanted to know.

"Since we no longer must wait for His Lordship, we might take the afternoon train. I believe it leaves in an hour . . . if that will suit the ladies."

"Fine by me," Aunt Nelly offered.

"Yes," Roberta said more lightly than she felt. "I shall be glad to get aboard the *Spiteful* and set out into the Channel on this evening's tide."

Lord Bond peered into the darkness outside the railway carriage as the Bristol and Exeter Railway train left Taunton behind on its way south. In half an hour the train should stop briefly to let him disembark at the end of his journey. His father had informed him a carriage and four would be awaiting to take him the rest of the way to Tiverton Castle.

He rested his chin on a hand as the faint glow of a lantern beyond the window penetrated the darkness. In less than a second, as the train rushed past, the eye registered a quick glimpse of a man crossing a farmyard beside the track. Perhaps a yeoman farmer with fertile land and no miserly landlord to call him to account. The Marquess had not included a reason for his own summons in the letter. It meant he expected his eldest son to spend time on the journey examining all of his recent activities for transgressions.

Lord Bond sighed and looked away from the darkened land. He had a strong suspicion he knew what had angered His Lordship.

A knock on the compartment door announced the arrival of the train's ticket collector. With a nod from Lord Bond, the man slid the door open and came part way into the opening. "Tiverton Junction halt, My Lord?"

"That is correct. Are we almost there?"

"Not yet, My Lord. If you wish, I can come back to inform you when we are five minutes away. Will you have servants to carry your baggage, My Lord?"

Lord Bond waved a casual hand upwards to the luggage rack. "A small valise. I can dismount with it in my hand. There should be a coach and footmen awaiting my arrival."

"Very good, My Lord. I will return as we commence slowing down."

Lord Bond returned to his ruminations. He doubted the Marquess' new tirade would return to disapproval of the perils involved in his son's journeys to the Continent. He seemed to take a quiet, unspoken pride in the fact that the family was well represented in the defence of the realm. As for the prospect of the loss of the heir to the title, his father's last words at the close of an earlier argument had been blunt—"die under a French guillotine if you will, Sir. I still have a younger son in reserve."

So he did, as long as James' feeble lungs did not give out before he departed Oxford and managed to produce a legitimate son upon a suitably connected young bride. The family dynasty of healthy bastards seemed as safe with the younger son as with the father and the elder.

And there resided the hint of the Old Man's summons. He must have heard the rumours from London about the buxom Miss Stephenson . . . either that or he was possessed of the arts of divination—an attribute Lord Bond had suspected more than once before. But, alas, a more mundane explanation always overthrew the supposition . . . the Tiverton fortune was more than sufficient to buy whatever spies its master desired. And he was never shy about casting judicious silver about in that manner.

About an hour later Lord Bond peered out of his coach window as the horses' hooves clattered into the stone tunnel of the castle gatehouse. In the light of the wall lanterns he glimpsed the low arched interior gateway before they emerged into the south courtyard. Tiverton Castle had been attacked but once, but that was by a Parliamentary force during the civil war, who had finished their business by levelling the walls and corner towers to prevent the castle from being held against them again. Later owners had accepted the destruction as permanent and built a mansion against the ruins.

Lord Bond alighted in the glow of a lantern held by Pearce,

his father's aged house steward. "Good evening, My Lord. So good to have you visiting again, Master Julian."

Lord Bond glanced around at the part of the house and buildings he could see—nothing seemed to have changed, but then why should it? "Thank you, Pearce. Your rheumatism being kept at bay?"

"Yes, My Lord. Thank you, My Lord." Pearce gestured for a footman to take the valise Lord Bond carried.

"Where is His Lordship? In the library?"

"I believe not, My Lord. He is reading in the Joan of Arc Gallery."

They entered the portico and into the front door where another footman stepped forward to take Lord Bond's hat and travelling cape. Pearce directed the footman with the valise toward the staircase. "You may take that to Lord Bond's old room." He then led Lord Bond to the rear of the foyer, remarking, "I had a fire laid in your room when I heard you were coming, My Lord. It's not a cold night, but these old stones need airing out when the occupants have been so long away."

"How does my father's mood seem?"

"Pensive, I might take the liberty of suggesting, My Lord. He is reading one of the histories written in French, I believe."

The Joan of Arc Gallery reputedly held a collection of paintings of the lady herself as well as members of her family. Lord Bond suspected they were not genuine, but an attempt at piety for the martyred Joan by an earlier, Catholic, holder of the castle. The Marquess, in a seat beside the fire, looked up from his book at their approach.

"So, you found your way home, did you?"

Lord Bond stepped to his father's side and bent to kiss the old man on the temple. "*Vraiment*, Papa."

The Marquess eyed him narrowly. "Hah! Sit down and tell me what you have been engaged in—I hear many rumours from my friends in the Admiralty. Pearce . . . bring some brandy for us . . . and some of those cheeses we had at dinner."

As Pearce left, Lord Bond seated himself on the other side of the fire and regarded the old man carefully. His father's face still held a ruddy glow even if his hair had long since deserted him. His hands seemed more gnarled than he remembered; the fist holding the book trembled slightly, and his eyes seemed excessively watery behind the spectacles perched on his nose. His tall frame looked bent over in the chair and the strong man's body became more gaunt as the years passed. Almost seventy, Lord Bond remembered, a very good age for the primary swashbuckler of His Majesty George the Third's new court in the 1760s.

"What's all this steam business, lad? It's too new for me to fathom. What is wrong with good oaken ships and a fine spread of canvas?"

Lord Bond took a deep breath; yes, the topic he had expected. Best he keep it to naval matters. "Napoleon is building himself a new invasion fleet. He has steam vessels preparing to haul his barges across the channel, and," Lord Bond could not help a glance around the otherwise empty gallery, "a possible steam powered battleship to keep our frigates and gunboats from scattering them."

"One battleship?"

"One very strong battleship with iron sides that may be invulnerable to our cannon shot."

The Marquess stared sightlessly up at the paintings above the mantel for a long moment. "What do we do about it?"

"I have to go to the Continent one more time. I learned when I was there last month that the vessel is under construction at Antwerp. I need to accompany an agent with expert knowledge of steam and steamships to learn enough of this monster to allow us to build a vessel to counter it."

The Marquess sat forward abruptly. "And this expert is supposed to be an engineman's daughter?"

"Good Lord. Where did you hear that?"

The Marquess glowered and would have launched into a loud tirade except Pearce and a footman appeared with their brandy and refreshments. The barrage had to be delayed until the two departed.

Lord Bond rushed in first. "The engineering firm of Stephenson and Partners is assisting the discussions and have a contract to build ten iron steamships of a novel kind. We are calling them steam galleys, as, like their namesakes of old, their chief weapon is their ram bow—"

"Very interesting, but I insist you tell me about this young woman. My informants told me that she had the temerity to lecture Their Lordships of the Admiralty about ships."

"Miss Stephenson was able to greatly assist the discussion of the steamships in the Admiralty boardroom. My impression was that Their Lordships were most gratified and pleased with her contribution to a technical discussion beyond their own direct experience."

"Miss Stephenson! Who is this girl?"

"Her father is Mr. George Stephenson, the steam locomotive and railway inventor. He it was who built the railway between Stockton and Darlington, and has designed and built many since—"

"The daughter. Tell me about the daughter."

"Roberta is the only child of the family, and has been raised almost as a son . . . as far as the family business goes. She is the manager of the shipyard on the Clyde where the first of these steam galleys has been built. She had considerable responsibility for the design and construction. I'm surprised you do not ask me about the sinking of my yacht by a French sloop of war in the channel. It must have been included in the stories you have heard. If she and her steamship, the *Spiteful*, had not arrived to sink the Frenchman I should be either drowned or a prisoner in France by now."

"*Her* steamship?"

"Yes. I was as surprised as you when I reached the *Spiteful's* quarterdeck and found a young woman in command—"

"My informant did not suggest that this young woman was actually the captain of the vessel."

"For reasons of secrecy, it was decided upon in the Admiralty meeting not to reveal such details. Neither would you have heard about the new steamship—it was decided to claim the rescue vessel was one of the navy's steam tugboats."

"I see." The Marquess sat back in his chair and took a draught of brandy. "This Miss Stephenson—she is a woman of beauty?"

Lord Bond took a deep breath. "I would not go so far as to suggest her to be of great beauty, but she is a very handsome young woman of about mid-twenties. She has, from my observation, a very bright and lively mind, and a degree of courage not often found in the fair sex."

"Courage? What courage?"

Oh. Lord Bond decided he had been too forthcoming. It would not be at all to his advantage and possible plans to let the Old Man know about her shooting the French spy. "Well, to sail boldly against the broadside of the French sloop and hold the course until *Spiteful's* ram smashed into the side of the enemy. We were not very well placed to see, and were very busy trying to keep *Foresight* from sinking, but from what we heard, the Frenchman kept up a continuous cannon fire until his ship was smashed."

"Yes," the Marquess mused. "Very admirable qualities; very admirable indeed, but only in a woman of low degree who has enjoyed a very strange and novel upbringing.

Certainly not ones to recommend her to be presented in the Prince Regent's court or in the drawing rooms of aristocratic England."

"My Aunt Caroline did not appear offended."

"My sister is not head of this family."

Chapter Nineteen
Night Navigating

Roberta took her place beside the quartermaster at the helm as she took over for the morning watch. The steady thump of the engine cylinders beneath her feet and the splashing of the paddlewheels astern attested to *Spiteful's* steady progress. The sulphurous reek of coal smoke drifted past on the wind of their passage. There were nearly two hours before sunrise, but a glance astern showed her the first glimmers of light streaking the eastern horizon. The Devonshire coastline was invisible to the north, but she fancied she could see the brief glimmers of distant lanterns on the cliffs as countrymen began moving about to prepare themselves for the day.

A slight noise of a closing hatchway announced the arrival of one of her passengers. Mr. Holmes appeared out of the gloom—his day of seasickness must have abated. His hatchet face seemed even more gaunt in the faint light of the binnacle, although his mouth seemed to be smiling. She felt unsure how to judge this man, seemingly foisted upon her by Lord Bond. If he was to be the judge of the fair price the Admiralty would pay for her ships, it was in her best interest to get on good terms, but her reserve was not so easily surmounted.

"Good morning, Miss Stephenson—at least I suspect it must be morning, although I am usually on my way home at this hour of the day in London."

"Good morning, Sir. I hope you do not intend to impress me with the details of your reckless city life." She smiled faintly. "I was brought up to consider the hours of darkness only appropriate to slumber, unless, of course, one's duties require earlier attention."

"Oh dear. I fear you have caught me out. In my defence, I must own that I have never spent every night of the week about town, but was merely relating the usual circumstances of my appearance in public at this time of the night. What hour is it, pray?"

"I was not aware that I was some vengeful fury appointed to pronounce upon your character, Sir. Please do not consider that I mean to improve your habits while you are aboard my ship." She laughed lightly. "It is the start of the morning watch, or a little after four of the clock if you find that easier to comprehend."

"I assure you that I see you as anything but a vengeful fury, Miss Stephenson, but as a most diligent and considerate hostess for this expedition. And you may consider my familiarity with nautical watches to be part of my profession . . . it's just that I am unused to their subjective application." He stared into the darkness over the starboard rail. "Is there land over there? I can see nothing. How do you tell where we are?"

"We are about four nautical miles off Prawle Point by our dead reckoning and will be able to confirm our position once we have sight of the Eddystone light ahead of us."

Mr. Holmes stared into the surrounding darkness, looking

not a jot reassured. "But you cannot possibly be navigating by compass. This is an iron ship."

"I have just relieved Mr. MacRae, and I assure you that it was no accident that I assigned him to this watch, the most exacting bit of seamanship of our voyage to Falmouth. I have complete faith in his navigation."

"The most exacting?"

"Leaving Lyme Bay and ensuring we have ample sea room as we rounded Start Point. But we do have some beneficial use of our binnacle. A judicious placement of some small magnets around the compass serve to supply a modicum of correction to our needle's errors."

"Hmm. Interesting, I have not heard this discussed."

"A practical, seaman's extemporization, Mr. Holmes, that has not had the benefit of educated consideration in the halls of learning. Perhaps you would care to give our method some thought—we may require more practical authority when several vessels of this class are steaming in company."

"I thank you . . . that I shall. But what sights can you take for measurement of our westward progress?"

"Only the sights of our machinery, Sir. Our engine room artificers keep a careful count of our engine revolutions during their watch. You may see here in our watch log." She opened the logbook under the faint light beside the compass in the binnacle. "We have been making between fifteen and sixteen revolutions per minute for most of the second watch. That is equivalent to a ship speed of eight knots, although of course, tide, wind, and currents will have a small effect upon that in terms of longitude on this course."

Mr. Holmes peered at the log and then into her eyes, a smile growing on his lips. "Wonderful. You have invented a whole new form of navigation. The Admiralty should award you a prize for your accomplishment."

"I assure you, Sir, that the accomplishment is in fact but a small part mine, but if a prize were to be offered I would be pleased to see that it goes in suitable proportions to everyone who has had a hand in the matter."

A call from the lookout forrard caused them to cease conversation.

"What do you have?" Roberta called, aware her voice would not carry so far. Another crew member of watch amidships relayed her call.

"A light. I see a light. 'Tis the Eddystone light."

A new swirl of the smoke from the boiler furnaces obscured their view forward, even though the tall funnels' purpose was to disperse the smoke away from the deck as well as ensure good furnace draft. "What bearing?" Roberta shouted.

"Two points off the starboard bow, Cap'n."

"Two points," she mused. "We must be farther south than we expected." She turned to the quartermaster. "Hold our course steady. I will go forward to con this light."

"Aye aye, Cap'n."

Mr. Holmes followed her as she made her way to the bow. They stopped beside the short foremast, its fore-and-aft sail furled on its boom beside them. They shielded their eyes from the stiff breeze.

"Can you see anything?" she asked.

"Not a thing," Mr. Holmes replied.

"I'll have to go up. The Eddystone light can only be seen above the horizon at about fifteen miles." She moved to the shrouds on the starboard side and took a pair of kid gloves from a pouch at her waist to slip on before taking a firm hand grip on the ratlines.

"Good heavens," Mr. Holmes exclaimed. "You mean to climb?"

"Yes. If I wish to see the light, Sir. Now you may understand why I and my lady engineers wear a boiler suit on duty." With that she pulled herself to the level of the bulwark and began to climb.

The breeze, damp with spray, became stronger as she left the slight protection of the hull, but she determined not to stop her progress until she reached the lookout position, where the fore topmast joined the top of the foremast, and climbed from the ratlines onto the narrow platform.

She held on to a rope brailing around the masts to keep from losing her balance in the gusts. "Where is the light?" she asked the young sailor crouching in the lee of the timbers.

He stood to point. "'Twas o'er there, Cap'n. I thinks a squall be hiden' 'en now."

"It was an intermittent light?"

He peered at her. "Nay, 'twere a white or a yellerish light."

"I mean it was by turns a clear light and then darkness . . . one giving way to the other but in the same place?" She thought a detailed description of the light had been given to all the deck crew, but clearly, nothing fixed the knowledge better than actual experience, and these lads had never sailed the Channel before this.

"Oh, aye. I was given ter think 'twas gone out, but then it shone agin."

Roberta nodded and turned her attention to the darkness before her eyes. The ship had been taking the sea smoothly from the deck, but up here every roll was magnified into a drunken lurch. Estimating the bearing to the light would be difficult.

"I say," came Mr. Holmes' voice from the deck below, "are you securely located, Miss Stephenson? Can you see the light?"

"We cannot see the light at present. Possibly a squall is obscuring it."

"Are you coming down? Perhaps I could come up to help."

"I think that unwise, Sir, though I appreciate your thought.

A brisk breeze at night in the Channel is not the time to make your acquaintance with a ship's standing rigging."

"There she be, Cap'n!" the sailor burst out. Pointing with his free arm. "O'er there!"

Roberta raised her head to catch the briefest wink of light before it went out. Judging herself against *Spiteful's* roll, she kept her eyes on the same area until it shone again. She watched a few more alternations before satisfying herself it was the lighthouse—the period of light was less than one fourth of that of darkness, playing out the motion of the clockwork mechanism that rotated the mirror. She estimated the bearing to be less than two points to starboard, but it was greater than one.

She stepped carefully to the shrouds and bent to lower her feet onto the ratlines—it was a more hazard-fraught manoeuver than climbing off them. The wet wood offered little secure hold for the hands' grip until the body's weight was supported by the shrouds. The descent to the deck was easy after this.

"God's grief," Mr. Holmes allowed as she reached the deck, "I should never make a sailor. What happens next?"

"I must go below to the chart room to check our course. By all means come."

Reaching the chart room, Roberta turned up the lamps to afford herself enough light to work. She plotted the direction from the lighthouse to the predicted course of *Spiteful* and shook her head. "This sight puts us twice as far from the coast as we expected."

"That's not good?"

"Hardly, Mr. Holmes. Your need for reassurance when you reached me beside the quartermaster at the wheel would have been betrayed if the error were to the north instead of to the south. We could have run onto the headland."

Mr. Holmes stared.

"But to present the whole sequence of possibilities for your education, I would suggest that our lookout on the foremast would have warned of danger as soon as we steamed close enough for the waves' erratic motions and the sound of breakers upon the rocks to have reached his awareness." She gestured at the chart. "This is intended to avoid such close calls with disaster."

"And to what do you attribute the error?"

Roberta studied the chart. "Probably the effect of a current that has affected our determination of distance covered, as well as drifted us off course. I must admit that steaming at speed through the night is somewhat of a controversial procedure among the maritime fraternity."

"Under canvas, continuing under full sail at night is also frowned upon," he answered. "You have the very good fortune to be able to invent your own seamanship here. I daresay a thousand young mariners of the male persuasion would envy the chance. Having seen your methods, I am assured that the Stephenson vessels are in competent hands."

Roberta did not quite know how to answer; he seemed quite extravagant in his esteem. She was pleased that he immediately turned his attention to the chart, making a response from her superfluous.

After some moments he frowned. "I must observe that the plotting you have carried out could as easily be duplicated with the application of the mathematical principles of trigonometry. Removing some of the need and delay of the watch officer leaving the wheel. Are you familiar with the procedures?"

Roberta regarded him with new eyes as she lowered the flames of the lamps in preparation to returning to the weather deck. "I have some familiarity, Sir, but not in this instance. I would be pleased to have you demonstrate what you suggest when we have more time. At the moment, I must supervise the changing of course necessary to return us to the track we had plotted for the journey."

Chapter Twenty
Stopover Falmouth

Symington Holmes stood at the port rail beside the foremast shrouds as *Spiteful* resumed steaming into Falmouth harbour under the guidance of the harbour pilot. He still smiled at that good man's concern as he attempted to convey the impression he was as comfortable with steam as were *Spiteful's* officers. The chief of them being a woman no doubt added to his distress.

Holmes had to admit a certain solidarity with the man . . . he had always been as uncomfortable around the fairer sex himself, as long as he could remember. He glanced up at the ratlines and pictured Miss Stephenson climbing them again, as she had done before daylight this very morning. He knew he could never have duplicated the feat . . . heights made him very nervous. The memory that he had given her a different impression still lurked in the back of his mind for all his effort to dismiss it.

He watched the unfolding picture of Pendennis Castle as

they steamed past the headland, thankful that the motion of their passage no longer caused him any gastric distress. The waters here were quite calm by comparison with the swell they had steamed into upon leaving Dover. Oh . . . ! Perhaps he had better not let the memory of that first day return.

The roadstead seemed well populated with smaller craft . . . likely fishing craft, as well as a larger bark anchored off the harbour being tended by a pair of Falmouth quay-punts, taking supplies and cargo to and from the shore. If he leaned over the rail, he could see the pilot's similar vessel following far astern of them. This was actually the second time he had been to the port, but the first time, several years before on Admiralty business, he had found little leisure to make himself acquainted with the surroundings.

Carrick Roads, the long inner harbour, was also alive with smaller vessels, and even a pair of naval frigates showing off their black and white colours and black gunports as they rode at anchor. A pair of 32s he surmised, perhaps preparing to take urgent Admiralty messages to English squadrons blockading Brest or Toulon. Or resting from the exertion of a stormy sail to England with urgent dispatches from an admiral of the fleet.

As they rounded the tail of Pendennis Point the town and port came into view. The new railway station at the docks was marked out with the columns of smoke from busy locomotives. Perhaps one of the columns of smoke came from the mid-day express from Exeter . . . he hoped Julian had arrived on it. His own first journey and arrival had been by mail coach from Launceston—the railway still under construction at that time. What had the Old Man wanted? His letter had seemed somewhat bad tempered. He felt glad not to have been the recipient of it.

When *Spiteful* anchored off the docks, several smaller craft and a quay-punt came out to them. This latter proved to have been engaged by Julian, who stood in the bow as the craft came alongside. Miss Stephenson and Lieutenant Worthington—fresh from the engineroom and smelling of heavy lubricating oil—joined him at the gangway to greet the arrivals.

"You made good time, Miss Stephenson," Julian said as he reached the deck. "Are my fellows ready to disembark? I've found our little Dutchman in Carrick Roads . . . . I'll take them there aboard this and be back in a trice. Will you depart again this afternoon?"

"If our messages do not give tidings needing a delay, My Lord. Did you bring us mail?"

Julian held out a small packet to her. "One for Lieutenant Worthington from the Admiralty, and one from Clydebank, my dear. I suspect from your father."

"Why, thank you. They were on the train?" she asked.

"I showed my Admiralty documents at Exeter and had the postmaster take them from the bag for tonight's mail train," Julian replied, then turned as Bloggins and his crew arrived on deck. "Ah, here you all are. Load your sea chests on the quay-punt and get aboard. I will take you to the *Nederlander*, off Mylor in the creek."

"Right yer be, M'Lord."

Julian turned to him. "Mr. Holmes, will you come with us?"

Holmes shrugged. "If you have need of my presence. I suppose I may look forward to a journey aboard the craft in due course, so it will be advisable to make its acquaintance." His thoughts, however, went in a different direction. What had transpired at the meeting in Tiverton? Did their father have some instructions for him, as well?

Roberta remained on deck as the quay-punt left for its run up Carrick Roads and the smaller craft announced their business. A keg of fresh mackerel from Cornwall would be a welcome addition to their diet on the run up the Irish Sea. Lieutenant Worthington went below to read his letter, so she checked with her watch officer before going below to her own cabin.

The letter was indeed from her father . . . he had arrived at the Clydebank yard just three days before. His news was not as welcome as his warm greeting.

"I have been about the local yards and find some lack that will certainly impact your building plans. In short, the supply of iron plate and bars will not be sufficient for your plans to build the ten galleys as well as the larger vessel if all must be accomplished by midsummer next year. In addition, the skilled craftsmen to build the required number of steam engines and boilers do not exist on the Clyde.

"I can supply some of the required boilers, connecting rods and cylinders from Tyneside, but that would necessitate towing the unfinished vessels to the Tyne for installation. I need hardly point out that the Firth and Clyde Canal will not accommodate vessels as large as the galleys you have sold the Admiralty, necessitating a hazardous tow around the north of Scotland in winter weather.

"No doubt many of these problems may be solved once we are together at Clydebank and the construction plans are set in motion. None of this in any way detracts from your triumph in convincing Their Lordships of the soundness of our design and securing the order. I feel the casualty of these difficulties will be our profits, as I see no recourse but to include even more subcontracting to other yards than your first plan envisaged."

Roberta lowered the letter and stared out through the

porthole in the ship's side. She should have asked for more solid reassurances from her fellow shipbuilders on the Clyde, but preparing *Spiteful* for its debut at Chatham had occupied most of her time. This *new* vessel, perhaps three times the tonnage of Spiteful, had completely set her plans—plans she thought were perfectly attainable—far out of the bounds of practicality. If she were not careful meeting their required improvements and alterations, they could bring the Stephenson shipyard to the brink of bankruptcy.

A sad circumstance for such a wonderful coup of but three weeks before. Now she felt the urge to leave the harbour and churn the Irish Sea to foam. The sooner she was back at her yard and with access to her design loft and her best assistant engineers the better. She must not despair . . . it required but fresh ingenuity and creative design to overcome this new setback . . . as she had overcome so many before.

Christopher Hoare

Chapter Twenty-one
Plans in Progress

Roberta stood aside until the chief stoker opened the watertight door in the iron bulkhead, then lowered her head to pass through. She waited for Lieutenant Worthington and Mr. Holmes to follow before she smiled and took the storm lantern from the man. "Thank you, Mr. Mishner. You may keep it closed; we will go up to the weather deck by the forward companionway."

"Right y'are, Cap'n."

Mr. Holmes, looking unusually seaman-like in a borrowed boilersuit, stood with his hand upon the ironwork of the bulkhead. "And what is the purpose of this structure, Miss Stephenson?"

"It serves more than one purpose, Sir. It closes off the boiler room from the forward part of the ship and keeps it from flooding if the ship has been holed forward by contact with the enemy; it also closes off the forward part of the ship from danger should a mishap with the boilers result in an explosion."

Mr. Holmes pulled his hand away from the bulkhead. "An explosion? Is that likely?"

"Not with complete observation and control by a qualified steam engineer, but I felt the structure a wise precaution for a ship in the chaos and confusion of a sea battle. I would also point out another purpose, in that it stiffens the hull at this point and so renders a structural service."

"You sees, Mr. Holmes," Worthington added. "That the whole engine room and boilers is isolated toward the stern of the ship; makin' enough weight to cause some hogging o' the stern structure in a heavy sea." He craned his neck and pointed where the bulkhead terminated at the weather deck level. "This big iron wall serves to carry part o' that load to 'elp the keel structure."

Roberta raised the lantern and Mr. Holmes' eyes travelled from the top, down to the slot in the deck where the iron vanished to meet the keel. "I see. I have never been asked to pronounce upon the structure of a vessel constructed entirely in iron . . . . Composite build, yes, with wooden timbers on an iron frame, but nothing like this."

Worthington seemed to consider a reply. "I say, Miss Stephenson. An idea have just struck me. This bulkhead divides the hull into two almost equal halves."

"Very close to that, Lieutenant. What does that suggest to you?"

"In your father's letter that you showed me, he mentions the *Spiteful* class hulls bein' too long to pass through the Firth and Clyde Canal. 'Tis a pity, cause wi'out engines and paddle wheels they would all but fit the locks."

Roberta looked again at the bulkhead as she visualized the ship's lines plan. "But half the hull might fit?"

"Exactly, Miss. If 'twere possible to send the hulls to Grangemouth in two parts, they could be joined together there, on this bulkhead, an' then be towed to Tyneside for the engines."

Mr. Holmes stared at the two of them. "Build a ship in two halves and join it together? Surely it cannot be done . . . the keel—"

"Is not a single piece of timber as in a wooden ship, Mr. Holmes," Roberta said. "We can insert a heavy iron plate to join the two halves and fishplate it to the existing keels in those halves. The bulkhead structure can also strengthen the joint. I think you have made an admirable suggestion, Lieutenant."

"Thank you, Miss Stephenson. I really do think that Mr. Holmes' presence and questions has brought us to a new and clearer understanding of our profession."

"I would rather have hoped that my contributions would have been something more sterling," Mr. Holmes replied with a somewhat lopsided smile, "but I'm pleased to help in any way that I can."

"I feel sure that when it comes time for you to regard our engineering and costs in your own professional manner, Sir, you will regard some of our eccentricities with a kinder eye," Roberta said. "The costs of building each vessel in not two but three—and perhaps even more—shipyards will add greatly to our building costs. The locating and hiring of engineers to even supervise such diverse operations will be a daunting task."

"Then perhaps I can offer a suggestion there," Mr. Holmes replied. "The Admiralty must supply engineer lieutenants like Mr. Worthington who must accompany each vessel through its multiple transformations and ensure that the whole is a perfect representation of its parts."

"A good idea." Roberta turned to Worthington. "How would that suit you, Lieutenant? Travelling engineering inspector . . . surely worthy of a promotion."

"I believes I have already received h'intimation of such a promotion, Miss Stephenson. Commander Ripley have suggested the need for an officer to inter'duce the new ship officers to their duties by makin' the *Spiteful* the floatin' school. The Admiralty wishes to purchase the vessel . . . as soon as the new dock work be done, and have myself command the vessel at Chatham. 'Twould be a Commander's post."

"Why, how gratifying for you, Lieutenant. But I must admit to some loss that we would suffer from your good fortune." Roberta paused to marshal her words. She had never considered him before as more than a congenial inspector of her work, but she had to admit that his down to earth good sense and encouragement had been of great value to her. "You have been more than an Admiralty inspector, you have been an engineering partner in many respects."

"Well . . . I . . . ," Worthington began. "Er . . . Shall we continue our inspection o' the ship? What would you see next, Mr. Holmes . . . the ram bow?"

Roberta smiled to herself, quite sure that if they were located in a brighter lit area of the ship she would see that his face was as bright a hue as it had been in the Admiralty boardroom. What did that signify? Was his deferential manner to her liking or was it not?

Lord Bond stood at the stern, as close as the splashing from the two paddlewheels allowed. They were mostly invisible behind a light iron shroud, that Roberta had explained had been introduced as a convenience, but now after their Channel voyage, would be strengthened into a heavier structure to prevent following waves from submerging the paddlewheels before they dipped into the sea.

She was somewhere below, conducting Symington on a

tour of the ship on this first day of their resumed voyage to Clydebank. They were somewhere near St. David's Head in St. George's Channel, about to pass from the narrows into the Irish Sea.

What was he to do about the Old Man's veto?

He felt certain that she was the only person confident enough to put together the information about the French behemoth and allow the building of a ship strong enough to counter it. She had devised the *Spiteful* on third hand knowledge of the pyroscaphes. But even Viscount Melville disapproved of his plan to take her to Antwerp.

He now had enough documentation to insert a team of four persons into the Netherlands—two escorts using the spies' papers and two intelligence gatherers using the American passport. Surely he could keep her safe with the extra help.

But the Old Man had refused his leave of even offering Roberta the security of a Platonic marriage to protect her respectability from the likely necessity of cohabiting with a "husband" on the journey. The Old Man had told him to use Symington. Symington! Clearly the Marquess didn't understand the personal reasons why such a suggestion would be meaningless. And at any event, he was the one who wanted to cohabit with the woman. *His* nights were the nights becoming troubled with dreams of her.

He noticed the master leave the quartermaster at the wheel and walk to the starboard rail, and decided to join him. "How is our voyage progressing, Mr. MacRae? Should we see St. David's Head?"

"Steamin' fair, My Lord. I sees the rocks called The Smalls droppin' astern so we should see the Head in another hour's steamin'."

"Rocks?"

MacRae pointed. "There, My Lord. Where ye sees the waves break, about eight cables' length distant."

Lord Bond stared, but it took several minutes before he fancied he could make out the place where the waves broke against the rocks. "We are clear when we see them astern?"

"Aye, My Lord. I jus' be lookin' fer confirmation afor I changes our headin' to starboard, and pick up the fifth degree of longitude as us be leavin' St. David."

"I see. You must have sailed this course before."

"Many times, My Lord. I were master of an East Indiaman, the *Berkshire*, afore I gave up the ocean to ply the waters of the Firth of Clyde. I had a wife then, y'see."

"And now you are away from home again in Miss Stephenson's service."

"Aye. She be a fine lady, and 'tis an honour to serve her."

Lord Bond had to agree, but with only an unspoken assent to himself. He stood watching the change of course and musing upon the benefits and drawbacks of the state of marriage until Roberta and Symington arrived on deck from below.

It was later that night before he found the time to speak his mind to Symington; they were preparing for the night in the cabin they shared.

"What did the Old Man have to say?" Symington asked as he sat on the edge of his cot unfastening his boots.

"About what?"

"You know very well what about, Julian. Do not try to play games with me. Did he ask about the ships, the next spying mission, or the young lady?"

"All three. He suggested that you should be the man to escort her."

"Me? I thought you were smitten by her."

"Smitten? Is that where he gained such an impression? You are his eyes and ears in the Admiralty—what did you write in your reports to him?"

Symington pulled off a boot and pushed it under the cot. "What's this? You are accusing me of spying upon you?"

"Somebody had passed him a quite thorough report." Lord Bond hesitated—the incompleteness of the Marquess' information about the *Spiteful* suggested he had received word of the official account; of the French sloop being sunk by a steam tug. Of course, Symington was devious enough to leave out the exact details on purpose. "Do not pretend that you do not pass on Admiralty secrets when he asks."

"Good Lord! Next, you will be suspecting me of being the Frenchmen's informer."

"No, we are closer to identifying him, I am told. Several of the King's German Legion officers suspect Gottliebe is the same person who betrayed two Line Regiments when the French created the Kingdom of Westphalia, in 1807."

"That is the puppet government ruled by Napoleon's brother Jerome?"

"Yes, but you have not answered my question about informing the Old Man."

"I tell him as little as I can, brother mine. Mostly about the doings of post captains and admirals and the back-room jockeying for promotion."

"Really?" In retrospect, he did not doubt the truth of the answer. They had grown up together once his mother had passed away and there was no one in the household to complain about raising a bastard son as a family member. Symington had always been a secretive sort of fellow. "Who do you think has sent the Old Man this latest report?"

"Ah, pure speculation will not answer your question, but I would suspect any number of private secretaries to Their Lordships. What did they tell him of Miss Stephenson?"

"Only that I was enamoured of her." Bond paused as the thought struck him. This feeling was nothing new, he had loved and fallen out of love before. "He has taken a very firm stance against that."

"You still want her to be a part of the spying at Antwerp?"

"Who else is qualified to make sense of the scraps of incomplete information we might glean from our observation of the shipyards? Do you feel a competent naval architect from your inspection this afternoon?"

"I feel I have a growing understanding, but confess it to be less that of our fine naval lieutenant's at this juncture. But he is already spoken for—the engineering department wants to place him in command of this vessel to school the officers and ratings who will be posted aboard the other ships of the class."

"You learned this from the Admiralty?"

"No. From Worthington's own lips this afternoon when we were on our inspection tour. I also learned one more thing— our Black Gang lieutenant is as smitten by our lady captain as are you; and she is very pleased with the quality of his engineering knowledge." Symington smiled slyly. "He proposed a valuable suggestion that might ease the difficulties with transferring the incomplete hulls to Tyneside."

"Did he, by damn?"

"She was very impressed—you have a very powerful rival for her affections there."

"Rival! What nonsense. I doubt he earns more than fifty pounds a year . . . and should be astounded if there were the slightest suggestion of a subsidy from a wealthy patron. All I need do is turn the Old Man's mind to a more accepting frame and the lure of the nobility will cast him into the nether darkness . . . ." Bond laughed shortly. "Back to the stokehold he rose from."

Chapter Twenty-two
Assessing the Gentlemen

Late in the morning of the next day the *Spiteful* steamed up the Clyde toward Clydebank. Symington Holmes stood in the bow watching their progress and smelling the mix of river weeds and heather from the hills. Almost all the river traffic seemed to be steam powered; the few merchant brigs in sight seemed out of place with the black smoke smears and higher wakes of tens of Clyde puffers bustling like ants around them.

He'd heard of the puffers, of course, but never visited their home waters to see them. So called because of their puffing one-cylindered steam engines, they were small vessels adapted from the traditional gabberts, single-masted sailing barges plying the trade routes of the islands in earlier years. Today, he felt sure more steamers plied the Clyde than the Thames at London.

"We'll be mooring at Clydebank within the hour," a voice behind him broke his reverie.

He turned to see Miss Stephenson had exchanged her

seaman's garb for sturdy travelling dress and even a jaunty flat-brimmed hat tied under her chin. It was not the first time he'd seen her in a woman's finery, but remembered the earliest occasion had been while she plied the corridors of the Admiralty, and he had been one of the curious who had found a reason to leave his office for a glimpse. He felt a slight disquiet; customarily, young women had never attracted this attention from him.

"Thank you for the information, Miss Stephenson. I have never been on the Clyde before and find it enough enjoyment to be pleased if our journey should even last longer."

She smiled, rather familiarly, but then he knew it merely a sign of her confidant manner. "I feel sure you will be sailing in the Clyde enough these next two weeks that you will come to know it as well as you do the Thames, Sir."

"I look forward to that. The town we just passed—what name would it have?"

"On the North bank? That would be Dumbarton. Mr. MacRae has his family there in a pretty rented cottage."

"I see you have let Mr. MacRae bring the *Spiteful* in this morning. He told Lord Bond he used to sail here with an East Indiaman."

"Yes, the *Berkshire*. He knows the river so much better than I that it would be foolishness for me to claim the command in his stead. I feel somewhat the truant, but it really is time for me to put aside my captaincy and resume the management role."

"And what honorific must we use to address you in this role?"

She laughed, her whole face lighting up with amusement. "Why, Mr. Holmes, I assure you that I claim no false dignity with the role. To friends and colleagues alike I will answer to Miss Roberta when in the works. The factory and the shipyard are no places for much formality."

"Really? I find that most unusual. In the Admiralty everyone is addressed either by his naval rank or as Mister. One soon gains an impression that the ceilings would fall in if anyone strayed into such informality . . . but then you are now acquainted with its ways . . . although I do believe you are the first young lady ever to enter the premises on business."

"I suspected as much, Sir. I was very glad of the kindness and support His Lordship offered me in those meetings."

"But I doubt if even he would go so far as to address you as Miss . . . ah . . . Roberta." There—he had done it. It felt almost like falling off a cliff, and he dreaded to think what would happen should he reach the bottom. No, he would take stronger guard and be sure that he should never fall that far.

Mr. George Stephenson arrived at the works jetty as the *Spiteful* completed tying up. The first down the gangplank was Roberta in a respectable travelling outfit spoiled by one of her frivolous bonnets; she came to him for an exchange of filial kisses.

"Welcome home, my dear. I hope *this* voyage was uneventful."

"Perfectly, Father. Is all well here?"

He smiled slightly and allowed his shoulders a slight shrug before the next arrival, his sister Nelly, whom he bussed with a slight peck on the cheek. "Comfortable journey, old thing?"

"Old thing yersel', I bin livin' the life of a duchess wi' a ship full o' grand gentlemen."

Roberta introduced Lord Bond in a marked reversal of etiquette. He vaguely remembered the young man from an Institute meeting a year previous. All parties pretended that nothing inappropriate had taken place. Perhaps it hadn't; he had set his daughter on her own course through society when he had agreed to make her a manager in the business. He should be glad and accept that Lord Bond had taken the novelty with good grace. Perhaps the young man was a stout heart and no fop for false dignities—he should be grateful for that. "Welcome to Clydebank and the Stephenson Shipyard, My Lord. Please consider us at your complete disposal. We are honoured to have you visit."

"Indeed, Sir, it is I who must express my fullest gratitude at your—and your daughter's—offer of hospitality, and perhaps some inconvenience with ignorant noses poking about in your premises."

"Not at all, My Lord. We would be no less pleased to place ourselves at your convenience than we are to do what we can for Britain in these difficult times."

Lord Bond smiled and turned slightly as another gentleman reached the jetty. "I must introduce you to this stalwart of the offices of Admiralty, Mr. Stephenson. Please meet Mr. Symington Holmes, an advisor to the offices of finance for the Royal Navy . . . and in the present moment a student of steamship design and construction for our investigations into the plans of the French."

"Delighted to meet you, Mr. Holmes. I must assure you of our most diligent assistance to your endeavours while you are here. My daughter's letter tells me that you have offered to speak of a number of interesting applications of mathematics of value to engineering. We are not well schooled in the science but are more than eager to learn as much as we may be able to absorb."

"Thank you, Mr. Stephenson, for your generous support of our affairs. It will be most gratifying if we find mutual interests and mutual benefit in our association."

Holmes seemed a rather strange fish to Mr. Stephenson, perhaps a slight function of the deerstalker hat he wore, but also in his rather offhand use of manners. He had not included Roberta for her share of the thanks when given the opportunity, which common courtesy would surely expect; but his daughter had seemed entirely unmoved by the omission. Did he sense something there? He would know better when he'd seen these visitors about the works . . . he was a common man who would rather make his judgements in familiar surroundings.

The last to be introduced was the naval lieutenant, Worthington, an entirely familiar object of interest in that he was a product of coal and steam worked upon in good Northern industries. His voice proclaimed him a man of modest upbringing and straightforward understanding and Mr. Stephenson was glad to walk in his company as they made a brief tour of the shipyard before leaving for the company mansion for dinner. The rear of the party was also a good vantage point to watch Roberta guiding the two gentlemen through the activity . . . and particularly to watch their attentions to her.

Roberta turned from the shipyard gateway as the carriage carrying her father and the guests clattered away over the cobbles. Her father said he would send the trap for her when they reached the mansion. She turned to Clara Brad, her number two in the shipyard. "Do we have enough coin in the safe to pay off *Spiteful's* crew, Clara?"

"I don't think so, Roberta. Perhaps half of them, but remember, men will be needed to unload the ship stores and coal before she goes into dry dock on Tuesday."

"I think enough live locally that we can expect to have sufficient help for that task. Let's go to the office. I cannot take the Admiralty warrant to the bank in Glasgow until Monday morning, but I can at least pay the married men who will need to take money to their families."

On the way to the office they walked past *Spiteful* and she called up to those tightening mooring lines. "I will need the married men to be paid off to come to the office soon, Mr. MacRae."

"Right y'are, lassie. I will leave the starboard watch aboard this evening to clean up the ship."

"You can have twenty-four hours at home, if you like. The ship goes into dry dock on Tuesday."

"Very good. I'll be back to make certain we're ready for that; Mr. Anderson can look after what needs done until then."

Anderson was the first mate of the deck crew. "Would you ask Miss Grandin to come to the office as soon as she's finished in the engine room? And please bring the crew log when you come, so I can see what is owed."

"Aye aye. Miss Elizabeth has already been pullin' the fires in the boilers."

She and Clara Brad looked over the records and shipyard orders for the period she had been away. Her father had done the same, but may have missed items he had not been familiar with before his arrival. She saw his entry about his visits to the shipyards she had arranged for construction of the contracted out spiteful hulls. One of them had proven difficult—claiming an unavoidable delay completing a vessel on one slip. Her father's note made her smile—he suspected the "blaggards" of inventing difficulties to demand more payment. She would make her own visit as soon as she could find the time.

When Elizabeth Grandin arrived at the office they discussed what engineering and boiler room artificers would be required for the dry dock work. "Those men we will need to start work on Tuesday . . . no, make that Wednesday. The ship will not be ready until the low tide has allowed the dock to drain . . . those men have their time off first. I'm short of coin at the moment, but will pay everyone who needs to leave tonight."

Elizabeth smiled. "Where do I go tonight? The mansion will be hard put to house all the new arrivals, but I can sleep aboard if I have to."

"Yes, you are likely correct—I will not know until I speak to Aunt Nelly about the arrangements with the housekeeper. Come with me in the trap when I leave. You can dine with us and if there is no room for you, you can share mine tonight."

Clara Brad looked up from her money counting. "I can ask about a vacancy in Mrs. MacDonald's rooming house—it is just next door to my digs."

"There," Roberta said, "By tomorrow we can make such arrangements as necessary. How are we with the cash, Miss Brad?"

"What large amounts do you need?"

"Mr. MacRae will need to take his two month's pay with him this evening—that's nine pounds. What about you, Elizabeth? You will be in arrears the same."

"If I'm to stay in the mansion for the weekend, I'll not need much pay until Monday—unless you expect to entertain the gentlemen with cards, tonight."

Roberta shook her head. "I didn't arrange to entertain them. This is a working visit. And do not play cards against Mr. Holmes . . . I'm told he is unbeatable."

"Is he?" Elizabeth said with a sly grin. "I wondered who held your fancy and now I know. *Unbeatable*, you say?"

"Oh, away with you! Don't be so silly. I have no interest in any of our visitors." Roberta felt irritation at her friend, who was usually so level-headed and reliable. She spoke the perfect truth, so why did her two companions exchange such furtive smiles?

Chapter Twenty-three
Popularity Contests

Sunday morning the house party and most of the servants went to church in Old Kilpatrick, but instead of continuing the Sabbath ritual, Roberta took her leave in the afternoon to prepare to go to the works. All of the gentlemen offered to accompany her.

"I thank you all, but I will be able to work better without the distraction. Elizabeth will come with me . . . if that is acceptable."

Elizabeth Grandin smiled and nodded. "It is. You need help with measurements?"

"Yes. You will know what to do. I must check on the lines for the next spitefuls to lay down."

"Do you want the carriage?" Father asked.

"No. I don't want to disturb the coachmen's day off. We will drive ourselves in the trap."

Lord Bond shook his head. "Such devotion to duty. You ladies surely do not need to work every day. When do you find the leisure to dance or attend entertainments?"

Roberta frowned at him. "When work is done, My Lord. You are well acquainted with the urgency of our construction and I must work out the details of the new bulkhead join before the yard men can begin cutting metal tomorrow morning."

Lord Bond threw up his hands as if in surrender. "Fainites! Mea culpa. I will offer no more obstacle to your mission, but I must offer to help with the driving, if nothing else. I promise to make no sound nor interruption while you work."

Roberta smiled. "Again I thank you, My Lord, but I will feel more at liberty to work if I am not preventing you from more interesting pursuits. We may be late back for dinner."

They had not gone far in the trap before Roberta turned to look at Elizabeth beside her. "What so amused you and Clara yesterday? Do you suppose I am expecting a proposal from one of these gentlemen visitors? They are colleagues and associates—nothing more."

Elizabeth regarded her steadily. "Perhaps you think you are not becoming involved with any of them, *ma Cherie*, but they are very constant in their attentions to you. You had best be considering their merits and trying to gauge who would best satisfy your heart."

"Oh nonsense." She did not need this distraction when she must have a clear head for her work. Elizabeth did not often lapse into French, a sign of her Émigré background and her closeness with her grandmother who spoke only French. Good Lord, perhaps she would have been better off with Lord Bond's assistance this afternoon.

"It is not nonsense, it is very much a matter of your good sense. Do you choose to be a lady engineer all your life or do you expect to marry one day . . . perhaps have children?"

Roberta busied herself with guiding the horse while she strove to dismiss the arguments. "What of you, Elizabeth? You quiz me, but you are almost thirty and still a handsome woman. Do you see yourself as a steam engineer for the rest of your life?"

They negotiated a crossroads in silence before Elizabeth responded. "I could perhaps refuse to answer your very direct question, Roberta, on the grounds that it is most unfair to throw a perfectly sensible and pertinent question back at the questioner. But I will answer it to this degree—I have received two very great disappointments in my earlier life. The young man I thought I might marry was carried off by consumption at the age of nineteen . . . then another man jilted me for another, mere weeks before our planned marriage. Do not think ill of me for deciding that the bowels of a steamship offered me a more prosperous and happy life than would any representative of the male gender."

"But if one offered you marriage now—what would you say?"

Elizabeth regarded her coolly. "It would depend upon his income and his reputation. I should regard his favours as I would any other offer of employment."

"Surely not. Is your heart quite resigned to not finding love?"

"It did, twice, and then lost it. I do not think the man exists who might kindle such hope in it again."

Roberta reflected quickly. "I was once offered a marriage, but it was very much a matter of business interest, and so turned it down. I became my Father's manager here precisely in order to avoid being married off to any ambitious engineer who thought my greatest charms lay in the factory I might bring him."

"Then perhaps you should be looking very favourably on Lord Bond. Doubtless he is worth much more than even the prosperous Stephenson enterprises, and does not need to marry an heiress."

"And you suppose he would marry a commoner?"

"It has happened before."

"In fairy tales, perhaps. I think him quite charming and very handsome, but fear he is accustomed to using his title as a means of getting his way."

"You think he has a bad reputation?"

Roberta hesitated. "I do not like to repeat false rumours, but there are stories about him being told in some of the best London households. I will merely say that the stories involve more than one engagement, neither resulting in a marriage union . . . and the more reliable evidence of a breach of promise suit brought before the Lords."

"If these are not false rumours, they are indeed a very grave indictment. So, what about Mr. Holmes?"

"Oh, really, Elizabeth, must we investigate them all?" Roberta flicked the pony's reins in irritation. "Very little is known about him."

"But you have investigated?"

Roberta shrugged. "I did ask some questions of people . . . friends of the Stephenson business and other connected trades-people in London when I was there. Of his family, only a mother is known . . . perhaps a widow . . . who lives in Kent. It is assumed that a wealthy patron paid his way at Cambridge."

"But he is a brilliant mathematician. That much is true?"

"Oh, I have no doubt about his brilliance, but it is perhaps the product of eccentricity. His only interest seems to be playing at cards, when he can find opponents, since he never loses. He spends nothing on his comforts or his dress . . . that odd hat he wore as we came up the Clyde yesterday. His Admiralty pay is believed to be sufficient to keep a good house in town, but he lives in a few rooms in an unfashionable part of London."

"Perhaps he sends the money to his mother."

"Very dutiful, I am sure, but no recommendation to a potential spouse."

They turned into the street leading to the shipyard gate. "So that leaves the stalwart lieutenant. He is to receive a good promotion, I hear."

"Ah, Mister Worthington. He seems to have only one fault, and that is his overpowering modesty. I do not know what upbringing might have produced that—except perhaps extreme poverty and an overbearing parent."

"Your father finds him very acceptable. He is the visitor he converses with most of all."

"Yes, I noticed. But I am not likely to accept a suitor upon my father's recommendation. Not again."

Lord Bond sat in the drawing room reading a newspaper for less than half of an hour before his pride urged him to trump Miss Stephenson's devotion to her duties with one of his own. Did he not have plans to put into motion? Did he not have people to speak with? Even on a Sunday, he might make a preliminary call.

Within the half of another hour he sat in the saddle of a riding mount he had borrowed from Mr. Stephenson's neighbour and galloped down the road toward Glasgow. The animal was of a rather inferior quality, but would serve his purpose. No doubt the rural squire found it suitable for expeditions around his estate but Lord Bond decided that he would make all arrangements necessary to hire a better mount while he resided in Scotland.

His afternoon project met with more fortune than he might have hoped. The headquarters of the regiment he wanted was easier to find than he had feared, and the Officer's Mess a hive of activity over the preparations for an entertainment that evening. General Auchtermuchty, whom he had purposed to meet, was kind enough to give him an hour of his time. All in all, a very satisfying turn of events.

Sitting in the General's private rooms in the Officers' Mess, they first discussed the war and its unfortunate turn over their brandies. The General looked at him keenly. "Am I to understand that you are on official business these days, young man?"

Lord Bond inclined his head slightly. "I am, Sir, but I fear I am at liberty to say very little about those duties. I may tell you that I am currently a servant of the Admiralty, who are desirous of information gained beyond the shorelines of Europe."

"The invasion preparations?" the General suggested, raising his eyebrows.

Lord Bond shrugged. "As a consequence, my purpose here is to ask for the loan of an infantry company for a week or two. I would like them to be assigned to guard duties at the steamship yards on the Clyde."

The General's eyes opened wide. "Good Lord, man. You think the French will strike here?"

Lord Bond shook his head. "No, General. My purpose is not to defend against the French but to teach some of our people how a shipyard should be protected. There are vital secrets in both ours and their shipyards—and the Admiralty charges me with the task of ensuring theirs are more likely to be revealed."

General Auchtermuchty regarded him with narrowed eyes. "Your words have veiled meaning, but I understand . . . you are hinting at something you cannot discuss. Verra good, laddie."

"I assure you that the time of your infantry company will not be wasted . . . and hopefully they too will derive new skills from the experience."

After dinner at the Mess, Lord Bond urged his borrowed

mount into a gallop and left the streets of Glasgow crowded with churchgoers on their ways to Mass and to Evensong. His mind turned again to his deliberations of the afternoon. Those persons who might be called upon to travel secretly to Antwerp to spy on the French steamships, particularly Symington and Miss Stephenson, needed some practical experience in entering forbidden locations safely. Luckily his interlocutor of the afternoon, General Auchtermuchty, had wholeheartedly acceded with his request for a military detachment for the shipyards.

The decision of the Admiralty to promote Worthington to the command of the *Spiteful* and station the vessel at Chatham to train naval crews to man the other vessels of the class had not sat well with his plans at all. He had intended to pair the lieutenant with Symington under the identities provided by the French spies' documentation; while he and Miss Stephenson travelled under the cover of the American passport. Now he needed another engineer . . . or at least a useful spy, to use the French identities. He must write to Their Lordships at the Admiralty this very evening.

With luck, very few days would elapse before the general came up with a suitable military force to carry out the guarding of the shipyards. Ostensibly guarding the yards against French spying, but in reality providing the venue for training his very amateur spies.

Chapter Twenty-four
One Embarrassed; One Lies

Her Monday started with a visit to the bank in Glasgow to cash the Admiralty draft. When she returned at noon, Roberta went immediately to her design office at the shipyard to begin some drafts for the proposed larger warship. Mr. Holmes accompanied her and proved most helpful in arriving at calculated numbers for the progressively larger ship designs that would be required to sink the French leviathan.

She looked up from her sketches to watch him filling pages of foolscap with notations and formulae. The recognition crept into her mind that Mr. Holmes would make a valuable helpmate in the Stephenson yards—perhaps enough to outweigh her concern of his more phlegmatic moods and manner in more social matters. She picked up a pencil. Better she keep herself upon the proper course to satisfy the needs of Admiralty and Britain and leave the unknown possibilities and destinations of herself to more suitable occasions.

He looked up from his figuring. "The ratio of inertial forces to viscous forces must be maintained in each enlarged design," he pointed out. "That way the performance characteristics may be kept constant and the engine power needed more easily determined."

Roberta moved closer to scan the last page of his figures and saw that they indeed did produce the characteristics she looked for. "Why, I thank you, Sir. I do believe you have saved me from many hours of trial and error calculations." She hesitated as Mr. Holmes turned enough so that his face came much closer to hers—close enough that she could feel his breath on her cheek. He seemed quite intense in his expression . . . almost as if he had the intention of . . . Surely not. Not in this manner. "Mr. Holmes, what are you doing?"

He jerked back. "Why nothing . . . nothing at all." His wide opened eyes gave him an expression of profound surprise—as if he had hardly been aware that he had come so close. "I . . . I was contemplating—er—some mathematical transformations."

Roberta pressed her hand to her breast. "Oh, I felt quite concerned that you had entertained an intention . . . an intention . . . Oh. Never mind, let me continue what I had intended to say." The words rushed out. "The Admiralty letter requesting the Stephenson Yard to submit proposals for their consideration suggest three designs should be submitted, of two thousand, two thousand three hundred, and two thousand six hundred tons, but leave it up to the tenderers . . . ourselves . . . to determine the proportions of the hulls as long as the vessel can maintain thirteen knots in a seaway."

Mr. Holmes took a deep breath and moved a few inches farther away. "And your enlarged spiteful design will do that?"

Roberta still felt the heat in her cheeks but thought to try to ignore it. "I think so," she said in a businesslike voice. "The engine designs are quite flexible at this stage. My father suggests using locomotive boilers from the Tyneside works to provide the required steam. The vessel's speed will be a factor of the steam supply, and so I merely need to provide accommodation in the hulls for the required number of boilers."

"They will all be of the same locomotive pattern?"

"Yes, and they have been proven over a number of years. I believe we have an advantage there over the Laird Shipyard at Birkenhead, who have also been asked to tender for the contract."

"Yes, I was surprised at that," Holmes said. "I thought the First Lord to be very confident of your abilities, but perhaps the full Admiralty committee decided on the more cautious approach of spreading the responsibility."

"And you will be one of the experts asked to pronounce upon the designs?"

"Yes," Holmes said with a smile. "I must admit it will tax my impartiality to the extreme, since I see many of my ideas could be included in your design, but I will not be alone in my pronouncements and am confident that the results will speak for themselves."

Roberta regarded his absorbed concentration as he looked down at the pages she returned to him and raised his quill to add some numbers. He really was a most agreeable man . . . as long as he was given a problem to occupy his restless brain.

The door to the office opened and Father and Lieutenant Worthington entered. "Making progress, my dear?" Father asked.

"Indeed we are. I believe that with Mr. Holmes' mathematical assistance we have arrived at some relationships that will allow me to determine the lines for the Admiralty's submissions before the afternoon is done."

"Wonderful, wonderful," Father answered. "And I have come to inform you of Lieutenant Worthington's generous offer—or would you prefer to tell her yourself, my good fellow?"

She and Mr. Holmes set down their quills and turned to face him.

"It is 'pparent that the yard is almost overwhelmed with the needs laid upon it, Miss Stephenson. Your father is occupied to the fullness of his time with supervisin' the buildin' of the contracted spiteful ships, both here and in they other yards. You are simil'ly engrossed in preparin' the submission of the Yard to the Admiralty tender . . . but amid all this activity the *Spiteful* itself is in dry dock and in need of supervision as the required mod'fications an' improvements are added."

"Indeed, Lieutenant. I must agree that I hardly know how we will be able to accomplish all our tasks within the time allowed."

"I have spoken with Miss Grandin an' with Mr. MacRae, an' offered to provide the supervisory inspections needed if they will act as the shipyard's assistants to organise the men at their work. They have assented. It seems a most satisfactory 'rrangement—since I also have the responsibility of accepting the delivery o' the vessel into the hands of the Royal Navy as its intended commander. Any defect would be mine own, an' I am sure that we will be able to avoid such as might escape a less involved supervisor."

Roberta looked at Father. "Do you approve, Sir?"

"Within reason. I told the Lieutenant that he must forward any difficulties involving engineering and cost decisions to either of us as might be most conveniently available."

"Yes. If you are away at one of the other yards, I can leave my plans and models to assist him. But it really is a most generous offer, Sir. How fortunate we have been to have all you gentlemen at Clydebank at this opportune time."

She saw Mr. Holmes hold the eyes of Lieutenant Worthington. "It really is a benefit, old chap, that we are able to thus prepare for our future duties in the actual circumstances that will surround them. I think Lord Bond will be impressed when you tell him of your suggestion . . . and if I may offer my own—if you invite him to accompany you on your duties and so afford him the practical experience he came here to acquire."

When he learned of the Lieutenant's offer, Lord Bond expressed suitable approbation, but it did not trump his irritation at the necessity for consulting the First Lord on the matter of finding another candidate to replace Worthington in the spying mission. After speaking with Miss Stephenson at dinner he learned he must direct two letters to London, not just about personnel but also about a technical question he had no expertise in.

When they returned to the topic in the library later, she confessed to the problem of determining the degree of protection that the crew of the new warship would need.

"Lieutenant Worthington suggested the use of thicker iron plates toward the bows of both the spitefuls as well as the larger vessel to protect the crew from the cannon fire of ships they intend to ram. However, I have no knowledge of the thickness of the plates that would be required. Has the Admiralty investigated the equivalent protection of iron as compared to twelve inches of sound oak timber?"

"Not that I know of, Miss Stephenson. Perhaps Mr. Holmes knows."

"I'm afraid not. I asked him and he had to inform me that Their Lordships of the Admiralty had given no thought to using the protection of iron for warships. They are wedded to the protection of wooden walls, and have no plans to supplement them with iron."

"We may have some yardstick once we penetrate the French shipyard and learn what armour thickness they plan."

She looked pensive. "I suppose that might answer, but it will be rather late. If we could borrow an eighteen pounder cannon, perhaps we might make a trial ourselves."

He frowned. "I would not recommend such an attempt, my dear. Not only would it add more work to your already full load—I fear it would prove a very hazardous enterprise. Only the most experienced gunners should attempt such an experiment. I do have a friend in the Royal Artillery at Woolwich . . . . I will write him for his knowledge of the matter as well as the possibility of *their* making a trial. Who would supply these iron plates for the experiments?"

"I had not investigated to that degree, My Lord, but I will consider the matter further. The best and thickest iron plates that I would hope to use come from Derbyshire."

"Then I will see what a few letters may answer, but I also have another matter to discuss with you. I want to place some soldiers in the shipyards as guards—not necessarily to ward off a threat but to act as participants in some much needed training for our putative spies. I would like you and Miss Grandin to take part—to evaluate the quality of their discoveries, of course."

"Really? How much time will this require?" Their discussion was interrupted at this point when her father arrived and she addressed her next words to him. "His Lordship has presented a request, Father. I hope you will listen to his intention and offer your assent."

Mr. Stephenson seemed a bit nonplussed at her words so Lord Bond quickly amplified upon them. "It concerns the matter of my imminent departure to prepare for my *clandestine* visit to the Continent, Sir. I wish to engage in something of a charade to test our fitness for the intelligence gathering expedition."

Mr. Stephenson seemed, if it were possible, to be even more confused, but his daughter came to the rescue. "Lord

Bond wishes to use our shipyard and works as a counterfeit replica of the premises in Antwerp where Boney's people are building their steamships. He wishes to conduct an exploration as if we were trespassers attempting to gather knowledge that might be otherwise forbidden."

"Ah, I see," Mr. Stephenson said with a much lightened expression. "You wish to learn how to spy upon our shipyard. I confess I know nothing about the arts of either spying or concealment."

"Then, in that case, Sir, my little masquerade may be of value to you should French spies actually attempt such a thing here. I expect to have a friend of mine in the 92nd Regiment of Foot loan us a company of soldiers for the exercise . . . to act as guards . . . perhaps as early as Monday next."

"What do you think, Father? He wants Miss Grandin and myself to be a part of the deception, as well as himself, Mr. Holmes, and Lieutenant Worthington."

"I do not understand why you and Miss Grandin should be a party to this," Mr. Stephenson said with a deep frown.

Lord Bond hurried to reassure the anxious father. "Mainly for their greater expertise in the shipyard. They may be better able to pronounce upon the value of the men's observations."

"I see, My Lord. Please excuse me if I felt an inclination to refuse your request . . . my daughter did mention the American passport in your possession that included the identity of a wife."

Lord Bond put on his most reassuring smile. "Indeed, Sir, that instrument is in no way connected to this deception. Rather one other thing—perhaps we might attempt an investigation of your recalcitrant subcontractor's yard as well. It may not expose anything untoward, but the owners of the yard will not know that."

Mr. Stephenson frowned as he looked toward his daughter . . . then he lightened a little. "I begin to understand what these deceptions involve, My Lord. But I should not wish to take any advantage from them. However, if they facilitate our nation's business I must not stand upon my reservations. What do you think, Roberta?"

"I do not like it, but Urquhart and McArthur really deserve to be treated with disrespect. Perhaps if the deception will allow the opportunity for us to examine this difficulty with them, we will not be judged badly. The prices we have offered them are already beyond generous, and it is mostly the Admiralty's money that is at stake."

"Indeed, I believe your judgment is sound," Mr. Stephenson said with a smile as he turned from speaking to her. "And if you can reassure me, My Lord, that there is now no intention to involve my daughter in this clandestine activity on the Continent, I will be doubly enlightened."

Lord Bond spread his hands wide. "The First Lord himself was disinclined to think the inclusion of Miss Stephenson appropriate, especially because her knowledge increases the need for her to be better protected. As far as Admiralty planning goes, the passport will not be used now we have the papers of the captured French spies."

"Thank you, My Lord. You have reassured me greatly."

"For that I am thankful, Sir . . . . I would not like to think your generous offer of assistance should bring your family and your enterprise any untoward outcome." He was glad that the reassurance seemed accepted at its face value . . . by the father at least. Miss Stephenson still regarded him with a marked expression of deliberation.

CHAPTER TWENTY-FIVE
IDEAS AND NEW BLOOD

Roberta puzzled over her drawings the whole morning. Designing steam engines of the required power for the new warship proved a more difficult task than she had anticipated—with so many variables involved, solving one problem merely led to another. She rose from her desk to pace the office floor.

She had gone back and forth a few times when one of her draftswomen poked her head in the door. "We are making tea, Miss Roberta. Would you care for a cup?"

"Yes, please." Perhaps relaxing over a cup might loosen the cobwebs in her head. She decided to go into the outer office to sit with the drafts-people. When she reached the door she noticed through the glass upper panel that Lord Bond and Lieutenant Worthington were already sitting there.

"Having a problem?" Lord Bond asked.

His words ignited instant irritation. His presence in the shipyard had elicited none of the interest in steamship engineering that had been his reason for requesting the invitation. Ostensible reason at least. His plan to involve her in the spying exercise made her suspicious. She hardly needed to lose valuable time from her work to sneak about the slipways—she could easily pronounce upon the spies' notes in the evening. "No. What makes you think that?"

"We could see you pacing the office floor."

"I needed to think. It helps if I walk."

Lord Bond smiled. "May I ask what you are working on?"

"The engines for our large warship. I have to send a request to the foundry for a mold of a trial cylinder this week."

Lieutenant Worthington looked at her sympathetically. "The cylinders for this ship must be very large, Miss Stephenson."

"Indeed they are . . . somewhat larger than our boring machinery can handle, I fear. It would be another critical delay if we had to order a new, larger machine."

"What might we suggest as a hol'ternative, Miss Stephenson?"

"Anything, if you know of one. Every thought of mine has led only to another difficulty."

They sat in silence for a few minutes as Connie, one of the younger girls, arrived with beakers of tea. Roberta sipped carefully at the hot tea while Lieutenant Worthington plied the sugar spoon generously.

Then he looked up. "When we had a similar problem with a Maudsley engine trial at Chatham, we was able to solve it by raisin' the boiler pressure."

"I thought of that, but the boilers we must use are too close to their limit for that. We would run the danger of one exploding."

"Can you increase the number of cylinders instead of making one larger?" Lord Bond asked.

Roberta frowned into her cup. How easily these problems

could be solved if one knew no engineering. "We then have the problem of transferring the power of another cylinder to the driving gears, My Lord. They must be kept in accurate synchronisation as they work."

"Hmm, I cannot quite visualise your problem, but I have seen it done in Cornish mines with man engines. Of course, there the power is that of men working treadles to raise or lower the device between different workings."

She had no experience with such things. "It would seem that men can adjust their effort with greater flexibility than can cylinders of iron, My Lord."

Lieutenant Worthington began to grow a pink hue, but nevertheless asked his question. "An' these man engines use the force of many men together, My Lord? What does the mechanism look like?"

Lord Bond raised his hands to imitate some particular shape in the air. "The treadles are connected to power shafts that drive the wheels of the device on an inclined track. As I recall, they each are connected through a crank . . . like those used on railway locomotives."

Roberta tried to visualise two steam cylinders operating a single crankshaft. "Unfortunately the strokes of shipborn steam engines are very large and each crank would need to be pivoted at a different angle so the steam demands do not coincide. It seems a promising idea but there are new problems. Come over here to the drawings of the *Spiteful's* engines."

They took their cups of tea and stood looking at the drawings pinned to the wall. Lord Bond seemed to see no problem, but Lieutenant Worthington pointed out the biggest. "If the connecting rods were required to follow the radius demanded they would collide with the upper walls of the cylinder."

"Then tilt the cylinder away," Lord Bond answered.

Lieutenant Worthington shook his head but flushed as he retreated from the fray. Roberta felt that she should say something to lessen his embarrassment at disagreeing with His Lordship—but then she saw how both of them could be right. "Perhaps tilting the cylinders on a pivot—keeping them all in the same plane—could prevent the connecting rods from striking the cylinder walls, Lieutenant." She ran her hand down the drawing as if describing the motion of the crank. "There could then be two cylinders working together, oscillating first this way and then that."

"Yes . . . I sees what you are suggesting, Miss. But would that solve the power problem?"

"Instead of single cylinders of almost ninety inches diameter, we could use double cylinders of . . . ," she thought for a moment, "sixty or sixty five. Well within the capacity of our machine tools to bore out."

They stood staring at the drawings as they drank their tea. Lord Bond looked pleased with himself, as he might be permitted—in the circumstances. Lt. Worthington seemed lost in thought but when he looked up his face bore all the signs of pleasant absorption in a fascinating problem. She smiled at the drafts-people—it would seem that many heads had turned out to be much better than one. She could hardly stand there sociably finishing her tea and joining in the happy conversation when powerful urges were directing her back to her office to plunge into the designs again with this new idea.

After lunch, Lord Bond waited at the mansion for the expected infantry company. He sat in the library with a pamphlet published by an office at Lloyd's on the permitted loads and pressures on cargo ship steam engines that might apply to be insured by the underwriters. Within fifteen minutes he had fallen asleep.

Miss Nelly Stephenson woke him. "There is a soldier at the front door asking for you, My Lord. The driveway is filled with soldiers."

"What? Oh, yes. I was expecting them." He picked up the pamphlet that had fallen to the floor, set it on the low table beside him and then rose to his feet. He turned his head to look out the library windows—indeed, there did seem rather a lot of soldiers drawn up on the driveway.

He walked to the front door where Mr. Stephenson's housekeeper stood talking to a tall, red haired redcoat officer in a kilt. "Here is Lord Bond, now," she said.

The officer stamped to attention and saluted. "Captain James McNab of the thirrd Battalion, the 92nd Regiment of Foot rreporting fer duty, M'Lord."

Lord Bond responded with a slight bow. "Thank you, Captain. Did General Auchtermuchty apprise you of the requirements of this duty?"

"I hae been ordered to bring the headquarters company to Clydebank to tak up defensive positions abit th' shipyards, M'Lord. Hae the defensive positions been scouted?"

Lord Bond frowned. "Hmm. There seems to have been a slight misunderstanding of the task to be carried out, Captain. I requested the General to supply me with a body of troops to come on piquet duty to allow the establishment of a guard around some of the shipyards. My purpose is to train some agents in the manner of gaining access to the premises. No expectation of hostilities is expected, Captain."

Captain McNab frowned and pulled at his long moustaches. "There is nae alarm of enemy intrusion then, M'Lord?" He seemed very disappointed.

"None at all, I'm afraid. Did the company bring everything they need to bivouac?"

"Ourr transport was left behind on the line of rroute, M'Lord. Ah can send a subaltern back to coorie them up . . . if you would be sae gude as to point out the location of our bivouac."

"I spoke to the town council about using some waste land adjacent to the Urquhart and McArthur Graving Dock Company premises. That will be one of the shipyards we wish to post our guard piquets in. I will have my horse saddled and accompany you to the location."

"Thank you, M'Lord. I will have the Sergeant Major start the men on the road immediately. Hoo far is it tae th' shipyard?"

CHAPTER TWENTY-SIX
CURT WORDS

Roberta and Elizabeth Grandin accompanied Lord Bond and the army captain to the Urquhart and McArthur Yard the next morning to help them decide on the location of sentries that might prevent unauthorised individuals from gaining access. While she felt her presence this morning a necessary aid for His Lordship's activities, she also hoped it might free her from participating in too many similar outings in the future.

They were met at the yard gate by Mr. Urquhart in a dark suit that bore the oily evidence of his closeness to the yard's activity. "What assistance do these soldiers need, Miss Stephenson? I do not want any work disrupted."

"This is Lord Bond, Mr. Urquhart. He is in charge of the sentry posting . . . with Captain McNab, of course."

Lord Bond gave a peremptory nod of the head in answer to the man's token bow. "We do not wish to interfere with the work of the yard at all, Sir. Your workers may ignore the presence of the soldiers. Captain McNab and I will select the sentry posts based upon two criteria . . . defensive value and field of observation."

"Defensive, My Lord?"

"While we have soldiers here, we will examine the ground for possible defensive positions, should there come a necessity in the future to keep French marauders out of the yard—not at all likely, of course, but a useful exercise for the soldiers."

"I see, My Lord . . . ."

"Perhaps you would be so good as to walk with us a few minutes, Mr. Urquhart, to give us a brief description of the buildings," Roberta said. "Some activities in the yard might be of greater interest to intruders than others."

Captain McNab addressed her. "I thought that ye and Miss Grandin werre tae assist us in that way, Miss."

She turned to him, as she deciphered his broad Scots accent. "That we will, Captain, but Mr. Urquhart has a better knowledge of his yard than we. He is his yard's superintendent."

"Och weel. Ah see the sense o't. Ah would expect tae post an NCO an' six men at an entry point, as mah tactical hinge, M'Lord."

They set out from the gate, following Urquhart as he led them between two fieldstone and wooden structures. "The warehouse to the left is for iron, that on the right for timber."

"Would either of these be of concern to the spies?" Lord Bond asked.

Roberta glanced at the left one, noting that she could glimpse some of the contents through broken planks in the walls. "The wrought iron plates brought in to construct the hulls would be interesting if they were of unusual thickness."

"What would be unusual?"

"Anything thicker than half an inch, as we discussed in the London meeting, My Lord."

Lord Bond frowned a moment but then nodded. Roberta hoped he recalled the need to determine the thickness of the French armour plate.

Urquhart stared. "Why would a yard need iron plates that heavy, Miss Stephenson?"

"I'm afraid I cannot explain at the moment. It has some significance for the ships we are planning."

They left the buildings behind and walked to a fork in the access road. "The building ahead is Steam Powerhouse #2," Urquhart said. "Over there is the Plate Bending shop, and behind it is the Forge. In the other direction are the Planing Mill and the Joinery."

"Ah might station twa sawjerrs here at th' vantage point, M'Lord."

"Good thought, Captain." Lord Bond nodded. "Where are the vessels still under construction, Mr. Urquhart?"

"You cannot see the actual building docks from here, My Lord, they are below ground level." He pointed. "Those hoists and cranes are between them."

"The ships are built in graving docks in this yard," Roberta explained. "Only the Stephenson yard is building on slipways at the moment."

As they walked she listened to the conversation behind between Elizabeth and Captain McNab. "Ah am told yer folk waur French emigres, Miss Grandin."

"Ah . . . yes, Captain. My father and grandfather escaped the Reign of Terror in 1792 and brought us to England."

"Sae ye speak French very weel, Ah suppose. Ah learned th' language when Ah guarded French prisoners transported frae th' West Indies."

"Then you understand and speak French, Captain?" Lord Bond asked.

"*Je comprend bien la lang, mon Seigneur*," the captain answered. Elizabeth caught Roberta's eye and the two quickly wiped the smiles from their faces.

"How much have you used the language?" Lord Bond asked.

"*J'ai e' très peu besoin d'elle en Scotland, mon Seigneur.*"

"Doubtless," Lord Bond said with wry smile. "Not many Frenchmen to converse with. You seem to be getting rather rusty."

"Indeed, M'Lord. It was th' reason fur mah interest in Miss Grandin's fluency. Ah wood appreciate th' opportunity tae improve it."

Roberta jumped in to answer as Elizabeth held a handkerchief to her lips. "I'm sure Miss Grandin will be pleased to help you, Captain. When she has time from her work."

"Over there is the blacksmith shop," Mr. Urquhart told them. "That's about it. You should be able to guide them from here, Miss Stephenson. If you will excuse me, I have some matters to attend to."

"Certainly, Mr. Urquhart."

"Thank you for your assistance, Mr. Urquhart," Lord Bond said with some coolness. "I will be sure to commend your cooperation to Their Lordships of the Admiralty."

Urquhart frowned as he turned away to leave them, but made no attempt to change Lord Bond's impression.

"Rather an ungenial person," Lord Bond remarked. "Are all your countrymen as reserved, Captain?"

"By nae means, M'lord, but there are some individuals tha' act as if Culloden waur only yesterday. A body disnae usually meet them in Glasgee."

"Hmmm. I suppose his manner might have some connection with the yard's quarrel with the Stephensons, Miss Roberta?"

"I think that may be the brunt of it, My Lord. If you do not mind, I will try to use your inspection as an opportunity to see if the delay in launching the new hull in the graving dock is genuine or a device to raise the payments we had previously agreed upon."

"Champion, my dear! I see you have quite embraced the idea and principles of covert observation. These are the very foundations of being a good spy. You will be able to see if their difficulties are in fact those they claim?"

"I expect so, My Lord." Roberta felt somewhat dismayed at His Lordship's readiness to praise her ability as a spy, but she extended her reply into details that might convey the impression that the purpose was more important to her than the means. "They claim to have been ordered by their customer to replace some rivets in the lower part of the puffer's hull—a contract matter. It will be easy to see if they have the necessary forge set up in the dock to heat replacement rivets."

Lord Bond smiled. "Shall we go there first? I should be pleased to have served your interests as much as you have served mine."

"I think it best to wait until Mr. Urquhart has quite given up such suspicions as those that soured his mood, and gone on to further business, My Lord. I think first we might look at the unloading quays on the river bank. Observing the material being unloaded from a distance could well be more productive than attempting to penetrate the centre of the yard."

"Excellent, my dear. Your good sense is already proving of great value. What do you say, Captain?"

"Indeed, M'Lord, th' lassie have a braw understandin' at th' shipbuildin' trade, but Ah see wee chance how sawjerrs stationed here micht prevent sic' observation."

When they reached the quayside and were able to look down at the barges being unloaded, Roberta gave a quick explanation. "The nearest barge is carrying iron plates for the hull of a spiteful class vessel. It has come as a tow all the way from the Lowmoor Ironworks in Yorkshire. The farther barge has just arrived from the Stephenson yard with heavy frames already cut and shaped for assembly into the keel of the ship to be built here."

Lord Bond seemed impressed and made many more appreciative remarks as they continued their inspection around the yard. In some ways, Roberta was also pleased, but had to admit that her wisest purpose was being betrayed by her contribution to the project. She had hoped to convince His Lordship that she might have very little to offer in the matter of espionage.

While the others were away at the Urquhart and McArthur yard Mr. Stephenson took the opportunity to look over the ship's lines his daughter had prepared. He was, however, surprised to find Mr. Holmes there already, apparently with the same intention.

"Well, Mr. Holmes, what do you make of our ship's lines? Is there a better mathematical method you might offer that would provide for greater accuracy?"

"I would not presume to know your business better than you and your daughter do, Sir. If my mathematics can assist you in what you have already accomplished I would be more than gratified. This object has been the instigation of my discussions with your daughter over the application of Newton's method of fluxions and fluents . . . that I earnestly believe she will find of inestimable value to her work."

"Indeed, I am most grateful for your interest in her engineering work and in our family endeavours, Mr. Holmes. It is not often that one can share in the knowledge of a Cambridge mathematician."

"As for devising a mathematical equivalence of the drafting work carried out here, I venture to suggest that the method for applying the results to the actual metal do not currently exist. I really do not see that I can do more than offer an imperfect method of testing certain segments of the lines for their correspondence to what was in the mind of the draftsman . . . or drafts-lady."

"I must express my sincere appreciation for your opinion, Sir. If I were a better proponent of theoretical figuring I might see where my questions are not as well considered as they might be—I'm afraid that as an engineman in my youth, a valuable part of my education was delayed to the point that any attempt to recover it sits poorly with the rules of thumb that have been my usual engineering methods. My daughter has the benefit of youth as well as a mind trained better by Miss Mather in her Ladies' Academy."

"I believe she received a very valuable grounding there, even as far as discussion of the disputation between Sir Isaac and Herr Leibnitz as to the true inventor of the system of fluxions. Miss Roberta explained that the main reason Miss Mather did not include more training in this mathematical method was a feeling of her own inadequacy as a tutor. Such intellectual honesty is as gratifying as it is unusual . . . certainly an attribute to the fair sex, Sir."

Mr. Stephenson responded with a thoughtful look, but did not quite fathom how he might extend the conversation into the conviviality he had seen develop from this common interest in mathematics between Roberta and the acuminous Mr. Holmes. "My daughter too has her feet firmly upon the ground in material things, Sir, but she is not ungiven to flights of fancy in some respects. The advantages given her by her gender also include some degree of sensibility along with the sense."

"Ah, Mr. Stephenson, there you threaten to pass from my grasp of sense into the tempting regions of sensibility—a journey I am loath to venture upon."

"You surprise me, Sir. I have seen your easy conviviality with your friend, Lord Bond, and marked it as a superior form of interlocution between . . . if I may be so bold as to suggest . . . between Whig and Tory, to the benefit of both."

"Yes, our circumstances would inevitably suggest our hearts are given to different social classes, but the accidents of birth do not entirely mark our careers as men. Lord Bond and I go back many years and have been tested much in the past. I believe that is as much as I may present upon the matter that also engages another who is not party to the discussion, and since we are both under the same degree of hospitality that you have afforded us here I would like you to accept my response as intended with the utmost degree of cordiality even as I must be about my affairs and leave you here to your weightier tasks. I bid you the most salubrious good day, Sir."

Mr. Stephenson did his best to hide the astonishment he felt for the other's response to his interest in both young gentlemen who displayed a degree of interest in his daughter—if he were not entirely misreading the situation. Surely as a father he might be entitled to a degree of inquiry into a matter that concerned his duties, but he managed a measured response. "Indeed, Mr. Holmes, if I may wish you an equally good day with as much cordiality."

CHAPTER TWENTY-SEVEN
ANOTHER SUITOR?

Lieutenant Worthington left his work crew in the engine room of the *Spiteful* and climbed to the weather deck of the vessel. His list of alterations and improvements was gradually being ticked off and he felt hopeful that they might float the ship out of the dock by the end of the week to prepare for a proving voyage of the work.

He glanced about at the other activities being carried out as he made his way to the gangplank to cross over to the wall of the dock. Mr. MacRae stood supervising the workmen here so he merely nodded a greeting as he passed . . . the man was an excellent seaman and he had no intention of second guessing his work.

"Good day to ye, Mr. Worthington," MacRae said as he passed. "Are ye away?"

"I am. I wish to find Mr. Stephenson. Do ye know where he is?"

"You'll likely find him on one o' the slips. I heard they

planned to set the keels for the ship to be built in twa halves this afternoon."

"Thank you for the information. I shall go there first." This would be the second of the new vessels they were to construct and the first to be built to negotiate the Firth and Clyde Canal. It would need to be towed to Tyneside for installation of the engines and boilers. Only one of the spiteful class ships would receive its engines and boilers here, before the resources had to be reserved for the larger, secret warship's construction.

He had not been told the reason for this larger warship, but assumed Miss Stephenson had received all the particulars in the Admiralty boardroom after he and Commander Ripley left. No doubt this secret was connected with the new spying mission Lord Bond prepared for. It was unusual for such great secrecy to be decreed for shipyard work, but he had no doubt but that the reasons were sound and the new threat most dire.

His duty would be to train crews for the spiteful class ships, and so he made sure not to appear inquisitive about this other, but he had to admit of some apprehension at the possibility of danger to Miss Stephenson in the project. His Lordship seemed to find every opportunity to include her in his spy training, and the impression created by the application of Mr. Holmes to the practices of shipyard work gave him the impression that the French were up to some new and novel devilry in their steamship plans. If she were to be involved he was quite prepared to volunteer as a member of the spy team to watch over her—even if it should mean the loss of his new assignment and promotion.

He walked between the plate bending shop and the foundry on his way to the slips. At slip number two he found a foreman and crew setting the first iron frame to the keel. This man told him that Mr. Stephenson was at the next slip.

He made his way between the iron posts supporting the track of a travelling crane along the length of the slip and walked across the lay down area for ironwork ready for working into the hull. He entered the next slip through a similar construction and immediately caught sight of Mr. Stephenson with some workmen laying out ironwork for the new vessel.

"Good day, Mr. Worthington."

"And a very good day to you, Mr. Stephenson." He felt not the slightest grievance for the omission of his naval rank—it was entirely otherwise. They accepted him here as an engineer and not a mere product of the Royal Navy's Black Gangs.

"What can I do for you?" Stephenson asked, glancing up from his task.

"Nothing that merits delay to your own work, Sir. Please continue. I see you are at a particular juncture, and we can speak o' my errand once these frames are set. May I assist?"

"If you will. I intend to build the two halves of the ship as if one piece, even though it will be taken apart again before launching. That way we will be certain of a good fit between the two halves of hull later."

"Very good thinking, Sir. So the bulkhead here will be of two walls of thinner plates bolted together?"

"Yes, until the final connection at the Grangemouth end of the canal, when they will be riveted."

They worked at setting the first iron of the redesigned bulkhead for half an hour before they might take a breather. While two of the younger workmen compared the measurements to the plan Mr. Stephenson carried, they stood back to watch. He felt honoured to be helping with the work, since it was the result of his own suggestion to Miss Stephenson in the bowels of *Spiteful* that day in the Irish Sea. Their measurements and alignments seemed satisfactory, as they well needed to be . . . no one had attempted to build a ship in two halves before, and so the whole exercise was carried out by a combination of experiment and practical experience—not at all unusual in these early days of iron shipbuilding.

"What did you want to see me about, Mr. Worthington?

"I hope to be ready for the new *Spiteful* trials this comin' weekend, Sir, but do not expect to see naval ratings here before then. May I ask for the ship's whole Stephenson crew to remain assigned . . . until such time as I can begin trainin' my Naval people? The Admiralty will pay, of course."

Stephenson smiled at him. "You have a warrant for that, Sir?"

"Not to hand, I confess, but I were given to understand in my orders that all such h'extempore arrangements and costs are approved while this urgency exists. I would hope to see your officers and crew aboard not only for the trial, but also for the voyage to Chatham."

"The contract documents Roberta received say that essential people from the yard will be required at Chatham until Naval personnel are adequately trained to take over from them. These costs are to be included in the contract as well. I see no problem in our providing everything needed to complete the *Spiteful* for commissioning pursuant to that time. We will accept your judgement of Admiralty requirements."

"Thank you, Sir." He lowered his voice. "I have another concern, too . . . if we may move away from the others a moment."

Stephenson seemed surprised at the request but walked with him to the edge of the slip. "What did you want to say?"

Worthington felt his face heat up but there was little he could do about that. "I am not sure how to express this, Sir . . . it may seem none of my business . . . it may seem superfluous to such considerations you have already entertained as father . . . in fact . . . it may also be too late for me to express my feelin's of concern for your daughter's wellbein' an' safety . . ."

"Yes," Mr. Stephenson said slowly. "Continue."

"I am not party to any details of this further shipbuildin' assignment . . . but it seems as if His Lordship wants a trained nautical engineer to take part in the spyin' . . . it seems to me that he have designs toward makin' Miss Stephenson that person . . . . I must express my concern that such an activity would not be appropriate . . . nor even safe for her. The incident in the train on our way to London from Dover leads me to suppose he have a very cavalier regard for dangers . . . to himself and even . . . to others . . . I must be rude. I know it rude . . . but I must ask you what he have said to you."

There, he had said it. He knew he had no right to ask Mr. Stephenson for permission to ask for her hand. He was only a poor naval officer and she had the makings of becoming a rich lady . . . but he could not stand by and watch His Lordship entertain designs upon her that might be to the detriment of her reputation and future.

"My dear chap, I must admit to surprise at the intensity of your concern for my daughter's wellbeing, but have to admit my gratitude for it. I too have been at pains to observe His Lordship's intentions and have spoken directly to him about them. My daughter has expressed her own suspicions, but it seems all too likely that she will be out of my reach when any further actions might be taken toward having her participate in this spying."

"His Lordship has expressed intentions toward her—?" He stopped abruptly in embarrassment. "I did not mean to be rude, Sir. I apologize. I had no right to ask such."

"No, my good fellow. Do not apologize. I feel bound to trespass on your own kind feelings in my turn. I must inform you that His Lordship's designs upon my daughter only appear to have been as a participant in this expedition to the Continent . . . although he tells me that the First Lord of the Admiralty is himself in disapproval of such an intention." Mr.

Stephenson reached out to take him by the arm. "But in all this, he has never once expressed a gentlemanly concern for her modesty and reputation."

"I feared as much, Sir. It have been my observation that Lord Bond shows very little regard for propriety, and a great deal of enthusiasm for his covert occupations."

Mr. Stephenson leaned forward and took hold of his other arm as well. "I would feel much reassured if . . . when she is out of my presence, and likely closer to yours, that you would keep an eye out for her safety. If it would be possible, I should welcome a communication from you imparting your concerns. Perhaps more . . . I might welcome your participation . . . as if a responsible member of the family . . . should there be no time for such a letter to reach me and be answered. Could you consider offering such . . . great . . . assistance?"

"I most certainly would, Sir. You may count on me." He felt almost uplifted by these words and expressions of trust— gratified that his honour should be so readily accepted. But . . . it did seem that the father's trust and good opinion regarded him in the manner of a blood relative . . . perhaps as a brother—while his own feelings were of a more passionate nature.

Chapter Twenty-eight
Spying Action

The parish church at Old Kilpatrick was unaccustomedly crowded on Sunday; accounted for by the presence of Captain McNab and his company of the 92nd Regiment of Foot. Roberta stood with Father and Aunt Nelly at the door watching the soldiers come marching up the road and then accepted the Captain's invitation to come with him when he inspected them before entering the church.

The soldiers seemed very smart to her, but somehow the Captain and his Sergeant Major found enough deficiencies to form a lengthy list of miscreants for extra duties over the next few days. She looked into about a hundred faces and felt it rather creepy how their eyes slid about to regard her while their heads aimed up at the far horizon.

"Are these soldiers all going to be stationed in the Stephenson Shipyard today, Captain?"

"Nae, Miss Stephenson. A third ay them are on duties in camp; anither third are awa' tae th' Urquhart Yard. We shall hae a single platoon fur yer yard."

"I see. What time do you want me to help place the sentries?"

"Nae at all, Miss. Ah shall use th' advice given at th' other yard tae guide mah placement of th' men. Laird Bond an' Ah agreed ye should nae expect where tae find them when ye come wi' us on th' day."

"Oh. I see." She didn't see why at all . . . unless Lord Bond expected to judge her own spy-craft in the exercise. But it explained the invitation for her to join Captain McNab in the inspection . . . now all the soldiers would recognise her again.

She left the soldiers as the Sergeant Major began to march the ranks into the church in single file, and stood with Father and the officiating minister at the door. "A fine congregation, Miss Stephenson," that worthy observed as each man doffed his bonnet before entering.

"Indeed, Reverend Sir. I trust the walls will withstand the power of so many lungs."

The minister chuckled. "The old kirk has stood a few hundred years; I'm sure the Lord's stormy winters have tested it as much before."

The following day Roberta barely had time to oversee the progress toward making a mock-up of the new engine before Lord Bond called for her. "If you have a warm cloak or a travelling cape, I suggest you bring it, my dear. We will begin our intrusion on the water."

"Indeed, My Lord? Are we to go fishing for our information?"

"In a way, we are." Lord Bond smiled. "Fishing makes an excellent cover for a spy, since everyone living near a waterway must of necessity fish for his supper. In this case, it will also lead to a certain degree of uncertainty among the defenders as to the intended site of our intrusion."

"I see. I must say I find your training of me as a spy to be very thorough, but I was given to understand that Lord Melville had expressly forbidden my participation."

Lord Bond laughed. "Do not fret, my dear. I must admit to being somewhat fanatical about my preparations for a spying mission, but I will be using the documents we took from the French spies to insert two men into the Low Countries. I think you would be equally distressed if I requested that you should be disguised as a cavalryman."

She paused to reach into her office cabinet for a weatherproof cape she used about the yard on rainy days. "I thank you for your reassurance, My Lord."

"However, I do hope that you will be, at times, close to our area of operations—aboard a Royal Navy vessel perhaps—in order to pronounce upon the value of our information. It would be particularly vital should there be some lack in need of rectification."

"But I shall be working here at Clydebank, My Lord."

His expression changed, as if he knew something she did not. "Yes. You likely will."

It was a cool day for August on the water, with a rain shower threatening to sweep up the estuary toward them. Lord Bond had his hired boatmen take them past both shipyards as they trolled over the stern. They merged with the other river traffic and had caught several fish before he had them turn back and land them between the yards.

She and Captain McNab were to set out on foot for the Stephenson Yard. Lord Bond did not explain what had caused him to change his mind but merely asked that she would accompany the captain to see the intrusion from the defender's perspective.

"Please give us half an hour before passing through the main gate, if you will," Lord Bond asked. "We will be taking a more circuitous route for our own entry."

Roberta felt she had been duped into preparing to engage in a covert intrusion and then asked to watch it from inside her own yard. He had not even informed her which of the two yards was to be subject to the exercise. "You will be spying on the Stephenson Yard, then, My Lord."

He smiled mysteriously. "You shall see what you see."

She turned away from him abruptly. Really! He could be so arrogant. "Well, we had better follow our marching orders, Captain. I assume you carry a pocket watch."

"Aye, Miss Stephenson. We micht make a leisurely stroll ay it. It being a short way."

She fumed the whole way to the main gate. How would this train people to spy on an actual enemy shipyard? They would have no knowledge of its name nor extent; Lord Bond had admitted being unable to approach it before at the meeting in the Admiralty. If this was a sample of his method, she was well out of it. She felt sorry for Mr. Holmes and Lieutenant Worthington, but the latter would surely not be involved in the actual mission—he already had his orders to command the *Spiteful* at Chatham.

Would His Lordship and Mr. Holmes undertake these tasks on their own? How then was she expected to receive word of their spying aboard a Navy ship offshore? There had been word of Dutch patriots opposed to Napoleon's rule . . . so were they in need of instruction in gaining information in a strange shipyard as well? He had the two young cabin boys on his yacht—they were either Dutch or Flemish, but they were not here yet and time was running out. The whole enterprise was far too disorganized for her liking.

They spent a little time in the yard's gate office, speaking with the Captain's sentries and her gateman and his clerk, who noted down all arrivals and departures of people and waggon loads. Captain McNab took out his pocket watch and opened it. "I think oor time is up, Miss Stephenson. Shall we inspect the sentries?"

"Yes, if you wish. I should like to watch the building slipways and the graving dock first." With a thought to the information from Antwerp she most needed, those seemed the most likely places in a shipyard to learn it.

Her workers all gave her little more notice than a hand to forelock as they passed them, while Captain McNab's sentries jumped to attention and saluted as he approached. It seemed that none of them had noticed any suspicious movement.

The slipways were a hive of activity. The construction of the two ships had been commenced a mere two days apart and the two construction gangs had taken it as a matter of pride to undertake the building as a race. The riveting hearths in the slip with the first spiteful being built whole were pouring out clouds of acrid smoke as the rivet carrying boys ran to and fro with their white-hot loads for the riveters. The banging of the hammers was near deafening. In the other slip the two parts of the ship were slowly gaining their keels as the double bulkheads were being set in place. Here, the riveting had not begun, but men bustled about with forge fuel and rivet blanks in readiness.

They walked to the riverside end of the first slip where Captain McNab instructed his sentries to be on their guard. "If ye see any comin' frae the river tae enter th' buildin' area, he main be ain of our observers."

"What main us do, Sirr? Seize him an' truss him up like a goose?"

"Heavens, no," Roberta burst out.

"Nae, laddie. Ye shall respectfully approach him an' ask his business. If he cannae answer, ye main ask him tae accompany ye tae th' sergeant at th' gate."

"The intruders are all gentlemen," Roberta said. "They will accept your questioning them as the completion of their tasks." She turned to McNab and gestured toward the men's muskets. "These are not loaded, Captain?"

"Nae, Miss. Powder an' shot has ne'er been issued."

A slight tremble ran down her spine . . . in the real spying mission the muskets would all be loaded and nervous sentries might shoot on sight. She decided to move to the graving dock, where the *Spiteful's* work was nearing completion. Perhaps it would be a good idea to quell some of the over-enthusiasm of the 92nd Regiment of Foot on guard there.

As they walked in that direction a corporal came marching rapidly to the captain. "There is a strange fellow bin pokin' abit in th' cargo barges, Sir."

"Have ye caught him?"

"Nae, Captain. He slipped awa."

"I would lay odds that is Lord Bond," Roberta said.

"Likely you're right, Miss. I will go there richt away."

Roberta continued to the graving dock and spoke to the soldiers herself. Some of the lads had seen a man enter the area from the river but had not been close enough to challenge him.

"Which way did he go?" she asked.

A very young soldier with red hair and a ruddy face pointed at the slips and made an answer in such a broad highland accent that she just nodded and said "thank you" before leaving in that direction. She pointed her steps toward the mid-point of the nearest slip and arrived just in time to see two soldiers half carrying a very wet and bedraggled man up the slipway from the river. She could not recognize who they had caught until she was almost close enough to lay a hand on the man's arm. It was Mr. Holmes.

"Good heavens, Mr. Holmes. You are soaking wet . . . quite covered in mud."

He regarded her soberly. "Indeed, Miss Stephenson. It seems that I have mostly learned that shipyards are veritable traps for the unwary. A careless foot might easily step off a plank and land in three feet of mud and water."

"Oh dear. Have you seen anything of the construction work?"

He nodded his head toward the hull slowly taking shape on the slip as they passed. "Only since the soldiers have rescued me. I hope His Lordship and the Lieutenant have more success."

"I believe Lord Bond has been seen among the iron shipments on the barge jetty. Captain McNab has gone that way to look."

Holmes scowled. "I hope they duck him in the river."

CHAPTER TWENTY-NINE
POST MORTEM

Roberta walked with the soldiers helping Mr. Holmes along, guiding them to the blacksmiths' shop where he might dry out in front of a red hot hearth. "I'm sure one of the men might find you some overalls to wear while your clothes dry, Mr. Holmes. I would caution you not to remove your boots, however. There could be red hot or sharp metal scattered about from the work at any time."

Even as she spoke, two men pushed a white hot ingot in front of a powered cutting wheel and a shower of sparks flew across the shop floor to the accompaniment of an ear-splitting shriek of tortured metal. They moved farther away and watched until the ingot had been cut in two.

Holmes regarded her gloomily. "Thank you for your assistance, Miss Stephenson. I think I will do as you suggest, once you have left. Where will you be going?"

"I believe Lord Bond suggested meeting at the gate office for a discussion. I will see you there."

She met Lieutenant Worthington strolling along the main shipyard artery as if out for his constitutional. He wore a tunic and breeches loaned by one of her father's gardeners, a flat workman's cap, and had an iron-workers' leather apron over his breeches and stockings. "Are we finished, Miss Stephenson? I think I has completed my part of the exercise."

"Soon, I believe. I just left Mr. Holmes drying his clothes in the forge . . . he was unfortunate enough to miss his footing and fall in the river."

Lieutenant Worthington looked at her with a grin picking at his lips, and they both quickly looked away from one another. "How unfortunate," he said, after a minute. "I suppose . . . he were unable to complete his assignment?"

"He was being assisted by the two soldiers who pulled him to dry land when I joined them. He said he had not reached the ships on the slipways."

The lieutenant pulled a straight face. "Have you seen Lord Bond?"

"Captain McNab was called by his sentries to the barge quay. They said some stranger had been seen there."

"Hmm. I thinks I had an easy run of it. Everyone who saw me assumed I was about my normal duties, I dare say."

Lord Bond, in the company of Captain McNab, arrived at the gate office about ten minutes after Roberta and Lieutenant Worthington. "Have some tea, My Lord," Lieutenant Worthington offered. "It is not Lapsang Soochong I'm afraid, but 'tis a welcome sup nevertheless."

Lord Bond accepted the mug and joined them at the office table. "Have you seen Mr. Holmes?"

Roberta felt a fit of giggles coming on and quickly hid her face behind the tea mug. Lieutenant Worthington gallantly stepped into the breach. "He is at the forge, My Lord, dryin' out. Miss Stephenson says he was unfortunate enough to miss his footing amid the clutter at the slipways and fell into the river."

Lord Bond scowled and pushed out a loud sigh. "Ah, he always was a clumsy child. No better now, by all accounts."

Roberta caught Worthington's eye. That was strange . . . it suggested they had known one another for many more years than she had assumed. Some of Mr. Holmes' comments about the Marquess took on an added meaning. "What did you make of the exercise, Captain?" she asked McNab in order to change the topic.

"I think my lads ha' done a good job, Miss. It has'na been an easy mark fer o'er intruders."

Roberta did a double take—she had hardly expected such a diplomatic reply. "What do you think, My Lord?"

Lord Bond had been staring at the captain with a calculating look. "Very mixed results, I fear, but we will take stock when Mr. Holmes joins us."

Mr. Holmes arrived fifteen minutes later and declined the offer of the tea. "The fellows in the forge have already plied me with enough to float the *Spiteful* away. Do you know how much tea they consume, Miss Stephenson?"

She laughed. "At lot—I see it in the accounts. But it is hot and hard work in that shop and I believe they work all the better for the refreshment."

Lord Bond regarded him down his nose. "What did you discover, Symington?"

Mr. Holmes squared his shoulders as if receiving a challenge. "I learned that shipyards are dreadfully confusing for fellows who do not know them; and that the Clyde is both dirty and cold. If I make such a walk again I will be doubly careful of planks that appear to have been dropped at random . . . and actually perform the duties of a bridge over a gouge in the mud of the riverbank. On the other hand, I have determined that for my part, I should learn far more from a conversation with a carefully chosen local workman than I might from a visit in person."

Lord Bond nodded. "That must be considered. But let us look at Lieutenant Worthington—who is every inch the image of a workman who belongs in the yard. What would you say, Captain McNab?"

"I maun agree, My Lord. I would'na taken more attention if he had walked past me than I would of a gatepost."

"So there is a valuable lesson we have learned. Did your disguise earn you a prize, Lieutenant?"

Worthington reached into his smock and withdrew a piece of paper. "It is a rather hasty sketch, My Lord, but I believe it shows all the particulars."

Lord Bond glanced at the paper and then handed it to Roberta. It was a very clear, if rough, sketch of the mock-up of the new engine design. She looked up. "You were in the tool room and saw the newly completed model?"

Worthington smiled. "That I was, and I must say I had to admire the design. I do not know how I would've been regarded in a strange shipyard, however. I feel those workin' there had seen me about the shipyard on other days."

"No doubt," Lord Bond answered, "but this offers another lesson. One day is insufficient time to learn what we need. I am looking for a way to insert a workman into our enemies' yards for enough time to gain the trust of the authorities."

"And what of your morning, My Lord?" Roberta asked.

"About as productive as Mr. Holmes'. I saw a great deal of iron bar, angle iron and plate, but could make little service of my knowledge. The longer I spent on the quay, the more notice Captain McNab's sentries took of me. I had to leave before I had satisfied myself of my discoveries."

After lunch Roberta and her father went to the Urquhart & McArthur Graving Docks to insist the dock be cleared and the subcontracted spiteful begun at once. Arriving at the head office, they demanded Mr. Urquhart escort them to the dock immediately.

"I did not see sign of the activity to replace unsatisfactory rivets when I was here three days ago, Mr. Urquhart," Roberta said. "There were no hearths working to heat the rivets."

Urquhart bristled. "Do you accuse me of dishonesty, Miss Stephenson? Do not suppose your gentle nature and gender should render you immune to a lawsuit or some other retaliation."

"Enough of that, Urquhart," Father answered. "Do not suppose you might not be dealt a thrashing and thrown into the river to learn gentlemanly manners. You will not speak to my daughter in that way."

Urquhart clenched his fists, but young Mr. Keiller, the son-in-law of the McArthur family, stepped between them. "Please don't, Angus. Fisticuffs will settle nothing. We must discuss this calmly."

"Calmly! When that little baggage snooped about the yard when she was pretending to occupy herself with assisting His Lordship?" He crossed his arms. "How do you know the hearths were cold three days ago? You smiled and charmed me to my face and then crept about the yard like a Gypsy. Did you ask the reason for the delay, perhaps?"

"Then you do not deny that no work has been carried out on the vessel in the dock?" Father demanded, his face reddening.

"You see! You see that they both call me a liar! I will not accept such treatment without demanding recompense. I insist you apologize before I utter another word."

"I have heard enough! I am leaving and cancelling the contract," Roberta said, turning to the door. "There are other yards in the kingdom where the vessel might be built . . . without the risk of deception and delay."

"Do not be so hasty," Mr. Keiller implored. "Let us all sit and drink tea together. I am sure we will come to an amicable understanding when tempers have cooled."

"I see no reason to stay," Roberta answered. "If every difficulty is going to result in a scene like this I do not want to do business with the yard."

Mr. Keiller urged Mr. Urquhart to take a seat and then came to her. "I do apologize most humbly for the senior partner's anger, but you must surely recognize that he has been sorely misjudged."

Roberta frowned. "Misjudged? How so?"

"There truly is a contract dispute with the owners of the puffer in the second graving dock, Miss Stephenson, but Mr. Urquhart is in the process of settling the dispute with legal action. Unfortunately, that requires the vessel not to be moved until the justice and the panel of shipwrights have seen it."

Father regarded Mr. Urquhart with a deep frown. "Why did you not explain this to me when I came originally?"

Urquhart turned away. "It is my yard's business, not yours."

"But did you not think we might offer to assist you with the problem," Roberta asked as she settled herself in the chair Mr. Keiller pulled up for her.

"I will not be beholden to another."

"Is that how partners in business are expected to act, Sir?" Father asked.

"Take the dock and be damned! I will order the puffer floated out on the next tide."

Mr. Keiller remonstrated. "But why? What about the . . . ?"

"We shall take the Stephensons to court for our losses in the first judgement, Mr. Keiller, that's why."

"Do you just need a dock to have the puffer inspected in?" Roberta asked. "When do you expect this to take place?"

"Three days hence," Mr. Keiller answered.

"Our own dock is to be vacated very soon," she went on. "The *Spiteful* is done. If you have your vessel floated down to us, we can take it in on the same tide. We have all the work crews busy with two spitefuls and do not expect to use the dock again for some weeks."

Mr. Keiller turned to his partner. "That sounds most accommodating, does it not, Angus? What do you say?"

Urquhart's eyes narrowed as he looked down at her. "What will be your fee for housing the puffer?"

Father looked at her. Roberta recognized his conciliatory expression. "A minimal charge for the work crew at the dock, and nothing for rental—as long as you are finished with the dock in time for us to lay the keel of our third contracted spiteful."

"And when might that be?" Urquhart asked grumpily.

Roberta smiled slightly. "Since your yard has all the iron not already being worked up, and all the available shipwrights to begin construction, we will delay its commencement until the present shortage of iron is eased by a shipload from Tyneside. Several weeks hence."

It would more likely be a month or more, but best she keep that extra time as leeway. Three vessels building at once would stretch their resources to the limit, and she had still to begin preparations to build the new, secret vessel. It would first require a new, longer slipway built, but that would be a job for a crew of local builders. "Is that a satisfactory compromise, Mr. Urquhart?" she asked.

"And all heated words forgiven?" he demanded.

"Overlooked, Sir," she answered. "No penalty to either side."

Christopher Hoare

Chapter Thirty
Subterfuge in Earnest

Next day, Lord Bond rode his rented mount at a smart trot from the mansion to the yard after receiving word at noon. His replacement yacht, the *Nederlander*, had been seen beating up the Clyde toward Clydebank. Miss Stephenson drove the trap beside him, wearing drab greys and tan in a thigh length caraco and petticoat. "How long will it take for Bloggins to reach your mooring, Miss Stephenson?"

She glanced up at the scudding clouds. "The wind can hardly be called fair for a run up the estuary, My Lord, but I would expect them to anchor within two hours."

"It would seem that the time nears for our paths to diverge, but I wish it were not so."

She seemed surprised and a little flustered. "It was surely always to be expected, My Lord. Your duty calls you to the Low Countries, while mine will hold me in this shipyard until my vessels for the Admiralty are built."

"You discount my mention of your presence off the Schelde

in a Royal Naval frigate, then?"

"It seems that Mr. Holmes is capable of offering the opinions you mentioned."

"Perhaps, but it was his assessment that I wanted confirmed. He will be in Antwerp, or somewhere close by."

She glanced at him as the pony negotiated a pothole. "You seem very critical of his ability to judge, My Lord."

"Symington, I'm sure, would be an excellent judge—given a few months more time to grasp all the technical details. But his very expertise and confidence make his words less valuable with his present degree of knowledge. He is, as I believe you have known from the day I introduced you to him, a gambler. I would be concerned to have him gamble with the vital information that could determine our ability to safeguard England's fate."

"You have known him since childhood, have you not, My Lord?"

His reply came out jerkily, that he put down to his mount's uneven gait on a rough place in the road. "Since my mother died. I was five years old at the time. Symington was seven."

She made no answer but watched him expectantly.

"Do you assay to delve more deeply into the Marquess of Tiverton's family, Miss Stephenson?"

"I would consider it very rude . . . if it were not for your propensity to challenge me with unwelcomed statements of some perceived entitlement of judgement over my own activities. Perceived only by yourself, I must add."

"You surprise me, my dear. I had the impression that we had become quite friends since our meeting upon the hazardous waters of the Channel. I have come to look upon your opinions as worthy of the utmost consideration."

"But you expect me to utter them even though I know nothing of the circumstances of the topic at play."

"Then I will make amends, my dear. The next time I will

have the privilege to speak of such matters, I will begin by bearing my secrets before you."

Now he saw her definitely to colour . . . not the brilliant display of a Worthington, but unmistakable. It surely seemed the time was near when he might progress to the next stage in advancing his interest.

When they reached the shipyard he went immediately to the quayside while she, with a rather distant manner, wished him a good afternoon and disappeared into her office. What a woman! She could change from girlish modesty to a shrewish assault upon the male race in the blink of an eye. He should put all thoughts of her from his mind . . . banish any idea of winning her to his bosom, but until this matter of the French ironclad was settled he had to make her his personal business. Yes, that was it. Everything he would do would be for England's sake.

He dismounted and tied the horse's reins to the pillar of a hand cranked hoist. Looking out at the river he peered at all the ship traffic until he saw a distant vessel with a very bluff, very Dutch bow. It had to be *Nederlander*. She was likely correct in her esti—Dammit, he was perfectly capable of making his own estimate of the time it would take before he learned who Bloggins had brought with him.

The last letter he had received from the Admiralty had informed him that the Hanoverian secretary Gottliebe had been apprehended. There was something in the letter that concerned Roberta, but he would wait awhile before informing her. Gottliebe had dispatched a letter to his superiors in France with the latest information from his man in the Admiralty before going into hiding. It had included something of their meetings with Their Lordships as well as a reference to a woman's presence. Interrogation revealed it had been dispatched through civilian mails that went through neutral Sweden.

The Admiralty also intimated that it had its own contacts in the Netherlands and wished to send some men with him. Since he had neither trained nor tested them he was unsure as to their quality. Would they be actual rivals, and even enemies, of the Dutch patriots he generally relied upon? Perhaps he had best align himself with his French Royalist friends for this expedition . . . at least it would make unsuspected dangerous hostilities within his team less likely.

The change would require another French speaker joining his mission. Holmes had a passing fluency, but no convincing accent in the language. At least the man would be able to work with some of King Louis' hopeful partisans. His own French had improved these past few years, and so had his Flemish with the benefit of Elise sharing his bed.

He had received the letter from her at last—he patted the pocket where it resided—relating how she had evaded a cavalry pursuit and reached her friends at Amsterdam safely. She must at all accounts be invited to meet him at Flushing . . . she had little loyalty to ambitious Dutch plans of freedom, and a strong attachment to him. Or to his money—to supplement the mere hundred gulden her absent husband in the Indies sent her.

The news he expected from his Amsterdam friends had still not arrived. If the Dutchmen the Admiralty promised were aboard *Nederlander* he might set out for Flushing and start building his network of allies upon arrival. It was getting late in the month and he wanted to be in Antwerp by September.

What to do with Miss Stephenson? Clearly she would never join his mission without the security of nuptials, and even if he went through the ceremony with good intent, there was always the Marquess waiting in the shadows, like a barn owl waiting to swoop upon an unsuspecting mouse. The Old Man had friends in the Church and in the House of Lords who would do his will to thwart the accession of a mere commoner to the title Marchioness. And Symington was well aware of this—would he betray the secret out of a sense of justice and gentlemanly feeling?

Worse, would he use the stratagem and its defeat, as a step toward gaining his own entrance to the lady's affections? What did Symington want with a wife? His mother would put up obstructions every bit as powerful as the Marquess. Good Lord! *There* must have been a love story worthy of Shakespeare when the two of them cohabited. But their son would never inherit a thing, and was even less likely to sire any issue.

By the time he turned his attention to the river again, the Dutch hoogaar had sailed much closer. It was almost time to go to meet it—he looked about for a small craft to hire, his eye lighting on a tiny pram with a mere boy fishing from it.

"I say, lad. Do you hear me?"

"Wha' have ye? Are ye speakin' tae me?"

"Yes . . . unless you have a fish aboard with a better command of English. Yes, I'm calling you. Come to the quay and let me aboard—there's a shilling for you to take me to the anchorage to meet my yacht."

Lord Bond seated himself in the flat bow while the lad balanced himself in the stern sculling with a single oar. They arrived at the mooring buoy almost at the same time as the *Nederlander* and he waited until they were securely tied before going aboard.

Bloggins met him at the rail. "'Tis sorry I be fer takin' so long, My Lord, but I had to put in at Pembroke Dock to rig a new suite o' sails . . . th' old ones was fit to rip at the slightest blow."

"Oh, no harm done. You paid on the Admiralty warrant?"

"Aye, My Lord. They accept'd wi'out a murmur."

Two strangers came forward as Lord Bond turned from Bloggins. "You are the Admiralty's picked agents, I take it?"

The taller of the two spoke. "Yes, My Lord. I am Cornelius van Ee, and my companion is Nicholas van Aa."

Lord Bond reached out a hand. "Honoured to make your acquaintance, gentlemen. Are you familiar with Flanders south of Breda . . . namely the Scheldt, Flushing, and Antwerp?"

The man identified as van Aa muttered something in Flemish. Herr van Ee spoke up, "My companion is from Neuzen, a small port on the south bank of the Westerscheld. I spent several years working in Antwerp when Bonaparte decreed the river be opened again and the port rebuilt."

"Your friend speaks no English?"

The two exchanged glances. "He understands well enough but chooses not to speak until he feels at ease with you."

"Oh, I see. Will I offend him if I address him in Flemish? I have a meagre fluency in it."

Van Aa answered in Flemish. "I should be grateful, your honour."

"Did the Admiralty explain what I needed from you?"

"To act as guides and as contacts with sympathetic locals," van Ee answered.

"That is correct. I will also be using some royalist French contacts I have . . . will that offend you?"

Van Aa smiled. "Not as much as having to put up with those arrogant pigs from Amsterdam."

"Good. I hope that means we shall get along very well."

"When do we leave, your honour?"

"In a few days. First, I have something to arrange this Sunday."

Chapter Thirty-one
Some at Sea

On Saturday morning, Roberta rode in the trap to the shipyard with Lord Bond driving. He told her he would be spending the day with his yacht crew making some final arrangements for his imminent spying mission.

"What are your plans for the day, my dear?"

"We hope to have the first of our new spiteful engines bench running today, My Lord. Its successful operation without a necessity for modifications will take quite a load from my shoulders."

"How does a bench run work?"

"We will connect its power shaft to the shipyard services driven by our stationary engine. It will be a good load, and if it succeeds in operating all day without showing signs of our earlier problems we will be able to build all the other engines with confidence. I wonder if Mr. Holmes will be available to witness the trial?"

Lord Bond shrugged. "He will move aboard the

Nederlander today. He believes he will gain more intelligence from the river side of the shipyards at Antwerp than from the land sides. He wishes to prove his theory over the next few days."

She thought his idea a good one . . . provided he didn't make falling in the river a habit. She had to turn her head away from His Lordship to hide the smile the thought brought to her lips. Looking toward the river from the vantage point they had reached revealed a growing pall of black smoke from the quayside ahead.

Lord Bond followed her glance. "Good Lord. What is that on fire?"

"I think it is the *Spiteful* crew starting the furnace fires . . . at least I certainly hope so. Lieutenant Worthington intends to take *Spiteful* to sea today on a trial run."

"Yes . . . I do believe the smoke comes from the river. Why do steamships produce this black smoke in harbour?"

"The furnaces and boilers are cold, and so the combustion is incomplete. As they heat up the smoke will lighten. Will you see Mr. Holmes? Perhaps you may ask him to visit the engine trial at the steam powerhouse."

"I will, if I see him. He seemed to be in one of his uncommunicative moods this morning at breakfast."

"Do you believe he has the qualifications for a spy, My Lord? He seems to be a very good observer, but not what one may call a very practical person."

"I believe you have made a perceptive judgement, my dear. Before we leave for the Low Countries I must team him with a more practical kind of fellow. It appears that I will need to use my Royalist Frenchmen as informers on this venture, so I need a man who can communicate with them."

"Mr. Holmes speaks the language, I believe."

"True, but both of the men operating under the cover of the French documents will need to speak the language . . . even if their ability is less than perfect."

Roberta did smile this time. "Like Captain McNab, perhaps?"

Lord Bond laughed. "Ah, yes. His French is certainly not perfect, but you do have a good point. His military training and initiative would make him an excellent team member. I will certainly go to Glasgow to speak with his commander, General Auchtermuchty, before I leave Clydebank."

"When do you expect to leave?"

Lord Bond's face seemed to withdraw all traces of expression. "Oh, I haven't decided. Someday next week."

Roberta made no answer since they were almost at the shipyard gate, but her mind worked furiously. His attempt to casually dismiss the date of his departure, as if unimportant, was surely anything but. His information that Mr. Holmes and one other would be using the French spies' papers meant that the American passport must surely be back in play if he was to go to Antwerp with them. How necessary was this mythical Mrs. Paine identified upon it? He had pretended that her presence was as unimportant as was the date of his departure, but she had to suspect that his pretence was intended mainly to withhold the information from her.

By nine that morning, the *Spiteful* had finished taking on coal and was ready to leave for its steaming trials. Lieutenant Worthington went down to the engine rooms and boiler rooms to give the order to raise steam and prepare to depart. This would be the first time he had ever prepared a ship for sea as its commander, but he did his uttermost to maintain a sober naval demeanor.

He spoke to one of the naval petty officers who had been drafted to the vessel in the past few days. "You are comfortable workin' under Miss Grandin, Mr. Cook?"

The young engineroom artificer looked as if he had a lot to say, but shrugged instead. "Aye aye, Lieutenant."

"You do not have to hide your opinion from me. I felt most uncomfortable when I first sailed in the *Spiteful*, but Miss Grandin is an accomplished ship's engineer. She has known the vessel since the first iron was laid down."

"As you say, Lieutenant. I'm sure you have satisfied yoursel'. That be good enough fer me."

"Good. But don't forget . . . you may speak privately to me at any time about difficulties . . . should they arise. Everything about the ship and its duties is unheard of in the Royal Navy before this time. We are as explorers o' darkest Africa and must mark out the way for our fellows to man other such vessels. Do well under me and you may hope for some good promotion in the days ahead."

"Thank you, Sir. I shall listen to Miss Grandin like her was yerself. You may count on me."

"Good man. Keep a good eye upon those crankshaft journals this trip . . . see your reliefs understand as well. They were redesigned after one failed in our Channel action, but this is the first time the new ones have gone to sea."

"Aye aye, Sir. I'll watch like an 'awk . . . . Miss Grandin already showed us what 'appened to pieces o' th' old one."

Worthington answered the young man's salute and went on into the starboard boiler room. Here were two more of his petty officer draftees, talking with Miss Grandin besides the steam pressure gauges.

"Once the pressure reaches ten pounds per square inch you must moderate the rate of stoking to allow the metal to expand slowly," she was telling them. "The safeties are set for sixteen, but if they blow they will set your haste back worse than steaming too slowly."

"Aye Miss. What if there be a real emergency for steam?" one asked her.

"While I'm chief engineer there will be no setting up the safeties and no jimmying them shut. I have seen the effects of a boiler explosion and never want to be in one. You can boil yourselves alive in your own boiler rooms once you have your own ships."

The young petty officers smiled sideways at one another. "Aye aye, Chief. Us will make sure us never does any such thing."

"I'm glad to hear that," Worthington cut in, and the young men looked around in surprise. He had once been a cocky young petty officer like these and knew he must take pains to rule them. Once they had shown respect for their responsibilities he might allow himself to unbend a little. "How long before we have steam, Chief?"

Miss Grandin smiled at him. "By three bells in the forenoon watch, Cap'n, you will have enough steam to loose mooring lines. We can give you eight knots by the time we reach Greenock."

"That will be good, Chief," he responded and gave her a regulation salute. The *Spiteful* had been an informal, easy ship under shipyard orders, but now he must begin to establish a Naval atmosphere. "I will go up and test the engine room voice pipes when I arrive."

"I will listen for you. Just give me time to speak with the stokers, if you will."

"Good." He looked at the young petty officers. "These boilers are little different than those you tended aboard the tugs you served in before. Just remember to treat them well— they may be your lifeline when full speed is demanded in action."

The two lads saluted as he left the boiler room. Mere boys . . . he'd bet his month's wages they had been the least experienced artificers in the tugs they'd been transferred from. No ship commander he knew had ever sent his best men on an

Admiralty draft. He hoped to have enough time to knock them into shape before heading north about to the North Sea and then south to Chatham—six or seven days before he needed to leave Clydebank—Lord grant that be enough!

Mr. Holmes, wearing his strange loose-flapped headgear and a seaman's tarpaulin jacket, arrived to watch the steam engine trials by mid-afternoon. He had two men with him who she had not seen before, and introduced them.

"Please meet Herrs van Ee and van Aa, Miss Stephenson. They are two new gentlemen sent by the Admiralty to join our expedition. Lord Bond thought it a good idea that they should witness a steam engine in action before we leave—if that is acceptable to you."

"Why, yes, perfectly. Welcome to Clydebank, gentlemen," she paused. "They do speak English, I hope."

"I apologise for my imperfect speech, Lady," one said. "I am Nicholas van Aa, who used to be the schoolmaster at Neuzen. I attempted to teach the language in my school, but some English laugh at my efforts."

"I find your English to be very good, Sir," Roberta said. "How did you lose the position?"

Van Aa scowled. "Napoleon's Chief of Police, the swine Fouché, thought me disloyal."

Roberta had to hide a smile, thinking the suspicion rather well founded. "Most unfortunate, Sir. I hope you find your position with more polite English people a suitable recompense."

"Miss Stephenson will explain to us what is taking place," Mr. Holmes said, offering her the twin to the smile she had to smother.

"Yes, these are the particulars since this morning," Roberta said, showing them the table of results; steam pressures, revolutions per minute, and bearing temperatures with some pride. The engine design was a success and now she could hand over the plans and specifications to the construction yards with confidence and devote more of her time to other duties.

When she sent the Dutchmen to see the boiler with the man in charge, she was able to ask Mr. Holmes about his own efforts of the past days. "You found the river an excellent viewpoint I suspect, Sir?"

"I did. While the land sides of the yards are walled and gated, there exists very little obstruction to one's observation on the water side. I believe it will be necessary to determine whether there are water-borne patrols to avoid, but I am more optimistic about this than I was after our attempts to infiltrate ourselves into the shipyards."

"Those were not very promising, I agree," she said. "But I thought you and Lord Bond were to travel together on the French documents. Today he speaks of needing another member of the party to travel with you, but what of these two Dutchmen?"

"I do not believe they have caused a change in his planning. But I really think he has not made up his mind at the moment."

Roberta thought the answer sounded sincere, but the way he avoided meeting her eyes as he said it aroused her suspicions. "The American passport seems to be a part of the plans again, is it not?"

"I really cannot offer an opinion on that, Miss Stephenson. Lord Bond has not discussed that matter with me."

Roberta felt that answer little more reassuring than the last, but felt it would be impolite to keep pressing on his discomfort. "If you have seen enough of our engine trial, I might suggest we go to the design office for some tea. I would like another opportunity to discuss the use of Sir Isaac

Newton's fluxions one more time, if you are agreeable."

She realized the change of topic pleased him by the smile it brought to his face. "I would be pleased to discuss the applications of mathematics with you, Miss Stephenson. I had never considered myself destined to be a pedagogue, but find you a very eager and promising student—and the offer of a cup of tea is equally welcome."

"Then we should go at once. I do believe I see the postal courier and his mount coming down the hill to the shipyard gate. We may be recipients of good news this afternoon."

"Really? You are expecting such?"

She laughed and shook her head. "Not really . . . the thought is just a fancy of mine. You must be aware that women are apt to get these premonitions from time to time."

"Really? I did not know that. I must admit that you are the first young lady I have come to know who is so easy to converse with. I have never found members of your sex to be worth more than a few mumbled words of greeting before now."

Roberta hid her surprise behind a smile. "And to what do I owe such improved reputation, Sir? My meagre aptitude for mathematics, perhaps?"

His expression turned guarded. "I must admit that your, decidedly not inferior, aptitude for mathematics plays a great deal in the matter . . . but only as far as I might consider you a worthy colleague in such discussions. But I do realize that I could value you as a sister, or as a sister-in-law, if that were to become our social connection."

"Good Lord! Do you see me suddenly married into your family, Sir?"

He frowned. "Perhaps I have said too much. I should speak no more upon it, but cannot avoid saying something with that connection—although it is not appropriate for me to apprise you of the whole matter. Just let me speak of Lord Bond's family in this one instance only. You should be aware that the Marquess holds absolute power over matters of the family and title, and that nothing can be accomplished without his express approval."

Roberta stared. "My dear sir, your words astound me—and in the same degree confuse me no less. How can Lord Bond's dependence upon the decisions of his noble father concern me? His Lordship has never acted in any manner toward me but as a gentleman who is conscious and careful of propriety. You must tell me more."

"That I cannot do, dear lady. Please consider our conversation over."

With that they left the steam powerhouse for the main office, walking together but now in a deep silence. After their candid conversation of a moment before, Roberta found his reticence to continue it quite baffling, as she did his serious expression. How was his admission of a lack of pleasing intercourse with other young ladies to bear a responsibility for his digression into the relationship between the Marquess and Lord Bond? And was that subject so dire as to be entirely responsible for his reversion to silence?

Perhaps not entirely . . . she had little insight into his deeper nature, and it might only signal a return to the incommunicative mood that Lord Bond had mentioned to her earlier. It seemed unfortunate that the introduction of this topic had completely ended any possibility of further conversation with him. She would have liked the opportunity to venture further questions about the *Nederlander's* passengers with a view to learning something more of the arrangements Lord Bond appeared to be keeping from her, but it was not to be.

Christopher Hoare

CHAPTER THIRTY-TWO
ADMIRALTY INSTRUCTS

Roberta was sitting drinking tea in the draughtsman's office with Mr. Holmes and Lord Bond when her father entered with the mail delivered by the courier.

"There's one for ye, lassie," he said, holding out two packets. "As well as one for His Lordship."

Roberta took the one proffered while Lord Bond rose to reach out for his. They both had Admiralty seals and he seemed surprised as he saw his. She didn't wait to see him open it before rising to fetch a pen knife with which to open hers.

It contained two separate packages inside, one quite thin and the other thicker. She opened the thin one first. It contained a short note and an Admiralty warrant that quite took her breath away. It was for an amount of thirty-three thousand pounds sterling!

Father's voice interrupted her consideration of the note.

"What's wrong, lassie?"

"Ah, nothing. Look." She handed him the warrant. "The message says that a formal copy of the transmission will follow, but this is the complete payment for the *Spiteful* and an advance on the construction of those vessels ordered from Clydebank."

She looked up to see Mr. Holmes and two of the draftsmen watching her father. Lord Bond appeared engrossed in his own missive.

Father smiled at Mr. Holmes. "Thirty-three thousand pounds. I must confess it to be more money than I ever expected to hold in my hands at one time."

Mr. Holmes peered at the warrant. "I suppose it would be rather wicked of me to suggest we take it to town for a celebration?"

"It most certainly would," Roberta admonished him. "I will take it to Glasgow on Monday morning so I may settle our outstanding accounts."

"I would suggest taking an escort of Captain McNab's men if you will be carrying that much cash," Mr. Holmes answered, a mischievous smile showing unabashedly on his lips. "Even in gold sovereigns that would be nigh on half a hundredweight."

"I do not expect to carry more than a small part of that it coin, Sir. And as for the bills of account, I will ensure that only the companies entitled to cash them will be able to do so. I would hazard a guess that we must pay out more than half of that amount for expenses already incurred." She looked him in the eyes and saw a rather vulnerable expression there. He was a strange fellow, and no mistake. She smiled slightly. "But I would suggest that—if my father approves, we might have a small celebration here at the yard tomorrow after church, that both we and our workers might enjoy."

"Rather!" he replied. "What do you say to that, Julian?"

"Say to what?" Lord Bond enquired, looking up from his Admiralty letter.

"That the Stephensons have offered us all a small celebration tomorrow. The Navy has paid their debts very promptly indeed. I must suppose it is because they do not have my own presence and lengthy deliberations to delay the accounting . . . . I say, you look quite vexed at your own missive."

"Vexed indeed. The Admiralty's information and Lord Melville's instructions have quite upset my plans. It seems that we must depart for the Low Countries at once." He caught Roberta's eye. "Your suggestion of this morning has proven most timely, Miss Stephenson. I will have to go to Glasgow in the morning to make arrangements with General Auchtermuchty for the seconding of Captain McNab."

The small party broke up soon after, when Lord Bond and Mr. Holmes left to find Captain McNab. Father left to return to the slipways and Roberta sat to finish her tea and read from the other Admiralty package. It contained instructions for her.

The letter upset *her* plans as well. The Admiralty wanted her to return to London with full sets of drawings as well as everything necessary to sub-contract a shipyard on the Thames to build two more vessels to the spiteful design. Apparently in his discussions with the government, Viscount Melville had found it necessary to ask for an order for two more vessels to station in the Thames, and the Prime Minister had demanded their construction begin as soon as possible.

While it meant extra profit for their yard, it was not as much as they would have made had they built the ships themselves under a less urgent requirement. She straightened her back—it meant but a small sacrifice for England, that she should be glad to make, but there was more. It seemed that Their Lordships of the Admiralty felt it would be beneficial to have her close at hand to assist in evaluating Lord Bond's information when obtained—perhaps even embarking upon a Royal Navy vessel of the coastal blockade to maintain a closer contact with the spying operation.

So Lord Bond had achieved the aim he had so constantly denied.

Early on Sunday morning, Lord Bond took horse for Glasgow to speak with General Auchtermuchty about attaching Captain McNab to his Admiralty enterprise. He had little time left to complete the arrangements, and worked himself into a foul mood as he rode along.

He did not consider the reasons Their Lordships of the Admiralty gave in the letter were sufficient cause to force him to change his plans and leave immediately for the Low Countries. Firstly, another person to travel with them aboard *Nederlander*, whose presence was so secret they could not write the name in the letter, and then the item he had relayed to Their Lordships from Elise's letter. She had found someone who could take a spy to Ghent to inspect the iron shipments from France.

Elise's person could well be genuine, but he suspected her enthusiasm to be greatly exaggerated. He knew her, while Their Lordships did not. Elise had only one loyalty—to herself—and one objective . . . to acquire a greater sum of money than her absent husband in the Dutch East Indies forwarded to her whenever he found it convenient. Bond doubted they were legally man and wife.

He was aware that her hundred gulden was only worth half as much in the Louis d'or that was the Low Countries' currency since Napoleon had removed his brother, Louis, from the throne of Holland and attached the land directly to France. She was likely anxious to receive a new subsidy from him, to make up the difference. Damn the woman. This time he would finish with her.

This whole day was a hostage destined to be wasted if he could not return in time for his appointment with Mr. Stephenson. He had at last come to the conclusion that it was imperative he speak to Miss Roberta's father before he left for Holland—and doubly important that he should become engaged to her immediately afterward. He had little fear that she would prove difficult, even though she had a mind of her own and already a strong suspicion that his designs were less than gentlemanly. Were they? He had to suppress a sigh as he kicked his heels into his mount's flanks. Of course they were not . . . well, they would not be if the marriage turned out to be a bargain, both economically and physically. He felt sure that once in his arms, the lovely Miss Stephenson would prove to be a prize worth crossing the Marquess to attain.

The Devil may take whoever should raise their noses in condemnation of a union between a peer of the realm and a tradesman's daughter. Stephenson was no ordinary tradesman. With the opportunity to invest in both improving the landed estates of the family and excelling in the new industries of steam, he felt sure the Tiverton fortune could grow enough to rival even that of the late Duke of Portland. With those thoughts returning his mind to a closer acquaintancy with equanimity he almost wore a smile as he reached the gate to the General's military headquarters.

The sentry marched forward, his musket at the port. "What be yurr business, gentleman?"

"Lord Bond to see General Auchtermuchty. Please open the gate and let me pass."

"Do ye have ident'ficatshun, M'Lord?"

"Of course I do. Open the gate at once."

"Well, Yerr Lordship, it do happen that the Generral be not at home."

Damn! That was all he needed. "Where has the General

gone? Please escort me to the officer of the guard at once."

The sentry's eyes and mouth worked together, one pair squinting and the other chewing imaginary cud as the man considered what he should do next. Luckily the inaction brought forth another figure from the guard house behind, this one with the epaulets of a lieutenant.

"What is the matter here?"

The sentry's face positively beamed as the need for a decision evaporated. "This genl'man wants terr see th' General, Sirr."

"Oh, does he? What is your business, Sir?"

"Lord Bond to see General Auchtermuchty. Please open the gate and let me pass."

"Lord Bond? I must inform you that the General is away hunting at a house party today. He is not expected back until Monday, My Lord."

"Could you please direct me to this house party, Lieutenant? It is imperative that I speak with the general as soon as possible."

"Hmm. I'm very sorry, My Lord, but I must ask you to show me some identification. There are rumours of French spies active in the area."

"If you will let me into the guardroom I will do so." Bond almost howled with frustration—the only spies this officer could have heard rumour of were his own teams practising in the shipyards. His sour mood descended upon him again like a Plague upon Egypt. That the officer promptly ordered the gate opened and escorted him inside did little to lighten it.

Bond reached into an inside pocket of his riding attire to pull out several closed packets of documents. "How far away is the General's shooting party? Can you give me directions?" he said as he selected one.

"All in good time, if you please, My Lord," the officer replied as he opened the papers to read. "I'm sure you would not want me to be careless in my duties."

Bond turned a growl in his throat into a hurrumph. "Of course not."

The officer read and then looked up with a frown. "This appears to be an American Passport. It identifies you as a Gideon Paine, a citizen of New Bedford. I need hardly remind you that we are at war with the American colonists—this is very serious. Please sit over there, if you will." The officer quickly detailed two soldiers to watch over him.

"Dammit, man! That is just an unfortunate mistake." Bond reached in for the other documents. "I have my warrant as a special officer of the Admiralty here, please look at it."

"I must ask you to keep both your hands in sight, Mr. Gideon Paine. I will call upon my commanding officer at once."

Bond punched a fist into his hand. Oh . . . this was ridiculous. "I was here just the other day to see the General. Look in the watch ledger, you will see my name and signature listed on August the tenth."

"I'm sure we will, Sir, but I must ask you not to make trouble . . . my men may handle you roughly. I will go to find my superior officer and we will examine your documents and the ledger when we return."

After returning from church, Roberta went to her room with two of the maids and Aunt Nelly to pack a shipping trunk for her stay in London. "First thing tomorrow morning we must get the carter to take this to the passenger booking office of the Firth and Clyde Canal," she told her aunt. "They may hold it there in readiness for my taking the steamship service to London that you did."

"I thoroughly recommend the steamships, lassie. I only wish I cude come with ye, but the offer of the Viscount's Lady must not be sniffed at."

"Indeed," Roberta answered. "The First Lord's lady is very kind to offer me her assistance and her protection while I am in the city. I should have no concern of being in the city alone without a chaperone while I reside under their roof."

"A Viscountess, Miss Roberta?" Heather, one of the maids asked. "I should be terrible affrighted in a noble's house like that."

Roberta smiled. "I'm sure I will feel much abashed, too, if truth were known. I hope I shall settle down quickly in such exalted company."

"Ah, but ye have had the attentions o' His Lordship for nigh on a month now," Becky, the other maid, said with a grin. "You must be near on a lady in yer own rights by now."

"Hush yure mouths now," Aunt Nelly scolded. "Dinna' be sae cheeky."

Roberta laughed. "Let them have some fun . . . 'tis grateful I am that they should work thus on a Sunday."

Aunt Nelly was not mollified. "Dinna cast yer good accounts about fer these hussies. 'Tis ainly the shillin's ye've promised that has brought them forth."

"Is His Lordship in love wi' ye, Miss Roberta?" Heather asked, wide eyed.

"Away wi'ye," Aunt Nelly said quickly. "Sic impertinence."

Roberta ceased pawing through her wardrobe, looking for her most fashionable dresses. "I wish I knew, Heather. Sometimes he seems very kind and bound to please—and then his manner becomes distant and I think he has no regard for me at all."

"Ah, that's jus' a man," Becky pronounced. "They be only at yer beck an' call when they want's somm'at."

"Aye," Heather said. "An' us knaws what they wants."

Aunt Nelly's expression darkened. "Enough, ye wicked trollops—sic language on a Sunday!"

Roberta warned them with a glance. "Let's get to work. Heather—take this dress please and lay it in the trunk."

"Yes, Ma'am."

"Do ye ken how lang ye'll be in Lunnon?" Aunt Nelly asked as they set out her underthings to pack the best.

Roberta shrugged. "A month at least." She could have said two, because this duty as a participant of the spying aboard the Navy ship would likely add weeks to her stay. She did not speak of that because she had resolved not to let her father know the details that had been in the Admiralty letter. She did not want him to worry—he was already fretting at Lord Bond's absence today because he had asked to speak with him in the library upon his return from Glasgow. She could not even tell Aunt Nelly, for she was certain to be unable to keep the secret.

Christopher Hoare

CHAPTER THIRTY-THREE
SETTING OFF SECRETLY

On Monday morning as Roberta prepared to take the new Admiralty warrant to the bank in Glasgow, another message arrived for her father. He interrupted her preparations to ask her to come into the library.

"What is it, Father?"

"Sit down, would you please, dear? I have not yet read the entire message."

Roberta sat close enough to get a glimpse of the writing—it seemed to be from the Stephenson Railway Works at Newcastle. That meant her old nemesis Martin Postlethwait had sent it—he was temporarily in charge of the works while her father was at Clydebank. She attempted to moderate her feelings of revulsion, but her memory of that unpleasant episode four years before when he had tried to claim her as if she were the spoils of . . . perhaps not war, but certainly of his devious efforts to ingratiate himself as the best man to manage the Railway Works in succession to her father. The old impression of being no more than a commodity . . . a convenient repository of the treasure that had been built up by everyone's sacrifice and effort over so many years—!

Men!

She began to reconsider the good feelings that had grown in her breast for the gentlemen who had shared her experiences and trials these weeks past. Who among them had been motivated by the same feelings of entitlement that had animated Postlethwait? Mr. Holmes seemed only to appreciate the feelings of superiority in education his guidance had engendered; Lieutenant Worthington no doubt valued her friendship as a path to advancement and command in the Navy; and as for Lord Bond—. How many of his expressions of kindness had been genuine? Had he really been there for her benefit in the Admiralty; and in the perils and tribulations since . . . or had he been using her as a stepping stone merely to achieve his own ends? Was he any better than Postlethwait?

"The engine works is in financial difficulty, Roberta," Father said, holding out the letter to her.

She accepted it gingerly, as if it bore some unseen effluent of its writer. She frowned as her eyes skimmed across the laboriously embroidered construction of its words and letters to grasp the import of its meaning. "He cannot meet the wages next week. Is that not a matter of his failure to properly budget for the company's expenses?"

"Do not be so harsh, Roberta. I will readily admit that I have taken a great sum of money from the Railway accounts to be able to finance our approach here to the Admiralty. I do not hesitate to point out that Clydebank owes him not a little in return. Please read on."

Roberta continued. She had to admit that several thousand pounds sterling had been tied up in preparing to build the boilers for her new warship. Further into the letter she found some accounts that indicated delays in completing and receiving payment for contracted locomotives could be attributed to much needed iron plates having been diverted to Clydebank. She set the letter aside. "What do you want to do?"

"I think in all fairness you will agree with me that when you deposit the Admiralty warrant today, one of the financial instruments drawn upon it should be a sum of money to recompense the Engine Works for their expenses incurred on Clydebank's account. I must take it to them myself."

The thought of Postlethwait receiving some of her Admiralty warrant was almost beyond bearing. "How much money, Father?"

"That is what we must decide before you leave for Glasgow."

She quickly focussed on the tasks this could add to her workload, even though the greater problems had been solved. "Are you quite sure that you can leave your work here at such short notice?"

"I am sure I can leave everything in your hands until I return. You will not need to depart Clydebank to answer the Admiralty's request that you go to London for another week, at least."

"Perhaps I could take the money to Newcastle."

"I do not think that a good idea—you and Mr. Postlethwait . . . well, I need not go on."

She thought it might be interesting to see his discomfort. "I can stand his presence for a day or two on a business visit—if he will not object to mine."

Her father raised a hand against her words. "There is one other matter that requires your presence here. Lord Bond has expressed a wish to speak with me. His intention had been to speak with us both yesterday, before he departs for the Low Countries, but he has not yet returned from his visit to Glasgow to speak to General Auchtermuchty."

Roberta tossed her head; she did not need to see him. What good wishes did she want to send him to Antwerp with? It seemed as if his desire to involve her would place her in a frigate off that very coast. Whatever she might want to say to him could easily wait until she met him there. "If Lord Bond wishes to have me see him off it can certainly take place when I return from Glasgow this afternoon. No doubt he will have returned by then."

Father stared at her perplexedly. "Well . . . if you think so, but I think you are being too flighty to treat his attentions so carelessly."

"His attentions are entirely his business, Father. Now I believe we should consider ours. How much money does the Engine Works need?"

Lord Bond rode hard until he reached the town of Paisley. The Laird of Ladyland, where the General had gone for the shooting, was almost twenty miles from Clydebank over difficult road, cut up by waggons hauling the local iron to Glasgow. He had been very lucky the Laird had room for him this past night, and perhaps just as lucky that General Auchtermuchty had readily agreed to write out an order authorising Captain McNab to join the spying mission to the Low Countries.

He trotted his lathered animal down Paisley's main street, looking for the turn-off to Clydebank. What he needed next was to find the Captain and deliver the orders, but that was not the end of the business. The senior lieutenant of the regiment must be located to take over the company . . . and that might take some time if the pay, company returns, and equipment accounts were not in good order. He would not involve himself in that business—he was a day late for his conversation with Miss Roberta's father. He did not see how he could embark on the *Nederlander* until Tuesday morning . . . he had best arrange to have draft horses rented at the Firth and Clyde Canal to tow the vessel to the North Sea shores of Scotland.

Should he go next to the *Nederlander* to ensure all the preparations for departure were in good order? He sighed. No, surely Symington could be counted on to deal with those matters in his absence. Then there was the matter of coin for their voyage . . . he doubted he could find French or Dutch coin in Glasgow. He should have arranged for the Admiralty to have that ready to be picked up at Edinburgh. Blast! This unexpected haste to leave had completely upset his planning.

His only motive in delaying the departure had been to secure Stephenson's approval to propose to his daughter—and then there should have been time to woo her with some appropriate gift . . . a piece of jewelry and an attendance at some function in Glasgow. Now, there would not be time for that. He put heels to the horse's flanks. If he did not ride hard he would not reach Stephenson's mansion in time to speak to either of them.

Roberta sat back in the barouche as Cam, her coachman, turned into the Paisley road from Glasgow. Her business had taken some time in the bank, but it had been most gratifying to have several clerks and an accountant bustling around to prepare the three money drafts she requested. The thirty-three thousand she had deposited now had large holes in it— enough for the next month's construction here, the eight thousand for Tyneside, and a thousand for her to deposit in a London bank to cover her shipbuilding business and expenses in the city.

She hoped to reach her destination in time to go to the shipyard to tidy her notes for the new building before returning to dress for dinner. Really, there was little work that could be done on the new vessel to counter the French ironclad until she had the information from Antwerp. As for the spitefuls under construction, she merely needed to be at hand to deal with difficulties as they arose, but the building was now in the hands of the construction superintendents and they had been remarkably free from requests that only she could deal with.

Lieutenant Worthington—soon to be Lieutenant Commander—would be at sea another day, she expected. The *Spiteful* had steamed down the Clyde early Saturday afternoon and would be gone until this evening or Tuesday morning—if they had no trouble. She was confident there would be none, and in any case, they had already proved the ship could complete a voyage on one engine if required.

Mr. Holmes had moved his kit from the mansion on Saturday and was now quartered aboard the yacht. No doubt he was dividing his time between ensuring the yacht's stores were in order and rowing up and down the river determining how much activity he could spy on from the water.

That left Lord Bond. What had been the topic of the discussion he had asked her father for on Sunday? How strange that he had not returned from Glasgow to keep the appointment. She had seen little of him of late, only the ride in the trap on Saturday morning. He had seemed pleasant but not effusively so at that time. Was he really attracted to her, as his attentions in London had suggested? Perhaps she had been mistaken . . . perhaps he was always gallant when in female company. But Aunt Nelly had thought him very serious in his attentions to her when she had witnessed them together in the city. Enough that she had cautioned Roberta not to get her hopes up.

Had she got her hopes up? She did not think so; she had merely been as amiable as she thought proper in the company of a very eligible bachelor. What were her hopes? Could she expect to maintain her duties toward her father and the business while being . . . ? She could not say it. A word danced in her head and seemed to blot out her vision of the countryside as she rode—the word was Marchioness. Surely a totally unattainable height, no matter what her feelings were toward His Lordship.

They turned off the Paisley Road toward Clydebank and drove to the shipyard. Roberta took the money draft and a pouch of sovereigns to deposit in the safe and then went to her office. Her father had not returned to the yard from lunch, and Miss Brad asked if she would inform him she needed his guidance.

A half hour saw her papers set in order and she had time to go over the set of plans she would need in London so two spitefuls could be built there in the yard the Admiralty had selected. She would need to clarify the payment her yard would receive from the arrangement with the Admiralty. This time she would be on her own, without Lord Bond's support. She could not help but feel apprehensive of her success without him.

She looked up at the clock in the draughtsmen's' office. Almost three in the afternoon—she had best get home to pass the message to her father. There was little more she could do here. Cam sat waiting in the barouche as she came out of the office and one of the passing workers gallantly stepped forward to assist her climbing in.

"Thank you, Thomas. How is your mother?"

"Still poorly, Miss. But her sen's her thanks fer the brace o' fowls."

"You were able to cook them? I believe Mrs. Hamilton sent instructions for making broth."

"Aye, all done right, Miss. Me sister Bessie cooked 'em."

"That's good then," she said with a smile as she closed the

door. "Drive home, if you please, Cam."

"Aye, Ma'am."

The ride to the mansion required twenty minutes, but they had only gone for fifteen when she saw their trap bowling down the road toward them.

"Stop, Cam. Who is that driving?"

"It be Miss Nelly, Ma'am.

Roberta raised herself in the seat to look. "Never. Aunt Nelly never drives."

But Aunt Nelly it was. They drew up alongside one another, to the annoyance and remonstrations of the driver of another carriage that barely had room to go around them.

"What is wrong, Aunt?"

"Nothing may be wrong eg'xacly, dear, but I thought you should know."

"What then?"

"Lord Bond have been in the library with yer father for nigh on an hour. They be waitin' fer you to get home—and drinking bumpers o' toasts a'plenty as they waits."

A cold fear gripped Roberta's heart. What had they talked about? What indeed—it hardly needed a Doctor at Laws to provide the answer. "Did Lord Bond ask Father for my hand?"

Aunt Nelly glanced at Cam. "I hate to admit t'my actions but I must own to listening at the door. That is exactly what he asked."

"And my father—? No, do not answer, the bumpers tell me."

"I hope you feel well composed to meet the gentleman," Aunt Nelly said with a sigh. "I did not want you to be discommoded at the surprise."

"I thank you, dear Aunt. I thank you with all my heart."

She smiled warily. "Nay. Not all o' it."

"I am not so sure, I must confess. I think my heart is happier with you and with this meeting in the road than it would be to continue with my journey."

"Pray, what are you saying?"

What was she saying? Did she really mean to refuse His Lordship? Why should she not? What right had he to sit getting drunk with Father before he had even asked . . . even heard her answer. Was she that transparent? Did he consider her no more than a grocer's daughter to have her head spun upon her shoulders at the mere thought of his address? She would show him.

"Go back home, Aunt, but do not immediately tell them you have seen me."

"What are you going to do?"

"I am going to London." There was nothing to stop her— her shipping trunk had gone to the Canal office this morning. The afternoon Puffer would leave in about two hours—ample time to be aboard. "No earlier than five of the clock you may tell my father that I have gone to take the money to Tyneside . . . and will continue on to London to speak with the Admiralty."

"But what about His Lordship? What is his answer?"

"Tell him nothing—. No, I suppose you cannot do that. If he asks you, tell him to write to me. Tell him that I cannot give any answer now. His conversation with my father has so distressed me that I must have more time to think before I should see him face to face."

"Good Heavens! Are ye sure ye knows what you'm up to?"

"My dear Aunt, you have been advising me to caution ever since you met His Lordship. Do not tell me he has quite changed your mind now. I had hoped you would approve of my decision—I am sure that my father will not."

"Well, that be true. But . . . but . . . You are a headstrong girl, but I loves thee all the more for it. Come, kiss me an' say farewell, for I shall hold thee dear in my heart until we meets agin'. An' never fear fer yer father—when he cools down I will tell him that you knows what you be doin' and will hope to take yer own time and give yer own answer to His Lordship when next ye sees him."

Roberta smiled. "If I see him?"

"Ah, dinna' try to play me fer a fool. I knows what be a goin' on. Play they gen'lmen fer fools as much as thee likes—bear in mind that once yer word is given, thee has become nort but a household chattel. If you mus' take the navy's ship to the coast o' Holland do tak' care. Oh how I wish thee were goin' to meet our Worthington—he be a steadier hand on the tiller than they what be goin' ter spy."

"Ah, hush, Aunt. Do not try to make my mind for me. Now kiss me again. Take care of yourself and Father. Tell him I am sorry to vex him so, but I must live my life my way."

CHAPTER THIRTY-FOUR
NO MEETING AT SEA

Three days out of Tyneside, the passenger steamer *Blyth* churned its paddles to reduce the waves of the Thames Estuary to spreading foam as Roberta reclined in a deckchair in the shelter of a midship's deckhouse. The late August sunshine valiantly made its most powerful demonstration of an English summer by propelling its warmth through the three layers of her travelling garb and possibly burning a lasting bit of colour into her unprotected cheeks. Her eyes sheltered in shade under the wide brim of one of her flamboyant bergere hats as she forsook the book in her lap to study the ships in the offing. They focused intently on a vessel destined to overtake them that she could not help but recognize—her own design, the steam ram *Spiteful*.

She had left Clydebank first, but with three days spent in Tynemouth, Commander Worthington and his first ship command had all but overtaken her. All it would need now would be a glimpse of Lord Bond's *Nederlander* and the embrace of coincidence would be completely full. Her own hasty departure from Clydebank had prevented her from hearing Lord Bond's plans, but he and his spy team must surely be far distant across the North Sea by now, since she felt it wiser for him to approach the Westerschelde from the east if the French authorities were to be free of suspicion.

"Good afternoon, Miss Stephenson," she heard close at hand, and looked up to see the friendly middle aged couple she had met on the voyage, Mr. and Mrs. Middleton, approaching.

"Good day to you both," she responded.

Mrs. Middleton stopped beside her, to smile as she reached down for the book. "Do I observe a deficiency in the charm of this novel that your eyes would rather observe the scenery? What are you reading?"

"A novel a friend of mine sent with the recommendation I read it," she answered, "but the ships . . . or rather one of them . . . is of considerable interest to me." She pointed. "The steamer on the horizon that rapidly overhauls us is no less than HMS *Spiteful*, built in my father's shipyard."

Mr. Middleton turned to follow her directions. "Jolly good show. I'm sure it must feel most gratifying to you that your family enterprise performs such sterling service for your country, my dear. What class of vessel is it? I must admit that its shape is quite unfamiliar to me."

"It is a vessel of a very new and specialized purpose," Roberta answered. "Its particulars are as yet of a confidential nature and it is best I not speak more of it."

"Good Heavens!" Mr. Middleton stepped back and shielded his eyes to take a better look at the vessel. "A dread secret I do declare. As long as it sends old Boney packing!"

Mrs. Middleton did not more than glance at the ship, and instead reached farther to pick up the book. "Why, the late Mr. Samuel Richardson's novel *Clarissa*. What advice do you follow that you should renew your acquaintance with such a sad story?"

"I'm afraid I was advised to note the wiles and trickery of Lovelace, the villain, in his attempt to besmirch the honour and modesty of the heroine during my sojourn in London, Mrs. Middleton."

"Good Heavens, is London such a den of iniquity these days?"

Roberta laughed. "I do not suppose that at all, particularly as I will be a guest of Viscount Melville at Admiralty House for much of the visit. I can only ascribe the choice of novel to the apprehensions of a gentleman friend who clearly wishes me to chart a safe course through turbulent waters." She spoke gaily to ensure her buoyant spirits would remove all trace of seriousness from her study of the ruination of a chaste young lady by a libertine.

It must have worked—the Middletons both laughed, and as they took their leave Roberta took up the book once more with the identity of the donor firmly present in her mind. What more perils did Mr. Holmes see for her in this waning summer?

She still deliberated unsurely over her reasons for escaping the mansion before Lord Bond had a chance to propose marriage . . . an intention that he had almost certainly designed. Sometimes she feared she would have refused him, and others that she would have accepted. The idea of a marriage into the nobility—and the eventual inheritance of a Marquisate—was too attractive to throw recklessly away, but her suspicion that he intended to hurry her into his bed so that he might involve her in spying on the new French warships at Antwerp would not be dispelled. The warning—it could have been intended no other way—of Mr. Holmes that the Marquess might oppose the marriage and perhaps have the power to undo it, reinforced her natural inclination to consider the situation more fully before giving His Lordship her answer.

Two days in the Stephenson Railway works at Newcastle in the company of Mr. Postlethwait were quite sufficient enough to incline her to refuse an offer of marriage from anyone . . . and all the King's horses besides. Postlethwait had been almost apologetic and perhaps chastened that her own status in the works was higher and somewhat more successful than his. Her coup in the Admiralty and the order for ten more vessels to spiteful design had deflated his arrogant self-assurance to a mere bubble in a teacup. His attempts at gallantry had been most gratifying . . . if a little difficult to accept without laughing—she almost felt sorry for his disappointment.

She should be turning her mind to the future meetings with the shipyard managements on the Thames instead of mulling over the past and other imponderables. She squared her shoulders and settled herself deeper into the deckchair as she picked up the novel once more. The copies of the ship plans had arrived by courier while she waited in Tynemouth and as soon as the Admiralty had decided upon the most suitable contractors she must inspect their works and listen to their propositions before handing over the construction of two of her prized spitefuls to their tender mercies. She herself must expect to return to the north to complete the building of the seven ships on order there as soon as the Thames yards were contracted—unless, of course, this reckless plan to have England's most original naval architect dare the French police and armies on a spying mission in Antwerp were carried out. Surely Their Lordships of the Admiralty must reconsider such folly.

Lord Bond had waited for the arrival of the First Lord of

the Admiralty in Chatham for two days with great impatience, two days that should have been spent sailing the North Sea, but Their Lordships had a new plan to put into action. In the interim he had received enough specie in Dutch silver guilders and gold French Louis d'or to bribe half the population of the Low Countries. He had also found enough time to visit the Archbishop of Canterbury, temporarily at his seat and not at Lambeth Palace, and receive a special marriage license that both dispensed with the need for calling the banns and also permitted the marriage ceremony to take place in any location that the uncertainties of war might impose. The one thing he had needed to deal with circumspectly, as Archbishop Manners-Sutton had minutely investigated him, had been the inclination of the future bride—he dare not admit that she had fled rather than hear his protestations of eternal love and fidelity.

He should be chastened, he knew, perhaps angered, but he could not help but admire her spirit and her independence in the flight. He was not inconvenienced by the chase—as an experienced hunter he allowed that it gave the eventual outcome and the prize all the more merit.

He hoped the First Lord might have come earlier, but apparently he was making this official visit to inspect the *Spiteful*; expected to arrive from Scotland any day now—at least that was the official story. The probable existence of a traitor in the Admiralty itself—and the visit to discuss the new spying plans for Antwerp—was to be shielded from any treachery by the ceremony of presenting the *Spiteful's* captain, the stalwart Alfred Worthington, risen from the Black Gang, with his new commission. What the First Lord needed to discuss with him must be connected with this sudden concern for a speedy return to the Low Countries.

Commander Alfred Worthington stood waiting with studied calm, if a few butterflies in the stomach, as the gig bearing the First Lord of the Admiralty drew nearer. With but an hour's warning of the inspection—from the harbour pilot as he came aboard at the River Medway's mouth—there had been too little time to wash the smoke and grime of four days hard steaming from the *Spiteful's* decks and paintwork. For the first time in his naval career he sympathised with innumerable captains who had cursed the steam engines and boiler fires that had besmirched the pristine white of sails and decks that was the prime evidence of a well-run ship.

His crew stood in lines amidships although he felt their bearing could hardly impress—fully half were Miss Stephenson's civilian crew that had been aboard the vessel during his first voyage—the Channel trial a month before designed to prove the adequacy of the vessel to meet its naval purpose. He formed the impression that he should introduce these people first to His Lordship, to establish the fact that this was not yet a commissioned fighting ship, and then he could expect to emphasize the degree of learning his naval newcomers had attained since leaving the River Clyde, and look to impress—for, indeed, he felt proud at how quickly they had formed a basic knowledge of their duties.

The gig disappeared from sight as it reached the ship's side and all waited with baited breath for the first sight of the First Lord's cocked hat rising above the rail—or perhaps he was not in uniform, being a civilian head of Admiralty. The bosun and his mate put their boatswain's pipes to their mouths in readiness and almost immediately sounded the call as Viscount Melville, in a dark blue greatcoat and tricorn hat, reached the deck. Worthington stepped forward to salute and then grasp the First Lord's proffered hand.

"Good to see you again, Mr. Worthington," the First Lord said warmly.

Worthington took a deep breath and hoped his colour had not risen enough to be noticeable as he smiled gratefully and answered, "And I am honoured to be of service to Your Lordship once more. Welcome aboard the *Spiteful*, My Lord, but four days out of Clydebank."

The First Lord stood aside as Lord Henry Paulit reached the deck. "Four days?" the senior admiral echoed. "That's good sailing. What did you log?"

"An average of ten knots for the entire passage, My Lord Admiral." He thought it appropriate to point out the vessel's deficiencies himself. "As you might tell from the soot and grime of the smokestacks that have barely cooled their fires."

Lord Paulit laughed. "Ah, do not take your accomplishments as excuse for your hard-worked appearance, Commander. I would not wish other commanders of steamships to learn such ploys in answer for their admirals."

The two Admiralty Lords and the next arrival, Commander Ripley, from the Steam Directorate, all joined in the polite laughter.

"Of course, My Lord, but I will put my naval ratings to work as soon as your inspection is done, and meantime present my civilian crew from the Stephenson Dockyard to you—starting with Mr. MacRae and Miss Elizabeth Grandin, the Chief Engineer."

As Lord Paulit spoke of seaman's things to Mr. MacRae, Viscount Melville stopped before the latter. "Miss Grandin. I am pleased to meet you after hearing about your sterling service on the trial voyage in the Channel."

Elizabeth curtsied and responded in French and English. "*Enchanté Monsieurs*, I am so pleased to meet zee Lordships that has so protect the country that gave my parents sanctuary when the terrors in France was so vile."

Worthington thought her French accent somewhat unexpected, since she rarely lapsed into it with him, but she surely had her reasons. The visitors took the time to ask how the engines had performed and how the new bearings stood up.

"The bearing, she are perfect, *Mes* Lords. I will pleased to show should you wish to visit below."

"Indeed, we will," Viscount Melville replied. "I want to see all the novel features of the ship."

And see them he did, from the stern paddlewheels to the ram, and he even crawled inside the rocket redoubt in the bow with Commander Worthington—the rabbit hutch as the matelots nicknamed it—where the Congreve rockets were loaded and fired to distract the enemy as they steamed in to ram.

The visitors seemed pleased and impressed as they took a glass of wine in Worthington's cramped cabin just ahead of the engineroom bulkhead below — no spacious stern cabins as they would be used to visiting in a sailing warship.

"I did wonder if Miss Stephenson would make the voyage south with you, Commander," the First Lord said conversationally. "We expect her any day to begin the preparations for building the two ships on the Thames."

Elizabeth Grandin, who was one of the party, answered. "Miss Roberta have to visit Tyneside on her way south, Monsieur Vicomte. There was an issue one of ze famille had to deal with."

"I expect you will find her in London when you return, My Lord," Worthington said. "We overtook the steamer from Edinburgh in the estuary as we arrived in the roadstead."

CHAPTER THIRTY-FIVE
CHANGING PLANS

Roberta spent the second day of her stay as a guest in Admiralty House going through the drawings she had brought for the yards who would build the two spitefuls on the Thames. The First Lord returned from Chatham on the second day, and after dinner he discussed his visit to the *Spiteful* and the plans with her in his library.

"Although in the past I have spoken with disfavour upon the acquisition of steamships for the Royal Navy, I must say that I was very impressed with your *Spiteful*, my dear. It is not a large ship, but you have achieved much with a great economy of space."

Roberta looked up in surprise. "Disfavour, My Lord? I had formed an impression that you had a favourable opinion."

"Of the use of tugs and other auxiliaries, yes. But not as warships—since I do not think it advisable to hinder our present pre-eminence in sailing warships. However, a special purpose squadron of your spitefuls for home defence in our present circumstance is quite a different matter. I was particularly struck by your coal bunkers forming enclosed spaces between the boiler rooms and the outer hull of the vessel."

"Thank you, My Lord. It is hoped that the coal will stop any cannonballs that come through the sides of the ship in action and prevent the boilers from being burst open."

"Good Lord, yes. A puncture would create a boiler explosion in the confined spaces of the boiler and engine rooms."

Roberta glanced at the shelves of books lining the walls. "Did Commander Worthington introduce my shipyard members of the crew?"

"Most definitely—he accorded them pride of place. I must say I found your Miss Grandin a remarkable engine room chief . . . she is French, is she not?"

"A daughter of Émigrés from the Revolution, My Lord. I believe she was but a child when she came to this country."

"I thought so. Her English is nearly perfect, with but a slight flavour of French."

Roberta tilted her head. "You noticed? Very perceptive of you . . . her English is generally flawless."

"Oh? Perhaps I noticed because I had not met her before. It made me wonder why Lord Bond did not consider her as a member of his covert intrusion into Antwerp. She seemed sufficiently proficient in the details of her trade that she could have made a fine contribution."

Roberta nodded. "Most likely, My Lord, but her experience will also be of prime value in the training of crews for the squadron of spitefuls."

"Yes. How are you coming along with them? I understand from my wife, the Viscountess, that you have been poring over drawings all day."

"I had to bring the plans up to date first, My Lord," she said, pointing out the engineering sketches she had added to the detailed drawings.

"Up to date, my dear? Surely the plans are only a few weeks old."

Roberta smiled. "We had to make a number of changes last month, Sir. Firstly, these 'A' version plans did not show the changes we had made to the original *Spiteful* as a result of our Admiralty trials. Commander Worthington was good enough to oversee our yard work and helped sketch the modifications. In addition, there is now a 'B' version of the spiteful design which covers the changes made to allow the vessels to be built in two halves and conjoined at Grangemouth for towing to Tyneside."

The First Lord shook his head. "I recollect what I was told about the reason for building the machinery on the Tyne, but was this drastic construction method really necessary?"

"It was far simpler and cheaper to move the halves through the Firth and Clyde Canal to go to the machinery than to transport the engines and boilers to Clydebank, My Lord. For the same reason I have proposed that the machinery for the Thames built ships should be wholly designed and built on the Thames."

"And the Stephenson works loses money on them. Your honesty and loyalty to the country should be recognized . . . I will recommend the government take note of that."

Roberta looked up at him from the drawings. What did he mean by that—some Royal recognition? A vote of thanks from Parliament? Her experiences were becoming more and more heady every day. "Thank you, My Lord, but we will come out quite well if we can hold the budget my father and I have set."

"So, where will you be during all this construction?"

"Between us, my father and I will supervise the building on the Clyde as well as the machinery installation on Tyneside. I really do not see how we can be involved in the construction on the Thames as well. I would recommend, if I may be so bold as to make a suggestion on Admiralty affairs, that Commander Worthington might be a member of the supervising board, since he was of such great assistance in supervising the modifications to *Spiteful*."

The First Lord inclined his head graciously. "I thank you for the advice and will certainly keep it under advisement."

"But the greatest interruption of my schedule will be the involvement this month or next with Lord Bond's spying. Are there really no other marine engineers who can take my place?"

The First Lord shrugged. "The choice was either to employ yourself or else an official of the Laird Yard who will be producing another design to our request for a ship to challenge the French ironclad. They really have no better expertise in steam engineering than you and even asked to use your assessment of the armour thickness needed. I discussed the matter in Cabinet and their preference was for you to be aboard the frigate of the blockading squadron." He looked up and smiled. "You see—you have quite dazzled the whole country with your accomplishments."

Roberta could feel the flush spreading from her neck. How would her modesty be possible to maintain with such a focus of attention on her? She had best beware lest she should get above herself, like a spoiled child. "Need I be at sea for long, My Lord? A week or two at the most?"

"Perhaps no more than a day to actually pronounce upon the stolen secrets, but between the sailing to the squadron, the waiting until Lord Bond reaches it with the information, and then the return to England, I would expect you to be gone at least two weeks."

"Did you know that he had spoken to my father before he left Clydebank, to gain his approval to ask me to marry him?"

The First Lord looked up abruptly. "Did he, by gad? And what did you answer?"

"I left immediately for Tyneside and London as soon as I learned of his intention from my Aunt. He has had no opportunity to speak with me on the matter."

"Good Lord. Do you intend—ah, no. Do not answer. I have no right to ask, but I must say I think your caution is advised. One should never rush into such a serious matter. I have always held that a young lady should have at least a year to consider a proposal of marriage—it is a decision not easily reversed."

"Yes, I know. But on the matter of Lord Bond's activities, do you know what answer he received from the artillery officer at Woolwich about the armour plate trials? I had six plates of two inch thick iron sent for them to shoot at."

"He did mention it to me, but at that time he had no answer. I will contact Woolwich officially and have you and an accompanying officer visit to see what they have discovered."

"Thank you, My Lord. And the Laird ship—since they will accept my assessment of the iron armour, I feel I should know something of their design."

The First Lord looked down at the table a moment. "I should not say much, because of your involvement in Lord Bond's activities, but they are proposing to take a two deck third rate and cut it down, plate the sides with iron, and provide steam propulsion."

"I see." Roberta frowned. "And the paddlewheels will be conventionally side mounted?"

"I understand so. I see you disapprove . . . the Admiralty also has reservations about the vulnerability of side paddles, but Lairds suggest your armour plate recommendations should be sufficient protection."

Roberta felt the weight of responsibility on her shoulders increase. Yes, and should the paddles be shot to pieces even with armour they would be able to blame her.

As evening fell, Lord Bond and the Count stood in the stern of *Nederlander* smoking clay pipes and discussing the night's plans as they slowly pulled away from the anchorage. The Count was Auguste, Comte de la Marck, a Royalist ally of England who had recently travelled from Vienna to London. His presence had prompted the Admiralty to change Lord Bond's plans and use the Royalists' prior arrangements to secretly enter the Low Countries.

"The code words for ensuring the landing party is not betrayed are—"

"A confidential Arenberg family secret, Lord Bond," the Count replied. "No one but my cousin will be able to offer the response."

"But if your cousin—"

"Is not there? It would be a great problem. I think we had then be better to use the method of your original intention."

"I see. All very well, as long as the landing party is not Napoleon's, and with a sloop of war at readiness nearby."

"It will be night. Your hoogaar should be able to sail farther inshore and escape even a small warship."

Lord Bond allowed a grunt to be his answer. This French nobleman had spent too much of the war in safety in Austria. He seemed to consider practical considerations mere trifles. He had complained about everything—even the time taken to reach the rendezvous for the full moon. They were now but one night after the full moon, and there would still be light enough to approach an unknown beach in safety.

They had spent the day in a cove under the shelter of a French artillery battery—having carried out a charade for the watchers ashore. It had been easy to outrun the weed-encrusted gun brig supplied by the blockading squadron; and its distant misses from a nine-pounder bow chaser had been enough to convince the local commander that his refuge had saved a small trader vessel on Imperial service from capture by the English.

Lord Bond had urged his Dutchmen to sing and to call loudly during the hours they spent at anchor, and the officer had not bothered to send a subordinate by small boat to examine them.

The Count set aside his pipe. "How many people do you wish to transport to Antwerp, Lord Bond?"

"Three will do. I have a Dutchman who has worked in the city in recent years, as well as two Britons who speak French. It would seem that the French Royalist I had expected to provide a safe house in the city for them is a member of your network. You will be staying in the city also?"

Monsieur le Comte did not answer this question directly. "My business is with many correspondents, Lord Bond. My purpose is to strengthen the Royalist cause sufficiently that the restoration of a Bourbon king to France will see these lands become part of a future, greater France."

"You expect to see Napoleon overthrown then?"

The Count laughed shortly. "I can tell from your own manner that you do not share the view. Perhaps understandable as you await a French invasion with great trepidation, but in Europe, we see the upstart hazarding his best army on an enterprise *tres dangereuse*—to which we ascribe credit to your ancestors who have foiled every such attempt since 1066. When Napoleon is sufficiently embroiled in England; Austria, Russia, and Prussia will stab him in the back."

Lord Bond did not share the Count's satisfaction. After years of sacrifice, his country would be the one to hold the line alone while its sometime allies seized the prize by stealth. Did Their Lordships of the Admiralty know of this intention? Did the Earl of Liverpool and his Cabinet know and approve the plan?

"And you, Lord Bond. Do you not wish to come ashore with me?"

"I have a member of my previous investigations in the Low Countries—who was left behind—to locate. Some useful lines of enquiry may already exist. I expect to use the *Nederlander* in the Westerschelde to search in several towns." He did not wish to admit to Elise's identity. Somehow he felt the admittance he relied upon a woman would only fuel the Count's already palpable derision.

"As you wish. I expect finding horses and a guide to escort your three men will already present an imposition for my cousin's followers. I will travel in a different party, of course."

Lord Bond wanted to retort that having to await the Count and convey him to this coast was already an imposition for his plans, but knew that it would start their association badly— and for all he knew they might come to depend upon these Royalists more than he had reckoned before they were done.

It was an hour past a moon-bright midnight before they arrived offshore of the beach the Count had named for the rendezvous. Lord Bond had Bloggins take the *Nederlander* into the shallows as far as they dared its flat bottom to keep from grounding. An hour past a high spring tide could take them farther inshore than was safe, and going aground on a falling tide would leave them high and dry for Napoleon's men to find in the morning.

One of the Dutchmen stood in the bow with a shuttered lantern to flash brief beams of light at the land that appeared to be no more than a cable's length distant. The third flash was answered by a brief light from ashore. They waited longer in a drawn out silence until they heard the muffled creaks of the rowlocks of an approaching rowboat.

The Count went to the bow to call softly into the silver gloom. Bond did not catch the words, likely given in a local patois, nor the answer, but it must have been correct for the Count then spoke in clear French. Bond released the hammer of the pistol he had been holding, gently lowering it onto the priming pan and nodded to the others to set their weapons aside.

When the boat came alongside, their luggage was transferred while the Count and his cousin embraced and spoke quietly together. Lord Bond shook the hands of Mr. Holmes and Captain McNab, and clapped Cornelius van Ee on the shoulder. "Good luck, you fellows. I will see you in Antwerp in two or three days' time."

Holmes looked at him gloomily. "I thought you knew where Elise is?"

"I have an expectation, and if it is correct we will arrive a day earlier. Try to find where Monsieur le Comte is going. It may serve us well to learn his business also."

He stopped speaking as he heard the Count step closer. "Are your men ready to embark?"

"*Oui, Monsieur le Comte,*" Holmes replied. "*Apres vous, Seigneur.*"

Chapter Thirty-Six
Discomfort with Allies

Symington Holmes sat in the centre of the six-oared beach tender as its rowers pulled strongly for the shore. His companions, clearly visible in the bright moonlight, did not speak as they worked, though they breathed heavily and sometimes spat overside. He would have liked to speak with McNab, sitting on the thwart behind him, but conformed to the unspoken caution of silence holding in the craft. Were there only French Royalists awaiting them on the beach, or were Napoleon's men also close at hand?

The Comte de la Marck sat in the stern with his kinsman, exchanging an occasional whisper that was drowned out by the creak of the oars in the rowlocks. All those not rowing looked about them continuously even though nothing could yet be discerned of the beach. He did not know whether their course was taking them closer to shore until a wave broke astern of them.

All at once, figures appeared on the beach. The breaking

wave slopped water over the gunn'les and slewed the boat sideways. The beach party rushed into the waves to steady the craft before the next wave could break over their side. With this wave's surge lifting them up they swept onto the beach and grounded with a clatter of shingle.

The guarded chatter of instructions and greetings in French from everyone heralded their arrival and disembarkation, and within a few minutes he found himself trudging up the beach with a Frenchman on either side. "Are the authorities expected?" he ventured in French.

The man to his right laughed. "The authorities are us tonight. *Mais*, speak not more until we reach the trees."

He could see no trees. When he turned to look back down the beach he could see McNab and van Ee similarly escorted up the beach behind him. He tried not to entertain any apprehensions, but the thought that they were entirely dependent upon these unknown men—and their true identities—for their lives and safety made his blood run cold. Le Comte de la Marck was accepted as an ally of England but was also a French aristocrat with the rank of general in the Austrian army. How many other loyalties and clandestine engagements did he have?

Holmes heard horses whickering before they reached the trees. All at once they were met by more men carrying muskets who greeted Monsieur le Comte, who appeared out of the shadows beside him, with enthusiasm and muted cheers.

"These men will take you to your transport," the Count said. "I will be leaving first with my cavalry escort."

"Will we have a guide, Monsieur le Comte?"

"The carter knows the way to Antwerp, but I can offer you a guide as well, if you need one." The Count turned to speak at length with the leaders of these musketeers. Eventually a tall young man with a cavalry carbine over his shoulder came to them.

"I am Henri. I am told you have French cavalry identification . . . . I am also a lieutenant in Napoleon's cavalry—and no more loyal to the Corsican than you. I will accompany you until closer to the city."

"I thank you," Holmes replied. "Do we leave at once?"

"I will take you to the farm where is the cart. We cannot begin on the road until Monsieur le Comte and his escort can reach the village Schoondijke. It is five kilometres in the French measure. We may rest and eat a little at the farm until depart."

"*Merci.* Will Monsieur le Comte and his escort be on the road ahead of us?"

Henri cocked his head before answering. "I think not. Does that worry you? It is better that we split into many parties and take different roads."

"Yes," Holmes said. "Yes, of course."

Once the beach craft with the Count and his three spies disappeared into the grey gloom, Lord Bond gave Bloggins instructions to get back into deeper water and head for Flushing, almost due north. He did not know if Elise had received his message to meet there, but it was the most logical place to start.

Nicholas van Aa came to him. "We sail north, when Neuzen is east south-east."

"That is correct. I look to find an agent in Flushing. Neuzen will be our next destination from Flushing."

Van Aa shrugged. "Flushing is no port today. Napoleon's money has made Neuzen a better one."

"Is that so? I heard he had ordered all the dredging and harbour work that restored Antwerp's ancient contact with the sea. I did not hear about Neuzen."

"The building of new docks and jetties were not only work. Neuzen was the port where much dredging on the Schelde was supplied. It has good harbour today."

"Then we might pick up a cargo for *Nederlander* to carry to Antwerp?"

"Very likely. You need cargo?"

"We need a reason to sail to the city. What might we find?"

"Canal barges bring building stone from inland. This hoogaar might carry twenty tons."

Lord Bond nodded. "Enough to pose as a merchant looking for a profitable cargo. You could arrange it in Neuzen?"

"I have contacts."

"What do you know of these French Royalists? They are not Flemish."

"The French and their siblings are everywhere. The Comte's family are Arenbergs—Belgian aristocrats with connections to Austria since the Low Countries were a Hapsberg possession."

"I see. I must say you have a good grasp of the subject."

Van Aa laughed. "I was a school teacher before Napoleon's king dismissed anyone who Fouché thought might not like France."

"Fouché, the Emperor's spymaster?"

"None other. He has been much to Bruxelles and Antwerp since the city regained its link to the sea. I was told your investigations are those secrets Fouché protects."

"Very likely. I am looking for information about the steamships."

"So we were told by the officers at the Admiralty, but they did not tell us why."

"The French steamships are very important to Napoleon's invasion plans. When we penetrate these secrets, the Royal Navy will be able to defeat the invasion at sea."

Van Aa smiled. "Now I understand. If we learn nothing,

England is invaded."

Lord Bond frowned. "Does that trouble you?"

"Any success of Napoleon's troubles me. When England defeats Napoleon, there will be a chance that Neuzen and Antwerp become Flemish once more . . . perhaps part of a new United Netherlands. Not that your fine friend Monsieur le Comte wishes that outcome—which makes his friends and ours poor allies to work together for you. But if we are freed from France again, I should have my school back."

Lord Bond had been aware that the French Royalists and the Flemish were only wartime friends but what van Aa said made him worry that neither were completely wedded to the plans the Admiralty followed. Lord Bond quickly tucked away and hid a renewed concern for the viability of his spying venture behind a ready agreement. "Yes. England will reward its friends, I am quite confident of that." His smile soon faded. He feared the government would find difficulty paying off conflicting debts to different friends and allies it had bought in the campaigns.

Christopher Hoare

Chapter Thirty-seven
Secrets of the Drawing Room

Roberta enthusiastically joined in the applause as the last strains of the second piece by the German composer Mozart died away. The whole company gathered in the music room of Admiralty House began to speak at once, as the Viscountess Melville herself rose to go to the leader of the ensemble to congratulate him.

It was a novel experience for Roberta to hear some of the most popular music of the age—particularly that of Herr Mozart whose work was considered somewhat sinful by the church in the north of England. She had heard some speak of *Don Giovanni* and of *The Magic Flute* in hushed voices and with pious expressions for their alleged devil worship and licentiousness—but the arrangements for the six piece ensemble here of some of those very arias had been delightful.

"What did you think of the music?" her seat neighbour, Lady Penelope Finch, asked.

"I thought it most moving and entertaining, My Lady." Lady Penelope was about Roberta's age and beginning to lose the bloom of youth. Her figure seemed quite plump under the exquisite gown she wore to the soiree.

"Will you rise with me and come next door to look at the refreshment table?" Lady Penelope asked. "I believe there will be a brief intermission before we return to hear the string quartet play something by the Viennese composer Beethoven."

"Why, I would be delighted."

They had hardly moved from their seats when a gentleman in a garish suit of velvet jacket and striped breeches approached them. "Hey ho, Cousin Penny. Going to raid the food, are we?"

"I will look at the refreshments and perhaps partake a little," Lady Penelope answered with a frown. She took Roberta's hand. "I suppose I had better introduce you to this ne'er-do-well relative of mine . . . since we are unlikely to be able to lose him in this small gathering. Miss Roberta Stephenson . . . please meet the Honourable Bertram Booster, my cousin not quite far enough removed, and the grand-nephew of the widow of the late Lord Doncaster."

Roberta dipped into a restrained curtsey in answer to his more casual bow.

"Oh, don't make an indictment of it, Penny, old thing. Miss Stephenson—" he regarded her carefully with his head cocked to one side, "pleased to meet you, I'm sure. Are you a member of the family here?"

"No, Sir. A house guest in London from Scotland."

"Ah, but another Scot by your voice. I'm sure you will have a pleasant evening here with all the city gossip from my cousin as well as the music."

"Oh, do not speak ill, Bertram. Miss Stephenson will suppose I do nothing but sit in drawing rooms and listen to scandal."

"I would hate to give her any such impression," he answered, "but not a word to my dear Great Aunt for the little contretemps of the other day. My tailor was quite pleased to make me another suit as soon as I wrote him a new IOU." He paused as they took their turn to leave the music room and follow the other guests to the anteroom beside it where the tables were laden with food and drink. He peered in through the door over the heads of those in front. "I dare say most of the refreshments will be in shells or fillets, as usual."

Roberta smiled. "Well, Sir, this is the Admiralty after all. Perhaps bounty from the sea is no more than appropriate— and no doubt quite delicious."

"Yes. Spot on. What entertainments have you found in London, Miss Stephenson?"

"I'm afraid I'm not here for entertainment, Sir. I came on an errand for my father's business with the Admiralty."

He leaned back and presented the palms of his hands in mock horror. "An errand of business? You must be bound to put me to shame. It is known all over London and the Home Counties that Bertram Booster has never been entrusted with an errand nor performed a stroke of what might be called business in his whole life. What business, pray, does your father have with Their Lordships of Admiralty?"

"My father is Mr. George Stephenson, the railway engineer and inventor, Sir. I come here on business for his shipyard on the Clyde."

The Hon. Bertram Booster's eyes opened wide. "Ah—the noise and wonderful smeech of smoke—railways. I do love trains, such power, such speed. And now ships as well? Do tell."

"We build steamships on the Clyde, Sir."

"Steamships. How delightful . . . I should love to sail in one of them. The very thought of all that steam burned out of the water by huge fires of coal sends me into ecstasies of admiration. But do not tell me you partake of the practices yourself; as your words . . . 'we build' . . . suggest. I really will not have you tell me that your part of the enterprise is any nearer to the . . . machinery . . . than to stand on the quayside and wave as the ships sail past."

"Then in that case, Sir, I will speak no other."

Lady Penelope stood between them as they reached the table. "Bertram, would you go to the other table and find some of that fine Amontillado Lord Melville keeps. Miss Stephenson and I will find you some delicacies in shells and in fillets, and meet you over in that vacant corner by the window."

"No sooner said than done, old thing. I will take possession of as much sherry as I can—I'm sure our host sends frigates full of that nectar across the briny continuously from the vineyards of Spain. How lucky we are to have the Marquess of Wellington's army taking possession of all the delights of the peninsula from those wretched French. More power to them, I say . . . ."

He was still talking as he left their side and made his way to the other table. Lady Penelope smiled. "Don't take any notice of Bertie, Miss Stephenson. He's a harmless ass."

Roberta laughed. "I think him most entertaining, My Lady. I am not used to such jollity in the North—we are far too serious in our activities. Should we take some of these oysters . . . were they harvested in the correct month?"

She assumed that the younger guests must be friends of the children of the First Lord's family. She had met two of the older sons and one of the daughters as well as the smaller children; the eldest was not yet twenty. The senior members of the concert party included several peers as well as the Bishop of London and members of the Board of Admiralty. She noticed Lord Paulit across the room and curtseyed as he acknowledged her. He seemed intending to join her but was hotly engaged by two richly dressed ladies in some voluble conversation as they circulated through the gathering.

When they rejoined the Honourable Bertram Booster, he continued to regale her with his ideas of steam and railways, and she did her best to listen with appropriate gravity to his fanciful explanations. "It seems to me that the railway companies are very wasteful, Miss Stephenson. Whenever I'm travelling and see the huge clouds of steam that escape from the workings I am almost apoplectic at the waste. I think the government should pass a law to oblige the engineers to collect the escaping steam and keep it in the boilers to use again—don't you agree?"

"That does seem a worthy desire, Sir. However, it does not completely take into account the difference in temperature of the steam in the boilers and that vented from the cylinders."

He stared at her as if she had suddenly transformed into a dressed up harlequin at a masque. "Temperature, you say? What do you mean, pray? Steam is all hot, is it not?"

A voice sounded from behind them, and they turned to see Lord Paulit. "I'm told that the steam in the boiler is at over two hundred degrees of Fahrenheit, while that blown out from the cylinders of a railway locomotive as it leaves the station is barely warm enough to more than cover the onlookers with a moist fog." He regarded Roberta with an ironic smile. "Is that what you meant, Miss Stephenson?"

She tried to keep a neutral expression. Poor Booster seemed dumbfounded. "Fahrenheits; what are Fahrenheits, My Lord?"

Lord Paulit took him confidentially by the arm. "Why, my dear fellow, I did not realize that you had such an abiding interest in steam propulsion. You may be very interested to know that the Admiralty has a great need of chaps like you to operate the steamships Miss Stephenson has designed. If you would come to the Admiralty tomorrow I could start you on a fascinating course of study. What do you say to that?"

The Honourable Bertram Booster turned pale and almost

dropped his glass of Amontillado. "Designed? Miss Stephenson? I'm really not sure, My Lord. Please let me look at my appointment calendar before I take up your generous offer."

Lady Penelope entered the conversation. "Why, Bertie, I think that is a wonderful offer. You must think seriously upon it."

"Yes. Perhaps so." The Honourable Bertram Booster spoke little more—merely dealing with a platter of various delicacies in shells and listening astonished to the rest of the conversation.

"I was hoping to have the opportunity to speak with you this evening, Miss Stephenson. The First Lord has asked me to accompany you when you visit the shipyard tomorrow to evaluate their proficiency. I do not pretend to be a source of great insight into the business, but His Lordship thought my presence would impart a degree of gravity to their consideration of the Admiralty's interest in any offer of theirs you might accept."

"Why, thank you, My Lord. I will be most grateful for your presence at the meetings. I have never met any of the Thames-side shipbuilding engineers. Would a departure at ten be too early—we have quite a journey to the Isle of Dogs."

"Yes . . . ten o' clock will be quite satisfactory. Has His Lordship offered a carriage?"

"Yes, he has. I am extremely grateful for all his kindnesses to me."

"No more than is deserved, my dear. I must express how much I was impressed by my visit to your *Spiteful* at Chatham. We are anxious to see the construction of two more begin on the Thames as soon as possible."

With that he made his apologies and left them to speak with another gentleman at the refreshment table.

"I believe that is Lord Liverpool's son, the Member of

Parliament," Lady Penelope told her. "Bertie, you seem quite green about the gills. You have probably eaten refreshments enough. Please be a dear and go back to the music room and see when the music will resume."

The Hon. Bertie Booster wobbled away across the room as if the technical discussion had completely upset his buoyancy. Lady Penelope guided Roberta to an even more remote corner of the room. "I do believe your business with the Admiralty means you must be the mystery woman who came to town with Lord Bond in July. Please tell me if that is so."

"I did not think I was considered any mystery, Lady Penelope. But it is true that I came from Dover on Admiralty business in Lord Bond's company at that time."

"Do call me Penny. All my friends do." She smiled as they seated themselves on a chaise longue beside a window. "You also went to Almack's rooms at that time?"

"Yes . . . we did. My Aunt and I accepted Lord Bond's invitation and accompanied him there. I'm astounded to consider that our presence was that well noticed by fashionable London."

"Ahah. Now you do, but the gossip was mostly focused on His Lordship. You are aware that he is forbidden entrance to Almack's since the difficulties of 1810?"

"I was not aware of any difficulties, Lady Penny."

That lady smiled and leaned closer to speak in a more confidential voice. "You have not heard of the breach of promise, then?"

"I was told something of the sort, but I doubted my informant's veracity."

"All true. It cost the Marquess a thousand pounds to settle the case, and the young lady in question is now the wife of a prominent member of the Commons. But there is more. Not content with that escapade, the following year there was the worse scandal of the . . . ," she paused to glance about them before leaning closer to whisper, "elopement!"

Roberta's heart jumped. "Surely not."

"It is said that they were apprehended before they had gone but a day's carriage ride from the city—so no harm done—if you see what I mean. But that was more than the Ladies of Almack's could tolerate—he has been barred from the balls ever since. That is why he waited until the City function before attending another ball in the premises. Did you meet his half-brother there?"

"Half-brother? Who do you mean?"

"Why Mr. Holmes, of course. Surely you did meet him—I was told he became a member of your party."

"Why, yes, he did, but I do not understand your calling him half-brother."

"Because that is what they are—although Mr. Holmes was conceived on the wrong side of the blanket. He lives with his mother in Kent when not in London. She is a veritable dragon, I understand."

At this moment Viscount Melville's butler entered the room and informed everyone that they should resume their seats as the music was about to begin. Roberta returned to her seat beside Lady Penny with her thoughts in a whirl. Were these stories true? From what she had already been told, it seemed all too likely that they were.

She hardly heard the next music. She had to change course from discounting whatever she was told of Lord Bond to attaining a stance whereby she might believe almost anything of him. And poor Mr. Holmes. How cruel the world was to innocents who suffered calumny not of their own begetting. No wonder his attentions to her seemed so marked with irresolution. She was told that such men were torn between an aversion to all women, and a fear of their regard being rebuffed.

CHAPTER THIRTY-EIGHT
CONTRACT DISCUSSIONS

Roberta rode in an open barouche to the Isle of Dogs with Lord Paulit and an Admiralty clerk named Wilson on a fine Thursday morning, the second of September. Once they left the city proper at the Tower of London, they drove through Wapping, Stepney, and Limehouse before turning south and crossing the lifting bridges over the exit basins of the new West Indian Docks to the West Ferry Road.

Lord Paulit pointed out the long line of five storey warehouses of the unloading docks, almost invisible behind a veritable forest of masts and yards of perhaps as many as two hundred vessels. "The north dock is called the unloading dock," he said. "When a ship discharges its cargo into the warehouses, it leaves the dock by the Limehouse Basin, where we have just crossed, and sails down the river to the entrance of the south dock—which is the loading dock. There it picks up a new cargo for its outward voyage. Of course, we could see more of the activity of the docks if it weren't for the twenty foot high walls surrounding the whole dock complex."

"The activity in the docks is secret?" Roberta asked.

Lord Paulit and the clerk laughed. "Secret from smugglers and thieves, most certainly. One of the incentives for the immense work of dredging and building was to reduce the amount of property stolen from cargoes unloaded at older quays along the river."

"Oh, I see. I'm afraid the thought of secrets and their discovery is very much on my mind these days."

Lord Paulit inclined his head sympathetically. "I'm sure it must be, but have no fear for your friends in the Low Countries. We have sent Lord Bond away with a powerful new ally to assist his discoveries."

"Oh. This has happened recently? I heard no mention at Clydebank before I left."

"Very recently. He would have joined Lord Bond's crew off the Medway at about the time you were arriving in London."

Roberta could not prevent a small gasp from escaping her lips. She had thought how far coincidence would be extended, should the *Nederlander* join the accidental rendezvous of the *Spiteful* with her passenger ship *Blythe* at the mouth of the Thames. What superstitious thoughts could be released now she knew Lord Bond and his vessel had not been far away. Could she sense some omen in it?

"Yes, you just missed him. The First Lord and I met him and his crew off Queenborough when we introduced him to the Count." He stopped speaking to reach across the carriage to take her hand. "Why, you look quite faint. The news distresses you?"

"It is nothing, My Lord. Merely some foolish thought that passed through my mind."

"It does not look like nothing. Wilson—are you carrying your flask today? I daresay you are. Pour a small measure into the cap, will you? Miss Stephenson looks as if she needs a small fortification."

"No . . . really. I am perfectly all right. Oh—well if you insist. Just the smallest drop."

"You are worried about your own presence off the enemy coast?" Lord Paulit went on. "Please be reassured that we expect a powerful frigate to join that squadron soon, and we will send you with her. We very likely will see the *Medusa* this morning, she has been in dry dock at the Thames Graving Dock on the Isle, here."

Roberta drank the small dram of rum and thanked Mr. Wilson. She took a deep breath and forced a gay smile. "I think that has done the trick. I do not know what ill thought assailed me—I really have no apprehension at being off the enemy coast in a Royal Naval blockading squadron."

Lord Paulit smiled, but he continued to watch her with a serious frown. She felt sure he intended to say more but had thought better of it.

As they rode farther from the docks toward Millwall they came to an area of crowded housing, teeming with running and screaming children and with roughly dressed and careworn women at the public water pumps. Roberta guessed they could be near her age, but bent over with loads and buckets of water they all looked like ancient grandmothers.

"I suppose these must be new homes for dockyard workers," Mr. Wilson said, pointing to a row of tiny houses in a street parallel to the road they followed. "I would suppose them to be conveniently close."

"Yes, I daresay," His Lordship agreed. "I did hear that all kinds of dubious tradesmen had rushed here to take advantage of the new docks. The cottages seem very small and ill found, but I would not doubt them to be no worse than the hovels the poor labourers and their families have moved from."

Roberta thought them possibly a shade better than the

homes provided for factory workers in the north of England. She watched the casual labourers' families as they passed, knowing that even the loss of a single day's wages would send all to bed hungry. The security of steady work was the only answer, but business owners preferred to hire by the day, placing every man in competition for the smallest wages possible.

When they reached the end of the houses, where new carpentry and incomplete rafters showed continuing construction, she turned her attention to the view intermittently visible across the river. Even in the midst of war it was apparent that England did not lack for the means to increase her works and her cities—if not her peoples' welfare.

They passed two piers and innumerable warehouses and workshops beside the river; all the clutter of industry and commerce as they rode along. Much of the industry seemed to take place in abandoned ruins—at least it would appear so except for the throngs of workmen carrying, hauling, and hammering as they built or moved whatever it was that brought their employers profit. The Clyde may have more steamships to boast of, but it had far to go before it could match London's volume of industry.

"Here we are," Lord Paulit said, as he turned to address the coachman. "Take the next gate to our right. This must be the Thames Graving and Shipbuilding Company."

They were delayed only long enough for Mr. Wilson to identify the passengers of the barouche to a stout fellow at the gate before they were waved on toward the river and a long low building with a sign saying "Office" above the windows. When they stopped beside the door, a tall, gangling man walking with a cane came out of the building to greet them. He bowed awkwardly as Lord Paulit climbed down from the carriage. "Lord Paulit? Very pleased to greet you, My Lord . . .

I am Charlie Napier, the proprietor."

Mr. Wilson dismounted next and stood close to help Roberta climb down. Lord Paulit reached out a hand to steady her. "And this is Miss Roberta Stephenson, the designer of the ships and manager of her father's yard at Clydebank."

Mr. Napier smiled broadly, his face twisting enough to reveal several broken teeth. He switched his cane to the left, reached out a hand to hers and shook it warmly. "I'm delighted to meet you, Miss Stephenson. I must own to have suspected your existence to be but a figment of some Admiralty attempt at secrecy, but instead find you to be not only real, but delightfully so."

Roberta laughed gently. "And I am pleased to meet the proprietor of a yard who is so full of gallantry—well met, Mr. Napier."

"Please call me Charlie, my dear. I'm just one of the workmen here." Napier turned and gestured to the building. "Please come into our inner sanctum. I'm sure I can clear a space where we might lay out the drawings." He gestured toward the map case Mr. Wilson lifted out of the barouche. "I hope you will forgive its clutter and grime, Miss Stephenson— it is but an old bachelor's abode."

The interior smelled of dust, of musty books, and of strong tea; it was every bit as cluttered as announced, and seemed too dark to Roberta to perform satisfactorily as a plans office. Very likely "Charlie" kept the plans for his vessels in his head and had little need to look at paper drawings. Not a promising situation for someone contracted to build an entirely novel ship for the navy. She sighed . . . was their day to be wasted?

Lord Paulit opened the discussions. "I and Mr. Wilson are here to look at the works buildings and the yard, Mr. Napier. Miss Stephenson is solely responsible for the business discussions and possible contract for the iron construction of a spiteful class vessel."

Charlie nodded. "I see, My Lord, but we are just completing work on a naval frigate in the graving dock. Admiralty surveyors have been here frequently."

"Would that be the *Medusa*? I thought she was at a different company."

Charlie shrugged. "There was a dearth of iron building and a deal of ships needing fitting out for war last year, My Lord. The graving dock was unused, so I bought it from the bankruptcy trustees and entered a tender."

"Then you have no ironworkers, Sir?" Roberta asked.

"Ah, that I do—iron workers and wood both. We are building hundred ton river barges in iron here, and I have loaned out some of my best ironworkers to the Ditchburn yard. I can have them back in a week."

"And where would you construct a spiteful?" she asked.

"In the graving dock—it will house a thousand ton ship, and has room for a length overall of 150 feet. *Medusa* will be afloat on the next high tide."

Roberta looked toward Lord Paulit, who seemed less disconcerted than she felt. "Mr. Napier did well on a contract for three tugs," he said, "and I understand the work on *Medusa* has been exemplary in quality and promptness."

She felt inclined to accept His Lordship's recommendation—after all, the Stephenson yard would neither be required to carry out the work nor manage it. If the ship was not completed within the time allowed, it was the Admiralty surveyors who would bear the responsibility. She would make sure that her payment for the patents and design would be included in the cost of construction, and instalments paid when the materials were purchased.

"Then perhaps we should look over the design drawings— is there a brighter room than this?"

Charlie shrugged. "There's a table outside overlooking the river. The day is fine . . . shall we go there?"

The table had to be cleared of tea and breakfast things by a pair of stout women in kitchen aprons before they could look over the drawings. To Roberta's surprise, Charlie seemed to have almost an instant understanding of details she thought she should explain. Within an hour, the only outstanding issue was the provision of the engines and boilers by another contractor.

"The Admiralty intends they should be built by the Maudslay works," Lord Paulit announced. "They have supplied a number of such machines for Admiralty contracts and our Steam Department think they will be completely satisfactory."

"But the machinery may not fit the baseplates and bulkheads laid out on these drawings," Charlie said.

"Indeed," Roberta answered. "I had already told Commander Ripley that we must supply drawings to Maudslay's immediately to determine what alterations were needed within the machinery spaces of the hull."

Charlie smiled. "And if I have a contract, I'd like to go along when ye take the drawings. Too many cooks can spoil such fine-fashioned broth as this."

"Indeed," Roberta said. "We must keep control over details as closely as possible. My father and I are the only two supervisors for our northern contracts."

They ate lunch with the proprietor and his senior workers at the same table an hour after noon and then walked along the riverside past a slip where one of the barges was being built until they could see the stumps of masts of the *Medusa* rising above the graving dock.

When they were able to look down into the dry dock they could see the shipwrights removing some of the timber baulks that kept the grounded hull upright and safe from warping. "Every third, mind," Charlie shouted down to them.

"Aye aye, Sir," one of the carpenters said with a wave.

Several more left the work and scrambled up the bracing.

A big man with hands as round as dinner plates stepped forward. "We're laid off when ship floats aht?"

"Aye, Reuben. If we have no contract to replace it," Charlie agreed.

"But we 'eard you want to build an iron ship in the dock next. What will us carpenters do?"

"There are many wooden working platforms and decks needed in the construction," Roberta said.

Reuben eyed her keenly. "Beggin' yer pardon, Miss, but that don't take as many as work 'ere nah."

She looked at Charlie—that was true. She had met the problem before—the more ships built of iron the more old-time shipwrights were put out of work. But she knew no way to prevent that.

Charlie took her aside. "One of our barges was built inside out, using wooden forms to hold up the riveted plates before the angle iron of the stringers were riveted inside. It saves the time taken to drill and fit the plates and uses more woodworkers. That means less cost than for the scarcer iron workers."

She had not heard of it before. "I suggest the method of building is yours . . . if you want to keep these shipwrights employed, I have no objection."

Reuben had moved closer and likely heard. "No objection to men earnin' a wage ter feed their families?" he said. "Is that yer finer feelin's?"

Roberta drew herself up. "No. I can offer more. I have employed redundant carpenters as riveters in my own yard. They do not take long to master the work—after all, the ability to swing a hammer accurately is the qualification for both trades."

Charlie smiled and put a hand on Reuben's arm. "Believe what the lady says. Ye were too proud to change last time. I'll give any man who wants it the chance now."

"Aye, but is the ship to be built?"

They all looked at Roberta. "Aye—if the Stephenson Yard gets its just dues. That means we both agree on the tendered price to the Admiralty."

Lord Paulit laughed shortly. "And I will no more speak to that upon the stonework of a graving dock as I would discuss the rum ration on the quarterdeck of a man-o-war, but England is in peril and will do its best for all men . . . and all women . . . who will do their best for it."

Christopher Hoare

Chapter Thirty-nine
One Uncomfortable,
One Very Comfortable

Symington Holmes stood on the corner looking over the heads of the passing crowds at the premises across the street—*Le Canard Noyade*. He glanced back at Captain McNab, who seemed to be reading an advertising bill pasted on a lamp post. McNab shrugged one shoulder toward the disreputable looking wine shop. Yes . . . he would have to go in to find out if it was the correct rendezvous.

Three small urchins stopped before him as he went to step off the curb. "*Sous, Monsieur?*" one begged. Good Lord—these little tykes must be really starving if they thought someone dressed as poorly as the disguise he wore had a coin or two to give them. He did have a piece of cheese . . . some of the last meal they'd shared with Henri and the carter before they dropped off the farm cart to walk into Antwerp. He pulled out the cloth wrapped wedge and broke some off. Three small hands grabbed for the hard and molding pieces and ran away.

He stepped into the street—here goes.

Pedestrians also overflowed into the street, hurrying this way and that. He crossed slowly against the crush, only reaching the other side as everyone made way for a passing waggon drawn by a swaybacked nag. He glanced back at the cart—was it his imagination or did it look an awful lot like the tumbrels that had carried the condemned to the guillotine during the Reign of Terror? Of course not.

He pushed open the door to the wineshop—the vinegary smell of stale wine enveloped him as he took a deep breath and went in. He had just a second to look at McNab, watching him from the corner, as he closed the door behind him. He walked through smoke and shadows to the counter.

"*Votre plaisir, Monsieur?*"

Holmes dropped a few sous on the counter. "*Vin primeur.*"

A half full glass landed on the counter before him. He turned to look around at the patrons as he took a first mouthful. New wine . . . grapey and still losing its sweetness. He counted three tables with patrons; one of old men playing dominoes, one with an old crone drinking from a bottle, and one of three workmen, smoking pipes and arguing over an empty wine bottle. No soldiers, but who might be an informant among these people?

He drank his wine while wondering if he should direct his question at the barkeep while these customers were here. He thought they looked as if they had nowhere else to go—he didn't have enough time to wait for them to leave.

The barkeep came back along the counter with a half full bottle in his hand. Holmes shook his head. "I'm looking for Monsieur LaGarde. Do you know him?"

The man didn't reply, merely made a small whistle, as if calling a dog, and raised a hand to the crone. She turned on her stool and leaned against the table to help her get to her feet. "Eh! I know. I know."

Holmes froze. Was this the signal for engaging an aged trollop? He wanted to run, but stood his ground as the hag approached.

"Yes, Monsieur. You ask for me?"

Holmes gulped. "Do you know where I can find Monsieur LaGarde?"

She smiled and her face transformed—not so old after all. "Monsieur LaGarde will be at home. I can show the way."

He let out the breath he'd been holding—that was the correct answer to his code question. "Can we go at once?"

"*Assurément*, there is just the price of my wine."

He turned to look for the barkeep, who seemed to have disappeared. The workmen pushed back their stools to leave. The old men looked up silently from their dominoes.

"Take no notice of them. Twenty sous is usual price."

He placed the coins on the counter and pushed away from the edge. The woman stopped at the door. "We will have to leave arm in arm. *C'est compris?*"

He opened the door for her and took her arm as they reached the street. "My companion will follow. Is that all right?"

"One companion? He will be discreet?"

"He is an army officer. He knows the routine."

They walked slowly in silence through the crowd that suddenly seemed the noisiest he had ever walked through. He tried to see the woman better as they walked, but it was difficult. She might be no more than middle age, and although she walked slowly he felt sure she could run fast if she needed to. Every shout from across the street sounded like a soldier's challenge, every loud conversation to be a discussion of his real identity. He had never felt so . . . damned English . . . in his life.

They walked the lengths of several streets and took short cuts through alleys and arched thoroughfares. He did not know whether they walked closer to the river—the only landmark he knew—or farther away. At length she stopped in a narrow alleyway where the crowd thinned, and turned to embrace him. She raised her mouth to his ear. "Tell your companion to join us."

He pulled away quickly and walked to the entrance of the alley. He arrived almost face to face with McNab. "Come with us," Holmes said.

When they reached the woman she stood in a low doorway. "Come. Speak not."

The door led into a smelly doss-house, the corridor thick with grime, and sleeping figures sprawled everywhere. The woman took them to a room, slightly cleaner and less crowded than the rest. A man looked up from an empty table. "You want LaGarde?"

"We were told to ask for him."

"Where did you meet this man who told you?"

"On a boat . . . from across the Channel."

"La Manche?"

"The very same. He must be in the city already."

"Perhaps. You are English, by your voice. Your companion?"

Captain McNab spoke up in his French and the man winced. "He is best to keep his mouth shut. He must act deaf-mute."

"But our papers identify us as cavalry officers . . . of *Le Troisième Régiment des Lancers*. We need to acquire suitable uniforms so we may walk about the city."

"Suitable uniforms could be possible—but your friend must have a bandage and a duelling scar that prevents him speaking."

Holmes looked at McNab, who seemed a mite put out. "You must do it for your country, Captain. Scots wha hae, and all that!"

Lord Bond awoke with someone's hair draped across his face. He raised a sleepy hand and lifted some locks to peer at—blonde—it must be Elise's. Yes, that was it. He had found her the previous evening in the best hostelry in Flushing, going under the name of Freiherrin Louise von Langenhorst— one of her usual false names.

He reached out to take one of her nipples in his fingers. After a little stroking and pinching she rolled away with a soft moan. His hand went down her body and strayed about until her eyes opened. He always marvelled how they shone bright blue even roused from sleep.

"Julian. What is matter? It is middle of the night."

"No, it's not. By the light against the curtains it must be the ninth hour."

"So? I am tired. Go back to sleep."

His hand slipped up the inside of her thighs. "How tired are you?"

"More than that. By God . . . did you not extinguish your desire last night? My body aches."

He ran another finger down her pearl-white cheek. "Surely not. You must have been in a nunnery since I left."

"I have no other lovers."

Lord Bond laughed and rolled over onto her. "Not by comparison—eh?"

"Ach! Get off, you great horse-cock. No more until tonight."

He continued to stroke her. "How long have you been Freiherrin this time? You have debts, of course?"

She shrugged. "A mere pittance."

"This hostelry does not own the word. How long have you been here?"

"Ten days . . . two weeks . . . something like that. I was

waiting for you."

"How much?"

"A hundred francs should settle it."

"That is more than the Admiralty allows," he said, pinching her labia between thumb and fingernail.

"Ouch . . . you beast. You never pay as Admiralty—I am personal a . . . assis . . . What is word in English?"

"Secretary? You cannot write. Associate? *As sociare* is the word in Latin. It means to join—a very good idea, my love. Let us join again."

She pushed him away and slid out of the bed. "No! Tonight." She walked naked to the window, pulled the curtain aside to look out. "I *can* write," she said wistfully, craning her neck to see down into the courtyard. "I can prove it by my letters to my dear husband in the East Indies."

"But not well in English. Perhaps you had better write to your husband for a hundred francs—or perhaps keep looking out the window like that. I'm sure you could collect enough admirers in a single morning to pay off your debts."

"Beast! That is why I hate you . . . what you say. You make me a trollop. Am I not good enough to be a Marchasa?"

"Perhaps in Italy, but the title is Marchioness in England. I should introduce you to my father—he might marry you."

"Pah. What would I do with an old man?" She turned with a pout. "Where is your ship?"

"What, indeed? Perhaps you could lead him to heaven in ecstasy. Perhaps I *should* introduce you. The *Nederlander* is in the harbour. We must go aboard this afternoon—we must be in Antwerp tomorrow to link up with my other companions."

"A Frieherrin does not sail in a hoogaar."

"This afternoon you will be Mistress Paine, from New Bedford. I think I will send you to see the American Ambassador."

"What is this New Bedford? I do not know it."

"I will tell you all about it—I was there in 1811 for the Admiralty . . . when I sounded out the appetite for the war."

Christopher Hoare

Chapter Forty
Cannon Fire

Roberta and Sir Joseph Sydney Yorke stood with a group of Royal Artillery officers on Woolwich Common as the twenty-four pounder cannon was prepared. They had arrived at Woolwich earlier that morning after travelling from Westminster by river steamer. Brigadier General Hopkins, Lord Bond's contact at the establishment, had met them at Woolwich Dockyard and arranged this final demonstration of the armour experiments.

"We have had quite consistent results," General Hopkins said, "that show us that at normal sea combat ranges the two inch iron plate is resistant to shot from a twenty-four pounder."

"What ranges have you considered, General?" the First Sea Lord asked.

"We understand that the French open fire at greater ranges than your people in the Royal Navy do, Sir Joseph. We found that at four hundred yards, the plates were barely scratched."

"Two cables length, then," Sir Joseph answered. "Not completely unrealistic for usual French crews, but when our ships press closer, the enemies' range, too, is reduced. What have you found at ranges as short as yardarm to yardarm?"

General Hopkins smiled. "That is what we plan to show you today. This will be the most demanding test of all. The target you see here will be forty yards distant from the muzzle of the gun."

"Before the cannon is fired, I should like to see the iron plate and the manner of attaching it to the target frame; if we might, General," Roberta said.

The General turned to her with an indulgent smile. "I assure you we have taken the utmost care with our targets, Miss Stephenson, but I am perfectly willing—indeed pleased—to show you the fastenings."

Sir Joseph laughed. "Lord Bond should have warned you how meticulous our Miss Stephenson is, General Hopkins. I do not doubt but that she has prepared herself with as much information as possible—the word among flag officers at the Admiralty lately has been amazement at her appetite for the experienced words of personal recollection."

"I have been most grateful to all the officers for their patience at my questioning, My Lord," Roberta answered. "They have given me a better understanding of the strength of solid timbers that must form our baseline for the assessment of iron."

The two senior officers exchanged a glance. General Hopkins then turned to listen to a short, stocky major who came to him from the direction of the target. "We would like you to show us the target before we fire, Major. Is there time to do that safely?"

"Yes, General. I have yet to inspect and approve the powder and shot before it is supplied to the gunners."

The General smiled at Roberta. "There, my dear. I'm sure

you will find Major Thurston able to answer all your questions. Miss Stephenson has the management of a shipyard in her father's business, Major. The query about the resistance of iron plates came to us from an Admiralty contract the Navy has with the yard."

"Indeed." Major Thurston both saluted and offered her a polite bow, and she responded by extending her hand . . . which after a momentary hesitation he shook. "If you would walk with me, Miss Stephenson, I will show you the target first."

They walked across the intervening grass, steadily outpacing the senior officers even though they began a technical discussion. "I was sorry not to have seen the two inch plates before they were dispatched to Woolwich, Major." Roberta said. "I did specify the order for them and made the delivery arrangements. Were you able to assess the strength of the plates? I was concerned that their strengths would show a difference between the direction of rolling and across the grain, as it were."

"I believe that was a phenomenon we have seen during the experiments, Miss Stephenson. You have some experience with iron, then?"

She smiled. "Since I was about ten, I'd suppose. I was as much about the steam engine workshops as I was in the drawing room. In those days we engineers had a great concern for consistency in the strength of the iron from which boilers were constructed. You must be aware of the number of serious accidents caused by boiler explosions."

"Indeed, I am. It would seem that standards have improved with time, though."

"That is due to a greater attention paid to the strength of the raw materials used. At our Clydebank yard I have ordered that all the iron supplied is visually inspected, and one piece of every ten has a sample taken and tested to destruction."

"Hmm, it seems you are as thorough as we must be when accepting a new cannon into the service. Iron is a fine substance, but apt to hide some surprises within its fabric," Major Thurston said as they reached the target. "You will see that the iron plate has been bolted to a wooden frame. This is to ensure the impact of the shot does not carry it away across the common. You may be interested to hear that we find the solidity of the wooden frame is a factor in determining the resistive power of the plate."

Roberta raised her head to look at the frame. "That is very interesting, Major. I thank you for relating the observation. It will have a definite bearing on the way in which we attach the iron to a ship. This backing timber appears to about six inches in thickness. Have you used other thicknesses?"

"Not in a systematic manner, I'm afraid. The carpenters were instructed to use whatever timber they had to hand in the woodworking shop." He stopped speaking and lowered his head in thought. "I can take you to see the remnants of the other experiments after this test. I have not ordered the disposal of any of the tested material to this date."

"The damaged plates, too, will offer me much information."

The two senior officers arrived to hear this last. "I hope you will not ask to have any of the plates carried back to the Admiralty," Sir Joseph said with a smile. "I can just see the expression on the First Lord's face when you set one down in his library."

The men all joined in the laughter, and she attempted to smile patiently at their male reactions. She hoped to be able to see every scrap of evidence that would provide her with necessary information, and had actually been considering having some of the samples brought to the city for closer examination.

"If you are ready, My Lord . . . Miss Stephenson . . . I will go and examine the ammunition next," Major Thurston said.

"And I will come with you, if I may," Roberta asked.

Thurston seemed concerned. "I will explain my procedure, Miss Stephenson. If you will stand at a safe distance from the powder."

When they reached an ammunition limber, some yards from the cannon, a sergeant jumped to attention to salute and open the caisson. The first thing Major Thurston did was to put on a leather smock to cover his uniform. "Not only a housekeeping matter," he called to Roberta who stood several paces farther away, "I must cover any metal accoutrements on my uniform to ensure they do not create a spark that might ignite the powder."

"Yes, I understand. We have had some experience with firing Congreve rockets from ships and have had to teach the rocketeers the safe handling of them."

The Major reached inside and withdrew a tall glass flask. "This is a testing device I have designed myself. It has holes of specific sizes through which I will allow a sample of powder to pass. A measurement of the grains too large to pass through, as well as the grains of less than the required size for the weapon will assure me that the charge is correct for this cannon."

"I see, Major. I can then be assured that the powder fired in all the experiments has been as carefully calibrated."

"Indeed, Miss Stephenson. I can assure you that the powder fired in every test has been the strongest possible." The major smiled broadly at her appreciation for one of the tricks of his trade.

They moved to the pyramid of cannonballs after the powder was approved. "These are all chilled cast iron, Miss Stephenson. We have found, over the years, that they are the strongest produced. These are the missiles we use to bring down stone fortifications."

"Do you have a method to pick the strongest?" Roberta asked.

"Only an accurate measurement of the weight. Lighter missiles could have inclusions of unwanted impurities. These have already been weighed, and I have no criteria for choosing between them."

"I see," she said. "I expect these cannonballs would be stronger and more consistent than those regularly issued to a naval vessel."

"I would agree that your expectation is likely accurate, but I'm afraid I cannot offer you any numerical assessment of the difference."

The next action was to issue the gunners with the powder and shot, after which Roberta and the Major walked to an earth berm behind and to one side of the cannon. When they arrived they found the General and the other visitors already there. The Major addressed everyone. "Once the cannon discharges, I must ask everyone to lower their heads below the rim of the earth berm. This is to protect everyone from the possibility of being struck by flying fragments. We have had metal ripped off a plate during the tests . . . which luckily did not fly in the direction of the watchers on that occasion."

Roberta watched as the gunners loaded the cannon. After the cannonball was rammed down the barrel from the muzzle, and the firing pan primed, all the gun crew except the sergeant with the firing lanyard withdrew behind the berm. Major Thurston stood at the end of the berm to look about to ensure no one had strayed into the firing range. The sergeant fixed his eyes on him and everyone tensed.

The Major raised his arm at the "Ready", and brought it down quickly at the "Fire!"

The sergeant jerked the lanyard and stepped away from the gun carriage. Roberta watched as the powder flared in the priming pan and then the roar of the explosion, the huge gout of powder smoke, and the recoil of the gun, made her duck down.

A metallic crash announced that the target had been struck. Everyone stood upright to see the result. The dispersing cloud of smoke made it difficult to see clearly, but Roberta thought the plate looked intact.

"If everyone is ready," Major Thurston said, "we can go forward to examine the result."

As they walked closer Roberta fancied she could see some change to the plate but was puzzled as to what had happened. Only when they stood beneath it could she see that the cannonball protruded from the plate like a cork in a bottle. The crater formed by the impact had jagged cracks spread around it in all directions, and at the rear of the plate a small swelling in the iron indicated the location of the impact.

"Good Lord," Sir Joseph exclaimed. "An excellent parlour trick, I do declare. I challenge you to repeat that, Major."

He laughed. "I doubt it would happen often, My Lord, but I'm afraid I do not know whether to call that a failure or a successful penetration, Miss Stephenson."

"I think that it might be our limit point for our successful armour," she replied. "Nothing less than a two inch thickness of plate can be called proof, and a lower standard of powder than the carefully selected charge used here would give our crews a measure of assurance. However, I believe I see damage in the rear of the plate that tells me some fragments have been spalled off. Any one of them could kill or wound a man unlucky enough to be hit."

The inspection of the plate continued and when they returned to the arsenal Major Thurston showed them the targets of all the previous shots. The detailed examinations lasted through the lunch hour and most of the afternoon. General Hopkins invited her and Sir Joseph to dinner and recommended they accept his offer of a night's hospitality rather than attempt a return voyage to Westminster pier after dark—which they gladly accepted.

The evening Roberta spent was a pleasant one with the army and the navy officers relating tales from their varied careers and amusing secrets of colonial administrations in widely separated outposts around the world. When she retired upstairs to the chamber assigned her she readied herself for bed and then sat a moment to reflect upon the import of what she had learned from her visit.

She felt she would use Major Thurston's observation of the effect of secure backing to the armour plates in increasing the resistance to the impacts. A thick wooden backing could prevent spalled fragments of iron from causing casualties inside the ship. As for the other matter, the proof of the French armour plates, she had no solution except the one Lord Bond and his team pursued. She had to know the thickness of the iron armour they planned to use on their ironclad.

CHAPTER FORTY-ONE
PROPOSITIONS

Lord Bond stood with the unilingual Bloggins in the stern of *Nederlander* as the canal barge drew nearer. He could see Nicholas van Aa standing in the bow of the craft but waited for him to hail before answering in Flemish. "You have the cargo, my friend?"

The barge slowed as the small deck crew, two young lads, lowered the lug sail to the deck. Van Aa tossed a line as they came alongside, which the *Nederlander's* crew caught and belayed to a cleat near the anchor before taking the strain of hauling the barge to a stop. "That I do . . . and better than rocks. Twenty bushels of turnips that should earn a profit in Antwerp."

Lord Bond frowned as he heard Elise, below decks, start laughing. Of course she would think his peddling vegetables to be funny. Perhaps he would let her sell them to see if she could earn enough to pay off her debts—if only he hadn't been obliged to pay them himself before they could leave Flushing.

Another problem preventing him from turning the joke against her was his need to start her spying on his Royalist allies—he had a strong suspicion that they had little interest in helping his people learn the secrets of the French steamships. The more they thought a new King Louis would rule in France after Napoleon, the more they would oppose English plans to weaken the country.

Van Aa climbed from the barge to *Nederlander's* deck. "Are the turnips to your liking, My Lord?"

Bond shrugged as Elise's imaginary market-woman's impersonation came to him from below. "It will mean we have a reason to trade in the market, closer to the city centre, I suppose. The purchasers of building stone would be harder to locate."

"If you will give me the fifteen francs to pay off the bargee, I will do so and then leave you before someone recognizes me near the Oostkade."

Bond looked around the canal basin and the few coastal traders taking on cargo. This was Napoleon's new harbour works, open to the Westerschelde and the open sea at one end, and leading through the first lock to the new Ghent Canal at the landward end. "Do not leave too soon. My agent who will be your correspondent in Antwerp will need to know how to contact you here." He turned to call down into the hoogaar's small cabin. "If you have quite finished playing the fool, Elise, please come on deck to speak to our Neuzen correspondent and arrange the passage of messages."

Elise came on deck, a mischievous gleam still in her eyes. "*Enchante, Monsieur.* To who am I speaking," she said to van Aa.

"I will use the name Schulemeister, with an address of No.3 Marke in Hoek. Who will I write to, Madame?"

"Do not use my identity," Lord Bond said quickly.

She looked at him with a smile before turning her attention

back to van Aa. "Very well. You may address your messages to Freiherrin Louise von Langenhorst at *Poste Restante* in Antwerp. We must arrange some secret code words to ensure our identities are not compromised. Let us walk to the other side of the boat," she said quietly.

Bond watched them move away. It was a good idea that no one but themselves knew this precaution. He thought he should object to the use of her alias again, but as far as he knew all the debts linked to the name had been settled. He was well aware she coveted a claim to nobility, it was what had made her such a reliable companion for his spying. The time was coming, though, that he must offer her something concrete in that direction.

When van Aa disappeared through the alleys behind the East Quay and the turnips were loaded in *Nederlander's* hold, they slipped moorings to return to the Westerschelde. As they got away on the fair wind from the west to make good speed up the estuary toward the entrance to the Schelde River he sat with Elise on the closed cargo hatch to plan their procedures in Antwerp.

"Who is the man you wrote to me about? What can he do for us?"

"He has a canal barge that brings iron from France for the shipbuilding. He would offer a place in his crew for a man who wishes to see what iron is being carried."

"I see. That will be a good opportunity. What does he want for his trouble?"

Elise smiled impishly. "A hundred francs."

Bond shrugged. This seemed to be her price of everything, but no doubt it included her cut. "We will use the dwelling that Cornelius van Ee has found for us in Antwerp, but we will not operate together. I will oversee what my two British spies undertake, but you must meet with all your contacts to observe what the Count does and who he sees. Can you do this?"

Elise smiled. "Of course, but why must I do it? Is not the Count approved by Admiralty?"

"I do not have a good feeling about him," Bond answered. There, he had committed himself to placing credence in mere feelings and intuition that he had chided Roberta about. She was beginning to influence whatever he thought. "Van Aa told me that you Dutch and the French Royalists were following different interests. I am concerned that my plans and that of England will be lost or betrayed in the conflict if I cannot have a means of advance warning."

Roberta followed the First Lord into his library after dinner, and sat with him to discuss her progress. "Your tests at Woolwich seem to have garnered much valuable information," he said.

"Yes, I am pleased . . . as far as the experiments go."

His face registered surprise. "But you are not entirely satisfied, my dear?"

"I would have liked there to be further tests. What would be the result of using two two-inch iron plates together . . . what difference would thirty-two pounder or even forty-two pounder cannon have made . . . how many successive shots at a single plate with the twenty-four pounder would have eventually defeated the armour."

Viscount Melville threw up his hands in mock surrender. "My dear young lady, you are a very Erinyes of Ancient Greece in your determination to wring every answer from your quest. I do not dispute that we have not looked at any of those outcomes, but did we not at our initial Admiralty meeting restrict ourselves to what is most probable in this French ironclad?"

"Probable, yes, My Lord, but not all that is possible."

"So you are not yet sufficiently informed to be able to design this larger steam ram that can defeat whatever the French put to sea?"

Roberta considered a moment. "I think that in the matter of armour plate to protect my ram and the protected third rate the Laird yard is building we are restricted to two-inch plate. That is the thickest that can currently be rolled. I would like to know whether doubling the plates will double the resistance."

"But you are doubtful?"

"The plates cannot be more than bolted together, which is not likely to allow them to act as a single four-inch plate."

The First Lord sat back in silence a moment. Eventually he picked up the brandy the footman had poured for him and looked into her eyes. "What more must you know before you may begin to lay iron?"

Roberta enumerated on her fingers. "The form of the French ship, heretofore described as two Third Rates coupled together; the engine power, and hence the speed; its seaworthiness in a seaway; the length of time it may stay at sea under steam power; the thickness of its own iron armour."

The First Lord took a strong draft of his brandy. "I must confess, that I am more persuaded that Lord Bond is correct when he asserts that you must be present to see these secrets truthfully uncovered. We have received some good news on that matter. The Foreign Office reported that one of its agents in Stockholm has intercepted the last letter sent by Herr Gottliebe . . . I was shown the letter at a Cabinet meeting. It is in cypher, of course, but apparently your presence in the Admiralty was noted."

Roberta put a hand to her mouth to stifle any dismay.

"Yes, my dear. It is always alarming when one sees one's own name in a hostile communication. But that threat has been extinguished, at least. There is one other matter I must speak about—it concerns a request that duty impels me to make. I have also learned something that makes me even more loth to hazard you in His Lordship's plans."

Roberta took a sip from her own glass, containing the First Lord's coveted Amontillado sherry. "What has increased the danger of his mission, My Lord?"

"The Government has received intelligence through our embassy in Switzerland that the cooperation and alliance offered by Monsieur le Comte de la Marke is not all that we were led to believe. Our ambassador has evidence from a reliable correspondent . . . that is, a secret agent informant . . . that the Royalists are betting both ways in this enterprise of Napoleon's."

Roberta's eyes widened in horror—this meant that all her friends could be in danger.

"This is only information from one source as yet . . . which makes it important but not completely reliable. This correspondent is French, and is in Paris, so it is possible that Fouché may have captured or turned him to his own purposes. However, because Lord Bond and his people are in the Low Countries as we speak, I cannot wait until we have confirmation. The *Medusa* will be ready for sea in a matter of days and I want to send another agent with you to go ashore to find His Lordship to warn him."

"How will he find any of them?" Roberta asked.

"I have not solved that problem completely, but I want to warn you that you are the only person we have who has met this schoolteacher from Neuzen who is a member of the party. He is the only person we know who can lead us to the team in Antwerp. Would you be willing to go ashore in Neuzen with the new agent to confirm the identity of Herr Nicholas van Aa?" The First Lord wore a very guilty expression. "You would not need to go farther, and would return to sea in the cutter that had brought you to land."

Roberta seemed to feel cold fingers down her spine. The

First Lord's request had suddenly started to sound too much like Lord Bond's, which she had been holding at bay for a month.

Christopher Hoare

Chapter Forty-two
Improvising Plans

Lord Bond stood in the centre of Antwerp's Grote Markt, the market square, looking around at the tall, ornate buildings that surrounded it . . . some as many as eight stories. The paper seller, from whom he had just bought today's newspaper, walked away, but standing beside the fountain that was their designated rendezvous, Bond took the paper from under his arm as if too anxious to begin reading to take it home first.

It was in French; all other languages being proscribed—even Dutch—since Napoleon's France had annexed the Low Countries. A few pedestrians walked past, but on this day, Sunday, the area was not crowded with market stalls crammed tight together. He read one column on each page, as if poring through the articles to find a specific story, but did not try to remember any. He was merely filling in time until Holmes or Captain McNab arrived—if they did . . . he was three days late.

Every few lines of text he raised his head to look around, noticing the passersby and keeping an eye out for anyone official who seemed to be watching him. His only concern was for the two men in uniform walking slowly toward him—wait! They were Holmes and McNab in their cavalry uniforms. Well, they had been spending the waiting time profitably, at least.

Holmes stopped before him. "Good day, Monsieur. Do you have time to show us around?" he said in French.

"Yes, I do, but we must go back to your house for you to change. The contact Elise has for you requires workmen's clothes."

"*Mais*, our documents require us to be sawjers," McNab said.

"Yes, but as a barge crew, you will have less need for identification. The barge and the bargee will be enough documentation. You must keep the rooms and the uniforms for your return to the city."

Before they could leave, some of the passing pedestrians looked askance at what appeared to be the apprehension of someone suspicious. Holmes seemed quick to note this and jovially slapped Bond on the back. "Well, let us move on then—we are waiting for you to buy us a drink."

"Where will this barge tak us, Monsieur?" McNab asked quietly.

"Up the Schelde toward Ghent. It is the direction from which comes the iron for the shipyards."

Their walk took them away from the market square and the river to a tall, narrow terraced house near the old city walls in a maze of narrow streets lined with similar houses. They stopped at the weather-beaten door for Holmes to knock. After a few minutes it was opened by a small girl of about ten. "Ah, Monsieur LaGarde," she said as she let them in.

Bond looked at Holmes in some surprise. Holmes shook his head and spoke softly in English. "The name seems to be a recognition signal for all activities. There is no Monsieur LaGarde as far as we have learned."

The girl led them up three flights of stairs to a narrow landing where she knocked on one of two doors that faced one another. The door opened quickly, letting a strong smell of boiling cabbage out into the landing. An older man stood behind the door, looking around the edge to peer at them with rheumy eyes. "Maria, gran papa," the girl said. At that, the man looked down at her and opened the door wide to admit them.

Inside, they followed the girl through three rooms, where the occupants looked up with dull expressions as they walked past. At the end of the third room the girl walked to a wooden cabinet with a few sparsely stocked shelves of fabric. Here she stood back to let Holmes and McNab take hold of the cabinet to heave it aside—revealing a narrow passage beyond.

"Welcome to *Chez Nous*," Holmes said with a laugh as he led the way. Lord Bond found himself in a long narrow room with a low, sloped attic ceiling. "Take a seat while we pull the 'door' closed," Holmes told him.

The room appeared to be sitting room, kitchen, and bedroom in turn as one looked down its length toward the blank wall at the far end. The sitting room boasted of one wooden chair and a broken down chaise longue; the kitchen of a bread bin and an empty table; and the bedroom of two pallets of straw on the floor. "It's nae a palace," McNab commented coming out of the passage, "but 'tis oursel's castle."

"Well, you may be lucky enough to find the barge more comfortable," Bond answered.

"What is this barge?" Mr. Holmes said as he returned. "I thought the young lady was to take us to a contact."

"This is the contact, and since I have assigned the young lady to keep an eye on our French allies, I cannot let them see her with you. The barge is employed with bringing iron from France and coal from Wallonia down the rivers to Antwerp. I'm hopeful that a few days of sailing toward Ghent and passing the nights in backwaters where other, loaded barges of friends congregate . . . you will learn what manner of iron is being transported."

"An' particularly, the thickness o' armour plates."

"Exactly."

"How do we find this barge?" Mr. Holmes asked.

"You will find it in the South docks. It is called the *Hortense*, of Baasrode. Elise has made the arrangements with the bargees . . . several barges owned by men from South Flanders will travel together. There is sometimes trouble between the Flemings and the Walloons, into whose provinces they travel to pick up the cargoes."

"I do not like the sound of that," Holmes said. "How many of these people will be your Dutch speaking allies from the north?"

"The bargee, for certain, and whatever other crew he has. Among the other barges will certainly be more. When you are ready, I will walk with you . . . and watch you go aboard the barge from the end of the dock. I'm hoping the Royalists—if any are assigned to follow you—will show themselves. I can divert them from seeing where you go."

Holmes and McNab looked soberly at one another.

"Cheer up," Lord Bond said. "You will be perfectly secure once you are on the river."

Not being too sure of the way through the winding streets of the old city, Lord Bond led them by way of the streets beside the city walls. Elise had told him the docks they wanted were located in the southernmost district of the city, most certainly at the southern extremity of the fortifications. They took turns to check whether they were being followed, with mixed results.

At one point they felt sure a well-dressed man was following, but he turned off their route to take a street leading into the centre from a city gate. If he was replaced by another agent, they failed to recognise him—or her, Holmes was careful to point out.

The two fake bargees looked quite disreputable compared to the well-dressed faux American, but Bond hoped they would not arouse suspicion among the soldiers stationed at various street corners and watching the crowds. "If we are stopped I will explain that you are leading me to speak with your barge skipper about carrying a cargo to Ghent."

Luckily, they were not stopped.

Arriving at the first basin of the docks, Lord Bond stood looking at the notices posted on a shipping company's window while the other two walked on. Here, they were the ones who blended in while he was the one looking out of place.

He left the window to follow just in time to see them clamber aboard a single masted sailing barge about half way along the quay. He decided to stay watching until he was sure they were not the object of attention for anyone else among the busy workers on the quay. He was beginning to feel satisfied they were safe when he saw Captain McNab clamber back onto the quay and walk toward him.

"Is anything wrong?" he asked when McNab reached him.

"There's nae room for twa bargees, M'Lord. They would'na tak me."

"Damn. Oh well, you can go back to your safe house—I know I can use your help while I'm in the city. We must keep Mr. Holmes' enterprise with the Flemings a secret from your landlords the French Royalists, which means we must concoct a new story—are you up to that?"

"Indeed I am, M'Lord. I was never easy in my ain mind fer our dependence upon them."

Chapter Forty-three
Alarming Information

Lord Bond crossed the cobbles near the double doors of the cathedral, walking slowly and wending his way toward the deaf and dumb beggar outside the portico. The beggar looked up, made animal-like grunting noises, and shook his wicker alms basket. Bond dropped a coin in the basket and quickly palmed a scrap of paper he found in the bottom. He tried not to make eye contact, but could not avoid nodding to Captain McNab—for a very fine performance.

He thrust aside his urge to walk quickly away, maintaining his zigzag, leisurely path until he reached the first of a line of shops facing the cathedral. One was a wine shop with tables outside where patrons enjoyed the early fall sunshine. He took a seat at one and didn't look at his message until the waiter had brought him a glass of wine.

The message was from Elise, in her mixed French and English script. "Letter for Paine at *Poste Restante*. Meet me there, noon."

Bond looked up at the buildings around him without seeing them; she had found a letter addressed to Gideon Paine in Antwerp? Good Lord, was he in the city? That might make things difficult.

He drank his wine quickly and placed a coin on the table before leaving immediately—it was but a quarter of an hour before noon.

The building where the post might be collected was adjacent to the horse barns where the motive force of the mail coaches and couriers were housed. He found Elise talking to the stable lads currying a pair of horses in the courtyard. "How did you find out about the letter?" he asked in Flemish.

"I ask if they have letters for Madame Paine," she said with a smile. "This is first time I get ze answer."

"For her husband. What do I need to get the letter?"

"You must pay ze postage, and show some proof who are you. Come with me—I show to you the office."

Lord Bond went to the counter and asked for the mail for Mr. Gideon Paine, an uncomfortable feeling running up his spine. He had almost ceased believing in the man's existence, wondering if he were as mythical as Monsieur LaGarde. No, not only could he be real but he could be in Antwerp, a real sot-weed importer. He could be here as well, coming for his mail—or have an agent looking to pick it up.

"Have you a proof *d'identite*?" the official asked, returning with a small package.

Bond unfolded the parchment that constituted his passport and held it out. The official glanced at it. "*Americain?*"

"*Oui.*"

"Six francs, *s'il vous plait.*"

Bond handed over the coins, pocketed the mail and hurried out. Elise stood outside and he took her by the arm to walk quickly into the crowd before anyone could challenge them. "We will return to our rooms to read this," he said.

At the *pensione* he locked the door before sitting at the table to break the seals of the package. Elise drew up the stool beside the bed to sit looking over his shoulder. "It will be in English," he said.

"So . . . you will explain."

Perhaps he would, perhaps he wouldn't. It depended upon what the letter said. He didn't answer as he drew the sheaf of pages from the packet, and then he was too startled to say anything.

"What means 'United States Minister Plenipotentiary to France'," Elise wanted to know.

Bond stared at the official letterhead. "It means . . . American Ambassador," he said.

"Why does ambassador write to Mistere Paine?"

Bond didn't answer—he hated to admit he didn't know. The first words of the letter didn't do any more for his state of mind than did the letterhead—"My dear Gideon . . ."

Not only did Paine exist, he was on first name terms with the American ambassador to France. This was getting worse, more alarming all the time. Where did his Dutch friends lay their hands on this passport? Did they know anything more about the man they had stolen it from?

He set the page down and turned to confront Elise. "Do you know the people who stole this passport? Do you know what happened to Paine after he left Amsterdam . . . ? He did leave Amsterdam, and not end up floating in the canal?"

Elise stared into his eyes defiantly. "I know nothing of this."

He slapped her hard across the face. "You must know something! We could be in great trouble. Search your memory—you must remember something."

Elise's cheek reddened, but she did not raise a hand to it.

Her eyes turned fierce. "All I know is a man was robbed coming from ze card game. It happen in early summer. No one knew where he went, after."

"I was told it was perfectly safe. That the man had left the city."

"Certain. The man was gone from Amsterdam."

"Yes—gone to Antwerp, by damn!"

"He is tobacco man—he could be in any port in France."

Bond stared into her angry eyes—quite true. The letter may only indicate that Paine was expected to arrive in Antwerp soon. He turned his attention back to the letter.

It continued—"I was glad to be able to replace your papers when you came to Paris, and must tell you that someone claiming to be you was in Flushing during the month of July . . ." Yes—he had been in Flushing then. Good Lord—his moves had been discovered.

He read the whole first page while still reeling from his narrow escape from discovery. It seemed mostly pleasantries and references to people in the Americas that both knew. It was only at the bottom that he saw something relevant. "Your wife is now in Paris and pleading penury. I have allowed her a small stipend, but need to learn from you if you intend going through with the divorce proceedings. I do not want to reiterate the reasons why I thought your matrimonial ideas were a grave mistake, but you could have found a better connected Frenchwoman than Mrs. Paine, or at least a more scrupulous one."

Bond ceased reading to glance at Elise—yes, he could understand what a mistake Paine had committed.

"What does letter say?"

"Mrs. Paine is in Paris, and the Ambassador has had to pay some of her debts. Paine apparently considers divorcing her."

"The beast! He bring *l'Americaine* to France and wishes to desert her."

"She is French, apparently."

Elise did not answer in words, but her expression signalled the information had struck a chord.

Bond set the page down and took up the next. It contained some correspondence about Paine's business interests, and information about other Americans in France who he might be advised to meet, and ended with the signature William Harris Crawford and below it a post script—directing him to a third, sealed page. He opened this to find—"Previous diplomatic messages have indicated that I can expect to receive a diplomatic package aboard the vessel *Reaper* leaving New Bedford before the end of August. It is very important that you should meet the vessel in Antwerp as the contents are highly sensitive and will be secured in the usual way. I must also inform you to expect Monsieur Le Duc d'Outrante in Antwerp in the first or second week in September on some official business. If you introduce yourself to him and inform him of the nature of our confidential papers he will dispatch them to me by secure messenger."

Elise's fingers on his shoulder dug in sharply as she exhaled with a gasp. "Outrante!"

"Yes," Bond answered her. "Joseph Fouché—Napoleon's Minister of Police—the spymaster who has caught almost every spy working against Napoleon. And I will be obliged to haunt the quays and dockyards to learn of the arrival of this American ship, *Reaper*, when I would prefer to be lying low."

Chapter Forty-four
First Class Cabin

When Roberta's Thames Packet steamer arrived in the Medway she saw not only her destination, the frigate *Medusa* moored in the river, but a column of smoke from the direction of the royal dockyard marking the berth of her *Spiteful*. She felt a warm glow as she thought she might see Commander Worthington again before she left the harbour.

Medusa had left London a day before she completed her negotiations for the sub-contracting of the second Thames-built spiteful. She had seen the frigate with new masts and yards, new standing rigging being tightened and adjusted, and new canvas gleaming white in the sun, as the crew took on victuals in the river from the Royal yard at Deptford, almost directly across from Charlie Napier's shipyard. She felt a thrill as she contemplated sailing in her—she had been told that Lord Nelson had once hoisted his flag in her.

The steamer blew salutes on its steam whistle as it passed between the naval vessels moored in the river on its way to the passenger dock on the quay at Chatham. On many of the ships, the crews responded, usually by climbing the rigging and standing on the main yard to wave their caps in answer. Roberta thought it a fine display of morale and seamanship. She had done her share of climbing the rigging, but *Spiteful* had a for-and-aft rig, and she had never walked out onto a yard of a square-rigger with no more than a single rope to hold onto.

Lieutenant Farley, the new addition to the spy team, came out on deck from the nearby companionway. He walked with a slight limp, the result of an injury sustained when his gun brig, *Marigold*, had been blown aground on the Goodwin Sands off the Downs. His seamanship had been sufficient to save his crew even in the teeth of a gale that threatened to smash the little ship to pieces, but losing one's command was a Court Martial offence in the Navy, and he had volunteered to undertake the spying mission while he waited for the Court Martial to convene.

"That *Medusa* is a real fighting ship, Miss Roberta," he said, staring across the water at the vessel—almost drooling at the sight, to her mind. "How I pine for a chance to command again and secure my promotion to post captain."

"Lord Bond has connections," she said, "but I cannot say what opportunities for advancement await us as we embark for the Low Countries. I must admit that I will feel out of place under sail, since my seafaring experience has mostly been restricted to steamships. Are you an ardent partisan for sail or do you have some good regard for steam?"

"I thought I was wedded only to the wind and sail upon a well found ship, but being helpless to avoid disaster when the gale chooses to play its worst upon a man's best efforts has inclined me to a more neutral opinion. The admiral had ordered the location of my mooring with an eye to adding security for the rest of his squadron at anchor. When we dragged our anchors, the steam tug near us raised steam and got out of the way of danger. How I would have preferred to do the same."

"The tug did not offer assistance, then?"

"The tug was ordered to help a seventy-four that was near to sharing my brig's fate. 'Twas a correct decision to save the larger ship, but a bitter lesson for us."

"But it seems the storm threatened enough vessels with the same fate that the captains at the Court Martial may not find fault with your actions."

"That is my most fervent hope, Miss Stephenson, but I shall not cease any apprehension until I see who will sit in judgement of me. I am not a favourite of all the captains in the squadron."

"Would you like to visit my *Spiteful*, Lieutenant? A word with our Commander Worthington might be worth your while."

"You expect to visit the vessel?"

"I hope there may be time for visits. Lord Melville gave me a letter of instructions for Captain Bell of the *Medusa* that may delay departure for another day. We will see what transpires."

When they disembarked from the steamer at Chatham a midshipman approached them. "Are ye the lady that is to come aboard the *Medusa*, Mistress?"

She smiled as she answered, thinking he must be all of fourteen and yet with the bearing of a man. "That is correct, Sir. And Lieutenant Farley has also been ordered to take passage with us. I am Miss Roberta Stephenson, what is your name, Sir?"

"I am Willis . . . very pleased to meet you, Miss Stephenson . . . glad to have you aboard, Lieutenant. Are you not joining the ship's company?"

"No, lad. I have detached duties. Do you have a ship's boat to take us?"

"I have the Captain's gig and four oarsmen, Sir. It is moored downstream of the passenger dock."

"Can you have the sailors carry my luggage, Mr. Willis?" Roberta asked. "I have probably brought more than was needed, but am unsure of my actual destination."

The lad smiled, quite wide eyed as he led the way. "They says you might go ashore—is that the truth?"

Lieutenant Farley frowned. "That is more than should be spoken of. We are on an assignment from the Admiralty—and that is all anyone should know."

Young Willis blushed and stared at his feet. "I will bear that in mind, Lieutenant. You may trust me."

They spoke little more as they descended the quay steps to climb into the gig, and only in polite commentary as they rowed out into the river after the sailors had loaded the luggage. They learned that vessels from no less than three Channel squadrons were moored within the harbour, some being revictualled, some delivering dispatches from or to squadron commanders, and some sending sick and injured ashore. *Medusa*, it turned out, was the only recently fitted-out warship present—a great rarity in a weatherbeaten and overstretched navy on continuous watch over the enemy coast.

As they reached the *Medusa's* side they found another ship's boat already moored there. Roberta recognized it. "That is *Spiteful's* cutter. Are men from *Spiteful* aboard?"

"That they are, Miss Stephenson. Commander Worthington has asked Captain Bell that the Master of *Medusa* might show his young men the frigate where our beloved Lord Nelson flew his flag when he commanded in the Channel."

"Indeed? I must own to the desire that I too might prevail on the Master that he give me the tour as well. Was he master when Lord Nelson was aboard?"

"That he was, Miss, but you shall have a tour that few others might share. I'm told the cabin assigned for you is the very selfsame cabin that the Admiral used."

"I do envy you, Miss Stephenson," Lieutenant Farley said, "but perhaps little of the furniture is the same as the Admiral used—it must be thirteen years since he hauled down his flag on *Medusa*."

Young Willis had another answer. "Thirteen years and two months, Sir. But the Master do say that the cot in that cabin be the same as Lord Nelson slept in."

"Really?" Lieutenant Farley said. "I'm sure you will sleep soundly there, Miss Stephenson."

"I'm not at all sure," she answered. "I should be fearful of not being fit to sleep in such hallowed accommodation."

"Ah, I doubts that," Willis said. "'Tis only the Chaplain that you be displacing today, and I don't doubt but that he have prayed so much in that cot as the Admiral his-self could hardly rate its shelter."

Lieutenant Farley glared. "Cheeky monkey! Get you about mooring your command here and do not speak so disrespectful of the Cloth."

Willis hurried to command his crew about mooring the gig and heaving them alongside the jack ladder, but he found the chance to exchange a covert grin with Roberta.

Midshipman Willis ordered his seamen to avert their eyes while Roberta climbed the jack ladder. Lieutenant Farley preceded her and helped from above, while she rued the necessity of wearing a travelling dress instead of the boiler suits she favoured at sea. She had ordered one packed in her shipping trunk and vowed to wear it when next she had to climb up or down into a small boat. When she reached the deck she was surprised to find quite a welcoming committee.

"Good afternoon, Miss Stephenson," Commander Worthington said, stepping forward to take her hand. "You caught us in the act of leaving *Medusa*, but if I may, I would be pleased to remain aboard to introduce you to all the *Medusa* officers."

"Why, thank you, Commander. I am pleased to be in your debt one more time."

He led her to a stocky man of middle height wearing a bicorn naval hat and a blue jacket with gold epaulets. "May I present Miss Roberta Stephenson, Captain? Miss Roberta, this is the captain of *Medusa*, Post Captain George Bell. Miss Stephenson is the manager and chief designer of her father's yard that built the *Spiteful*."

"Welcome aboard, Miss Stephenson. I trust you will find us a gentlemanly lot, for all the necessary exigencies of war."

"I'm sure I shall, Captain Bell, but I expect Commander Worthington has spoken in confidence that I am not unaccustomed to living on a warship in the Channel."

Bell smiled. "He has intimated such, but I regret our need to prepare for our own departure means I cannot avail myself of his invitation to inspect your father's craft."

Lieutenant Farley stepped forward to introduce himself to Captain Bell while Worthington took Roberta around the commissioned and non-commissioned officers, introducing her with great relish as a particular friend and benefactor. By the time the introductions were over she felt she could hardly have been paid more compliments if she had been royalty. She did walk with him to the jack ladder as he prepared to join his crew members below in the cutter.

"I am deeply concerned to find you have been sent aboard a warship to join the blockading squadron, Miss Stephenson," he said *sotto voce*. "Indeed I am beside myself to find His Lordship's designs so furthered. Please tell me that you have not made any undertakings toward him."

Roberta was taken aback by his manner, but felt inclined to reassure him rather than dismiss his impertinence. "I have not seen His Lordship since my departure from Clydebank, my dear friend. You may calm your fears as far as my own intentions are concerned. My presence here is merely to fulfil the task of safely introducing Lieutenant Farley into His Lordship's party if the *Nederlander* fails to make its planned rendezvous with the blockading squadron."

"Then, despite the Admiralty's orders to keep the *Spiteful* away from the enemy coast, I will do all that I can to ensure the *Spiteful* is nearby at sea at that juncture, Miss Stephenson. I will never desert you . . . you may count upon me." With that he took her hand most forcefully and kissed it before turning to set foot onto the jack ladder, leaving her somewhat flushed and flustered, looking out across the anchorage until she could compose herself sufficiently to contemplate rejoining the officers.

Roberta watched the departing cutter before she moved away from the jack ladder. Would her dear friend turn for a departing look at her or maintain his stiff forward looking stance from his seat in the stern? She had to admit that she had not awarded him the attention and regard she should have while the other gentlemen used their positions to the fullest. She made herself a solemn promise—if it was in her power when she returned from the shores of France—she would rectify her mistakes.

END

Steam and Strategem

ABOUT THE AUTHOR

Christopher Hoare was born in Britain three months before WWII started. Later, that resulted in a scholarship place for secondary education under the Butler Education Act and eventually to some engineering training at a Ministry of Supply establishment. While he appreciated the training, he really wanted to be a writer so he left halfway through the course for a stint in the Artillery, and then in the N. African oilfields, followed by a move to Canada and work in the Arctic and Northern bush. He had intended moving on but met his wife of 43 years and is still here—diligently writing at last, and turning all the life experience into somewhat contrarian fiction.

Most of his published novels four out of six have early steam power as a factor in the plot, and he claims his previous work experience with gear manufacture, steam generators, and steam powered utilities makes him almost a founding father of Gear-heads.

CPSIA information can be obtained at www.ICGtesting.com
Printed in the USA
LVOW06s0935311013

359142LV00003BA/86/P